THE GOD RESURRECTION

THE GOD RESURRECTION

A DAN KOTLER THRILLER

J. KEVIN TUMLINSON

KNOVELTON

For Kara—
Doing any of this without you
is just an absurd notion

PROLOGUE

THREE NIGHTS AGO | *Göbekli Tepe, Turkey*

ACCORDING to everything the man had read, it was the oldest temple in the world.

Older than Stonehenge. Older than the pyramids. Older than anything the man had ever known or read about or seen before in his life. Older than anything he'd ever before put his hands on. He was touching history. True history.

The man, shrouded in darkness and hidden from the view of guards or archaeologists or anyone else, rested both palms on a stone pillar and felt the gritty texture of the stone, the embossed and carved designs of bulls and lions, and that of a human figure with the wings and head of a bird.

So much history in this stone. Ancient and enigmatic. And so well preserved, buried for nearly twelve-thousand years, here in "Potbelly Mound"—the English translation of the Turkish name, *Göbekli Tepe*.

The site had been a series of large, bulbous mounds that

had lain untouched for eleven and a half millennia, until the 1990s. During that decade, archaeologists discovered that the stone slabs and lithics found on the surface of the mounds only hinted at a deeper secret—of a temple built in a time before recorded history. And now, section by section, mound by mound, it was being excavated, cataloged, and then reburied to continue its preservation.

Some sections—such as the one the man found himself standing in at this moment—had been uncovered and reburied once before.

Simply by existing, *Göbekli Tepe* had upset the apple cart of modern theories on human development. It had also become an inspiration for dreaming about what new and incredible things might be discovered—what hints of bygone cultures might be uncovered, layer by layer within the Earth, or perhaps under its oceans. There was more history hidden right beneath our feet than we ever imagined possible.

The man could understand why this site was so intriguing. Such grandeur. Such beauty. Such *history*.

He stepped away from the stone pillar, bowed his head slightly out of respect for that history, then gripped the wooden handle with both hands. He raised it above his head, and brought the head of the sledgehammer down with a solid, immutable strike directly to the base of the pillar. It took three more strikes to rend the stone to rubble, and to break through.

The man glanced around. This was noisy work, and he needed to remain unnoticed and undisturbed.

The site was protected by a contract security team—not much better than mercenaries for hire, in the man's opinion. But they were currently being distracted on the site's far perimeter, pulled away by the antics of children using American fireworks to put on a spectacular show. The man occasionally heard the pop and bang and saw the burst of colorful light from a bottle rocket exploding in the Turkish sky. It was like American Independence Day. Glorious.

The noise and the spectacle, as well as the cunning of the Turkish children in evading arrest, would give the man the distraction he needed, and more than enough time to complete his task.

His employer had given him precise instructions, and so far everything had been exactly as described. The man liked for things to go as planned. He was prepared for any contingency, of course, but this was better.

He knelt before the rubble that now lay at the base of the pillar. All that history, reduced to so much chipped stone, dust and debris. A shame. The man felt a twinge of regret over it, then brushed the stone aside to reveal the chamber.

This space was ancient beyond reckoning—but its contents were not.

The man hadn't been given every detail about the origin of the package, but he knew that it dated to no older than perhaps the early '90s, when *Göbekli Tepe* had first been unearthed. Here, among the carved stones of the ancient temple, lay a modern artifact. Something that was also ancient, in its way, despite being only three decades old. Something that would change the course of human *destiny* just as much as *Göbekli Tepe*, itself, was redefining human *history*.

Again, the man didn't have every detail. But he knew enough. He knew his employer, and he knew what went on in that lab, buried in its own secret place. The man knew a lot of secrets, and he was good at weaving the bigger story from small fragments.

This small fragment—a remnant from decades past, buried on the site of thousands of years of history—was one more piece in a larger puzzle that the man's employer had been putting together for most of a century.

So many measures of time, overlapping, influencing each other, and wrapped up in one little package.

Another burst of fireworks from above, and the man's work was briefly lit by shades of red and green.

"Hey!" someone shouted from behind. "Hands where I can see them!"

The man hesitated for only a second, then left the package at his feet as he stood and turned, slowly and cautiously, his hands raised.

This was an unfortunate turn of events, and the man regretted what came next.

The guard turned on a flashlight, which kept the man from seeing any details, but it was obvious there was a weapon.

"Put the hammer down!"

The man glanced at the sledge hammer, still in his left hand, raised above his head. He'd nearly forgotten he was holding it.

He stooped to place the tool on the ground. As he had anticipated, the guard tracked his movements with the light, and likely with the weapon as well.

The man stood, leaving the hammer at his feet.

"Put your hands on your head and turn around," the guard said.

The man did as he was told, putting both hands on the back of his head, then shifting his position, pivoting on his right foot while raising and stepping with his left. The maneuver placed the handle of the hammer between both of the man's feet, woven between them at an angle. The toes of the man's left foot slid under the wooden shaft. The segment of handle just under the heavy hammer head pressed against the man's right ankle.

The guard approached and put a hand on the man's right shoulder. "Do you have any weapons?"

"No," the man said. Though this was technically a lie.

The guard started to pat the man's sides, his pockets, the folds of his clothing. He would find nothing of interest. "What are you doing here? Did you... did you just *destroy* that pillar?"

The man saw no reason to lie. "Yes," he said. "I was hired to do so. To retrieve the bundle at my feet."

The guard shifted the light to the ground. "What is that?"

"Something old," the man said. "Not as old as this temple, but in today's world it may as well be."

The guard peered at the man. "Something's not right about you. I'd better call Sarge."

"Unfortunately," the man said, with genuine regret, "that will not be possible."

He twisted suddenly, kick backwards with his right foot while pivoting on his left, bringing his ankles together to hold the handle in a pincer move as he spun. This caused the hammer to swing around in a tight, controlled arc, slamming into the guard's ankles with brutal force, toppling him toward the ground.

The guard screamed in pain and the man's hands shot out with lightening speed, gripping the guard's wrists, tilting them upward just as the guard's weapon fired. The man crouched quickly, using his bodyweight to bring the guard's wrists down with him. He spun, twisting and crossing the guard's wrists over each other painfully.

The guard cried out and released both the weapon and the flashlight.

The man rolled, dragging the guard forward and slamming him face-first into the ground. It was a brutal impact, as the soil here was covered with fresh shards of broken stone as well as the native gravel and rock. It seriously dazed the guard, and his nose and mouth were dripping blood.

The guard dropped to the ground in a heap as the man released his wrists.

The man stood over the guard, who was slowly struggling to regain his senses.

Wanting to give his enemy some sort of hope, some sort of chance, the man hesitated. This gave the guard a moment to recover, then to notice his weapon and flashlight near at hand. He reached toward them, grasping, frantically trying to regain the upper hand.

The man had picked up the sledge hammer by this time, however, hefting it against his palm. As the guard crawled toward the weapon, his hand stretching and grasping desperately for it, the man brought the hammer's heavy head up, letting it hover for a moment in the air. He adjusted and tightened his grip, then brought the hammer down in a perfect arc to smash the guard's right hand.

The guard screamed in agony.

"I regret this, my friend," the man said. "You sound American. Are you American?"

The guard was screaming and cursing, rolling onto his side and holding his pulped right hand against his chest as he fumbled with his left for something in his pocket.

"As a fellow American, I want to say that I respect you as a brother. But you serve a purely capitalist regime, my friend. And the consequences of a life spent uncaring and unfeeling toward the plight of others... well, I want you to know that I will personally redeem you for this. I will take on the burden of your sins, and I will balance the ledger on your behalf. God will see you in paradise, my friend, do not worry."

The guard was fumbling with a small radio, holding it close to his face with a trembling hand. "S-sarge! Dispatch! Anyone!"

"Farewell," the man said, raising the sledge hammer a final time, dropping it in a quick and controlled swing, bringing an end to the guard's suffering and fear as the hammer struck his skull with a brutal, sickening impact.

The man dropped the sledge hammer then, letting it fall to the ground inches from the quivering body of the guard. He stooped, retrieved the bundle, and tucked it into the inner pocket of his jacket. He zipped the jacket up, pulled the dark hoodie over his head, and then sprinted away from the scene.

An alarm sounded, likely the result of the guard's final defiant act—his call for help.

Good for him, the man thought, smiling. *His final act was not in vain.*

As floodlights were brought to bear on the site, as the body was discovered and a search team was hastily organized, the man made his escape. He leapt and scaled the side of one of the trailers used as personnel quarters, then jumped to the security fence, swinging deftly over it and landing in a crouch on the other side. The maneuver would have been worthy of an Olympic medal, but it was routine for the man. His fitness and readiness regime would have put any Olympian to shame.

Now on the outside perimeter of the ancient site, beyond the security measures and far from the eyes of the search team, the man set a pace that would put miles of distance between him and this place. He would rendezvous with his transport in sixteen klicks. A brisk run over rough terrain, but he could handle it easily.

He ran, and the Turkish night was still filled with the sights and sounds of fireworks as the man became indistinguishable from the darkness enveloping the hills and terrain surrounding *Göbekli Tepe*.

CHAPTER ONE

NOW | Historic Crimes Headquarters,
Manhattan

Dr. Dan Kotler—anthropologist, author and speaker, pseudo celebrity and occasional FBI consultant—was not a fan of meetings. He was also less than fond of bureaucracy.

Especially *pointless* bureaucracy.

Though, as he considered it, any other kind might be as rare as comets.

This bit of governmental side show playing out before him, however, was very necessary.

Kotler was but one among many, in a gathering of representatives from both the private sector, the echelons of government, and the entire alphabet of US law enforcement agencies, all surrounding an immense, ring-shaped table that would have sparked envy among King Arthur and his knights. Which, as Kotler thought about it, was a somewhat appropriate analogy for what was happening here.

Or maybe the "Council of Elrond" was a better metaphor. The assemblage in this room was representative of all the dwarven and elvish kingdoms of US government and law enforcement, powerful corporations, and leaders in academia, with a mission statement as fantastic as the premise of any fantasy novel Kotler had ever read.

Seated next to Kotler, on his left, was FBI Agent Roland Denzel: Kotler's partner for the past five years. Though for six months, recently, Kotler had ducked out of his consulting work with the FBI, on a furlough of sorts. The events of the past month, however, had brought Kotler back around. Literally and metaphorically.

To Denzel's left sat Agent Danielle Brown, the new head of Historic Crimes—formerly a fledgling division of the FBI. Brown was Denzel's replacement for the leadership position. The verdict was still out on whether this was a good thing or a bad thing, but Kotler suspected the reality wasn't as black and white as that.

To Kotler's right sat Dr. Elizabeth Ludlum, the new second-in-command for Historic Crimes... and Kotler's ex.

Though he wished, very much, that this last part were not true.

Kotler had no small measure of responsibility for the current state of their relationship, however, and he accepted that responsibility, and the consequences of his decisions, with as much resolve as he could muster. He was the one who had put things on pause. He was the one who had gallivanted off on a Don Quixote-like quest to tilt his lance toward the windmills of the Jani and the Novensiles. It was Kotler who had swung a wrecking ball into their romance, and he was willing to accept that he may just have lost her forever. Best to move on.

Still, she smelled wonderful.

Standing at a podium at one end of the room was Kendell

Young—a rare bird in halls such as these. Young was famous worldwide as a YouTube and social media influencer. In a very short span of time, Young had gone from broadcasting out of his bedroom, chatting about books and politics and marketing as practically a religion, to attending A-lister parties and dining with heads of state, influencing everything from fashion trends to government policy.

Young's net worth was effectively incalculable at this point. But "unbelievably wealthy" wouldn't have been a wasted description, from Kotler's assessment. In fact, Kotler suspected that Young's wealth was quite a bit higher than any public records might indicate, and that it was not entirely dependent on his social media influence or his diversified holdings.

More than financial wealth, however, the one thing Kendell Young seemed to cultivate and draw to himself most was power.

Or perhaps *influence* really was the better term.

Young seemed to have the sort of influence that allowed him to ask for, and get, anything he wanted. He could sway public opinion, making or breaking a business with a casual comment or errant expression, or galvanizing his followers to a specific cause or goal or political candidate with a soft plea and a charming smile, accompanied by a few words of almost folksy common sense and wisdom. Though, as Kotler saw it, that common sense and wisdom was tinged with misinformation and dubious conclusions.

Kotler, however, seemed to be in the minority.

In the brief span of time between Young entering the public eye and today's notably heady meeting, the influencer had amassed a fortune and an army of supporters, with friends among the most elite and powerful personalities on the planet. He held a position of sway and power—albeit unofficial— among nearly every major government of the world.

Including the United States.

Perhaps more disturbing, however, was a fact that was not public knowledge.

It was something that Liz Ludlum and Agent Brown had discovered about Young, and a fact that Kotler found both plausible and immensely problematic.

Kendell Young had taken over as head of the Novensiles, after its former leader—Richard Kotler—had been forced to cut ties and flee.

Richard Kotler. Dan Kotler's own grandfather. A man whom Kotler had thought was dead and buried for decades, but who turned out to be very much alive. And possibly in better health and with a greater level of physical fitness than Kotler himself.

The Novensiles were a rogue faction of a secret order known as the Knights of Jani. For centuries, the Jani had accumulated and amassed power and wealth, using both to nudge history in a general direction, toward some hidden goal no one but they could fathom.

The Order had tendrils in every world government, and likely every major corporation in history. If any item, action, or institution represented the power to sway human destiny, the Jani likely had a part in it. And certainly had an interest in it.

The Novensiles had emerged more recently, within the past couple of hundred years at most. Dissatisfied with the Jani's quiet, hidden influence over the world, the Novensiles wanted to use the amassed power and wealth of the Order to *reshape* and *redefine* humanity. History—always determined by the winners—would be their *product*. They would craft and reshape and engineer it to favor them, to empower them to rule, and to usher humanity into a millennium of service to their goals.

Their moniker—the *Novensiles*—wasn't even the only

name they used. In fact, the faction used several names in a variety of languages: *Novensiles, Alihat Iadida, Diathan Ùra,* and many others. A string of names in a plethora of languages, modern and ancient, all translating to a single idea that drove everything the Novensiles did.

All of their names translated to the same thing: *The New Gods.*

Over the past seven months Kotler had withdrawn from everyone and everything he cared about, in pursuit of the Novensiles. He wanted, more than anything, to find a string to pull that would unravel the fabric of the organization. He was aware that this would effectively be an attack on the Jani—an organization that was powerful and influential beyond belief. But there was a lot driving him to pursue this.

Not the least of which was Kotler's own grandfather.

Seven months earlier, Kotler had learned that his grandfather was alive and well. A little too well, in fact. Richard, a member and leader among the Jani, was also the secret head of the Novensiles, until he was ousted and sent on the run, as a result of Kotler's interference with his plans.

Richard was forced to go underground, leaving a void in the Novensile's leadership that, it was now obvious, Kendell Young was more than willing to fill.

It was difficult, however, to decide which was worse: Richard Kotler's role with the Novensiles and their plans, or his role in manipulating his own son's research in the most vile way imaginable, for his personal benefit.

For decades, Richard Kotler had used his power among the Novensiles to coerce Cristoff Vellar—the former business partner of Kotler's father, at Vellar-Kotler Genetic Research, and the ersatz guardian of young Dan and Jeffrey Kotler—into using the business as his personal healthcare provider.

More than that, Richard had turned a section of Vellar-Kotler into a mad scientist's dream.

In violation of any number of international and US treaties and laws, not to mention every conceivable form of ethics and morality, Vellar-Kotler had engaged in an off-the-books human cloning program. Richard Kotler had used the technology emerging from this program to prolong and even enhance his own life.

At 94 years old, Richard was almost in better physical shape than his own grandsons, thanks to the miracles of fringe science.

And now, Richard was out there, somewhere, with 36 genetic samples, taken from the tombs of gods and kings, extracted from archaeological sites all over the world. Kotler had inadvertently assisted in handing those samples over to Richard and his people, and now he lost sleep wondering about the consequences.

There was no way to know for certain Richard's plan for the samples, but it was a sure bet that he intended to use the Vellar-Kotler cloning technology. From there, Kotler could conceive any number of ways in which these clones could be used as symbols and tools that would allow Richard to complete whatever plans were running through his twisted mind.

All of that had, in part, contributed to what was happening here and now, in this very conference room, located in what had become the official HQ for the newly reinstated Historic Crimes.

"When I look around this room," Young said, smiling and scanning the people seated around the conference table, "I'm really impressed by the potential I see. I'm also impressed by the accomplishment. This could be one of the biggest inter-departmental task forces in the history of the United States. At least, that's what they tell me," he flashed a sparkling grin at some of the higher-ups in the room, who all nodded solemnly.

Everyone in the room was aware of how unusual and unlikely this was: A fellowship of representatives from disparate organizations, many of which might have conflicting goals and protocols. It shouldn't have worked. It shouldn't have been possible. And yet...

Kotler scanned the table, marveling at this gathering of people who held sway over so much power on the world stage: Senators, CEOs, the uber wealthy, and of course agents from among the most powerful law enforcement agencies in the US.

It was quite a collection of power and money. But not everyone present was impressed by Kendell Young.

Seated just to the right of the podium was Senator Arania Acosta.

Agent Brown had filled Kotler in on Acosta's role in all of this, as well as the things the Senator had learned and revealed from her interactions with Kendell Young.

Young's involvement with the Jani had become obvious once all the pieces came together. And it wasn't much of a leap to figure out that he was a Novensile—his methods and philosophies practically demanded it.

Acosta, on the other hand, was still a mystery in progress. As one of the Senators who had been abducted from the Senate floor in broad daylight and on live television, Acosta had become embroiled in something well beyond her seat and position. And particularly beyond her experience. Someone was using her—manipulating her by keeping her isolated and dependent on the people who had helped her rise to power. She'd been systematically isolated since the abduction, her every public appearance carefully controlled and contrived to shape public opinion, and her work within the Senate itself compromised and dictated by an outside influence.

She had turned to Liz and Dani for help.

That, by extension, meant that Kotler was obligated to help her, as well. By his own choice, of course, but he would take that responsibility and commitment no less seriously. He owed that much to Liz.

How he would be able to help, of course, remained to be seen.

The other familiar face on the Oversight Committee, and another that was not merely smiling and nodding at Kendell Young's every word, was Ethan Patterson, the industrialist billionaire and founder of Athena Astronautics, among hundreds of other businesses and corporations.

Patterson had reached out to Kotler a month earlier, recruiting him to help investigate the murder of an archaeobotanist who had been working for him out in the Mojave Desert. Patterson had contracted the man to search for a rare plant—the source of a drug that Patterson could use as part of his mission to liberate humanity from its dependency on the Earth, and to carry colonies out among the stars.

It was the sort of lofty and ambitious goal that bordered on science fiction, but by Kotler's estimate, Patterson was just the sort of man who could actually pull it off.

The plant—known as *makry ypno*, or "long sleep"—had been an import. It was brought to ancient America by an errant crew of Greco-Roman sailors and shared with the local indigenous tribes. The plant had grown, hidden, in a network of lava tubes in the mountainous region of the Mohave Desert. Kotler and Denzel had been instrumental in finding it, and in defending it from a team of mercenaries, bent on harvesting it to sell to an unknown party.

Though Kotler suspected he knew exactly who that party was.

Shooting, bullet dodging, and scaling precarious rock faces

without the proper gear had ensued, but ultimately Kotler and Denzel had survived, and rescued a severely injured FBI agent to boot. It had been a win all around.

Patterson had informed them that he'd been approached by the Jani multiple times over the years, in an attempt to recruit him into the Order. He had also revealed that he'd been invited to join the Oversight Committee for the reboot of Historic Crimes.

None of this, Kotler suspected, was a coincidence.

Judging from the passive, almost bored expression on Patterson's face as Young spoke, however, it seemed clear that Patterson was not beguiled by Young's charms. Or, at the very least, he wasn't buying whatever Young was selling.

Kotler's relationship with Patterson was a bit untried, but both Kotler and Denzel agreed it was better to keep the billionaire technologist close, to see if he could be an ally. Or to mitigate his impact as an enemy, if it came to that.

Likewise, Agent Brown and Liz Ludlum expressed a similar perspective about Senator Acosta. It was unclear how much they could trust either Acosta or Patterson, but it was very clear that either could be an invaluable resource. And it was better to keep an eye on them, either way. Friends close, enemies closer, and the undetermined closest of all.

Kendell Young had chattered on all this time, and Kotler refocused, mentally coming back to the room, turning to hear what the influencer had to say.

"As we move forward into a new era," Young said, his tone weighted with metered gravitas, "I feel confident that the resources we've dedicated to Historic Crimes will allow us to not only preserve history, but to make the entire world a safer place. The record of Historic Crimes, to date, has been impressive. As just a small division of the FBI, it has aided in the prevention of numerous world threats. Terrorists have been stopped. Harmful viruses have been halted. Dangerous technologies have been safe-guarded. What started as a means of solving crimes involving arti-facts of historic significance has evolved into something that makes the world a safer place to live. And that is something we all need."

Young smiled as he looked pointedly around the room, taking in each face, assured of everyone's agreement.

He hesitated when he came to Kotler.

His expression flickered briefly, and there was something there that Kotler couldn't quite read, but it hinted that Young wasn't a fan.

Or was that Kotler's imagination?

Kotler had never met Kendell Young before today. He'd watched him on YouTube a few times, but his content wasn't what Kotler typically enjoyed. Young was very marketing focused, to the point of treating it as a life philosophy. It was clear that marketing was something of a religion to the man—both a lens for viewing the world and a tool for shaping it.

If Young disliked Kotler, he'd hardly be the first. But given that Young had usurped Kotler's own grandfather among the Novensiles, it wasn't hard to figure out what the problem might be.

Of course, names and family relations were generally kept secret in the Order. It was entirely possible that Young had no idea that Kotler was Richard's grandson. He might have a completely different reason for disliking Kotler, though there was no real way to know what that reason could be. Not yet.

Given the number of off-the-board pieces that nevertheless influenced the whole game, Kotler had to assume Young had information he was keeping close to his vest. Information that, Kotler knew, was probably dangerous, and would likely rear up to bite them all in their collective butts at some point.

Whatever it was, Young's expression passed so quickly that

it almost didn't register. If not for Kotler's well-honed ability to read body language, he might have missed it entirely. So perhaps it was nothing more than a struggle to remember Kotler's name, or some other innocuous thing.

One could only hope.

"But it's time we take things to a new level," Young continued. "Historic Crimes, as a small division of the FBI's White-Collar Crimes department, has never had the sort of reach or resources it needed to tackle global threats. It's remarkable how much the division was able to accomplish, given its limitations. But that brings us to here and now."

"With the establishment of this Oversight Committee, and the inclusion of experts, academics, and agents from the entire spectrum of law enforcement and beyond, we have now assembled the most elite team of resources in the history of the planet. And the scope of Historic Crimes has evolved as well. The charter has been extended and expanded. We no longer settle for merely policing theft, we now actively search out potential world threats, particularly those that leverage historic sites, artifacts, or historical documents to tip the balance of power. We have become guardians of history, and protectors against the dangers that may be hidden there. Ladies and gentlemen, welcome to the new Historic Crimes."

He raised his hands and smiled as he said this, the sort of polished-white grin that would have made Tom Cruise blush with envy. Most of the room erupted into applause, and Young soaked it in, nodding and waving, thanking everyone.

Kotler watched.

Young's eyes flicked to Acosta and then scanned across the room to Liz. He passed his gaze, then, onto Kotler. For that brief instant their eyes locked, and something was transmitted. Something Kotler wasn't yet sure about, and couldn't quite translate. But it was the first real slip in Young's well-crafted demeanor.

Kotler recognized it instantly.

Young knew who Kotler was. It was now a certainty.

What that meant, however, and would it lead to, remained to be seen.

"WHAT CAN you tell me about Kendell Young?" Kotler asked, sipping coffee from a ceramic mug.

Kotler, Liz, and Agents Roland Denzel and Dani Brown were all seated in a local coffee shop, just blocks away from the Manhattan FBI offices. Or, Kotler mentally corrected, the floor of the FBI offices that was now officially Historic Crimes HQ. At least until it was moved somewhere new. Young had made it clear that he wanted the whole thing to be completely autonomous, expanding the unit's footprint in addition to its charter.

"Wildly popular YouTuber," Liz said. "Though he's built kind of a media empire from there. He has a whole staff of people who produce content now, but he's still a pretty constant part of it all. He posts on Instagram more than most teenage girls."

Kotler smiled at this, and Liz returned the smile, briefly, before reverting back to a neutral expression, eyes averted.

Things were still a little uncomfortable between them. Kotler's fault, he remembered.

"He's got tendrils in everything," Agent Brown added. "He's in thick as thieves with basically anyone who has any influence over people. Celebrities, government types, even a handful of Saudi princes."

"Do we know his agenda?" Denzel asked.

Dani shook her head. "Not fully. But Senator Acosta has been helping us gather intel."

Kotler considered this. "Dangerous for her," he said.

"Same danger she was already facing," Liz replied. "She's been through a lot."

"The kidnapping," Denzel said, nodding.

"More than that," Liz replied. "Young has had her increasingly isolated for months. Her own people are working for him. Cameron Michaels included."

"Her boyfriend?" Kotler asked.

"And her campaign manager, head of staff, you name it," Liz said, nodding.

"Wasn't he one of the abductees?" Denzel asked.

"Yes," Dani replied. "A mole. We think he helped orchestrate all of it."

Kotler shook his head, wondering at the layers of complexity and duplicity that had to have gone into the abductions. Having people on the inside was a given. It was something that the task force still running the investigation had been looking into. Cameron Michaels might have gotten a pass, inadvertently, because he'd not only been one of the abductees, he'd been one of the "heroes" of the event. His relationship with Acosta might also have played a role in camouflaging his involvement.

How far back did Cameron's part extend?

"Do we think Young had anything to do with Acosta getting elected?" Kotler asked.

"I'd put money on it," Dani replied. "He's using her. She's popular. Cute. And she has a lot of sway with the younger crowd. Especially the would-be socialists."

"Interesting," Kotler said, thinking and sipping his coffee. He glanced out of the coffee shop's large front window, taking in the bustle of the Manhattan street. People moved along on the sidewalk at the usual frenetic flow. Life in the city moved constantly at pace, with no real concern over the secret machinations of a social media influencer turned global powerhouse, or anyone else, for that matter.

"What do you think it means?" Liz asked.

Kotler glanced up, meeting her gaze.

She was looking at him as she used to. Curious, maybe a little admiring, though that could be wishful thinking on Kotler's part. She had always respected his work, and the way he thought. It was their personal lives that Kotler had wrecked.

Still... he'd take any olive branch.

"I think Young has been playing a long game, and I think Historic Crimes has always been a part of it."

Liz nodded. "We agree," she said, glancing at Dani. "But I'm not so sure he had such a direct role in the original charter. Your grandfather used his own pull to influence the founding of Historic Crimes, but we're still not sure why."

Kotler sighed. "I think I know." He looked at the faces gathered around the table, all watching him intently. "Richard has been hunting for certain historical artifacts and documents, as part of whatever he's planning. I believe his role with the Jani was becoming compromised as his leadership of the Novensiles forced him into certain decisions and series of events. His access to the Jani's network for finding and procuring ancient artifacts was being narrowed. Having me tied to the FBI, with the Agency's resources, helped to open things up a little. I think our caseload for the past five years hasn't been as random as we might have thought."

Denzel was holding his coffee mug in both hands, letting it hover just under his nose. "You're saying your grandfather has been influencing our caseload all this time?"

Kotler shook his head. "Not all of it. Not every case. But yes, mostly. I feel pretty certain that our work has been nudged, at least. So many of our cases... well, to be frank, they've involved me, directly."

"It's been noted," Dani said. "It was something I was asked about dozens of times as I went through the vetting process for... my new role." She glanced quickly at Denzel, who waved the whole thing off and continued to sip his coffee.

"I was asked about this a lot, too," Denzel said, lowering his mug to the table. "And what could I say? I kept telling them what I knew. I thought for sure that someone would put the nix on having Kotler as part of Historic Crimes, and that they might even launch a criminal investigation. But it just..." Denzel waved a hand and made a sound, indicating things had fizzled out. "Never happened."

"Yeah," Dani added, "I'll be honest, Dr. Kotler, I couldn't understand why you were getting off so easy."

Kotler winced slightly, as much from Agent Brown's formality as from the implications of her statement.

Like Kendell Young, it was clear that Agent Dani Brown was not a Dan Kotler fan. Despite sharing similar names, Kotler had resolved himself to the sad fact that they would not be "name buddies." A tragedy, of course.

But in some ways Kotler could understand why Dani didn't care much for him. He represented an outside influence on the agency she'd dedicated her life and career to serving. From everything Kotler knew about Agent Brown, she liked the rules and structure of the Bureau. She liked bringing order to chaos. And Kotler could be a disruptive, chaotic influence. He didn't think or behave like an agent. He wasn't under any chain of command. He was a free agent, completely self-sufficient and capable, even insistent, on determining his own course. Orders or no orders.

So, pretty much the antithesis of everything Agent Dani Brown stood for. Conflict was inevitable.

"I wouldn't say 'easy,' exactly," Kotler replied. "Every time something happens, I get grilled and pestered and restricted. But yeah, I take your point. By now, I figure I should at least be in a cell somewhere, waiting for someone to finish scouring every pixel of my personal history. Especially after everything that went down at Vellar-Kotler. The company has violated more international treaties than I even knew existed, and my name is on it. But beyond some pretty uncomfortable questioning, there didn't seem to be much scrutiny over it. No real consequences. Even when they restricted my travel, they removed the restriction after barely any time had passed. I had a guardian angel out there, somewhere."

"Your grandfather," Denzel said.

Kotler shrugged. "Maybe. It seems like the best bet. But then, here we are again. Richard is in the wind, but I'm still being brought back into Historic Crimes, even though I'm not sure Kendell Young really wants it that way."

"We had a little to do with that," Liz said, exchanging glances with Dani. "We made it a condition for the two of us to come onboard."

Kotler glanced at Dani, who wasn't making eye contact. He suspected she went to bat for Denzel, out of solidarity for her former boss, but may have only included Kotler for Liz's and Denzel's sakes.

"I get the impression that Young would have pushed back," Dani said. "But couldn't."

"Couldn't?" Denzel asked.

"I think we had him over a barrel, for one reason or another," Dani replied. "I'm not sure how." She shrugged. "There's still a lot about this we don't know."

"At least now we're starting to see who some of the players are," Liz said. "I think Dani and I were put in charge of Historic Crimes so Kendell could keep an eye on us."

"And use us," Dani said. "He has an agenda, for sure."

"So we'll have to keep an eye on him right back," Denzel replied. He glanced at Agent Brown. "I know you're in charge..."

She held up a hand. "Consider yourself the lead on the Kendell Young investigation," she replied. "I have my hands full with running this new joint effort. I'm buried in bureaucracy. Coordinating with other agencies is enough of a headache, but dealing with the civilians makes me want to shoot someone."

"Let me guess," Kotler grinned, "Ethan Patterson?"

Dani made a sour face. "He trusts no one, dictates all terms, and I'm not sure putting a gun to his head would force him to compromise if he doesn't see a benefit to it," she said.

Kotler chuckled and nodded. "That sounds about right. We're still working out whether we can trust him, but if we can take him at his word, he's not one of the Jani. And he seems to have some pretty pure motives for the work he's doing. That whole thing in the Mojave Desert—finding the *makry ypno* plant—Patterson legitimately wants to use it to help humanity get out among the stars. The drug his company is refining and testing from it is going to make that possible, along with a ton of other benefits to humanity. I'm in the 'sort of trust him' phase."

Dani nodded, accepting this, and then turned to Denzel. "And you, Agent Denzel? What was your impression of him?"

Denzel considered before speaking. "I don't trust him yet," he said. "But he hasn't lied to us so far. Everything he's told us has checked out. But he's more Kotler's asset than mine."

"*Friend*, Roland," Kotler said. "When civilians connect with someone we say 'friend,' not 'asset.'"

"Whatever you want to call him," Dani said, locking eyes with Kotler, "we need to get him figured out. And soon. I want to know who we can trust on that Oversight Committee. And who we can't. So far, the trust list is very, very short. We can't afford wild cards."

Kotler nodded, draining his coffee and standing. "Alright. I'm meeting with him this afternoon. I'll find out what I can."

He was about to turn and leave, but hesitated. He looked back to Liz. "Hey, can we... would you want to come with me?"

Liz glanced at Dani, then back to Kotler. "Ok," she said. "I'd like to officially meet Ethan Patterson, anyway."

Kotler nodded, exchanged a quick and knowing glance with Denzel, and then escorted Liz out of the café.

On the street, Kotler called for an Uber, which arrived in minutes. So far, he and Liz had simply stood beside each other, mostly in silence, and this continued during the Uber ride.

It just didn't seem like the right time to start talking. Not yet. Things were still awkward.

But the conversation was coming.

CHAPTER TWO

ETHAN PATTERSON's Manhattan apartments were not far from Kotler's own. The difference, as far as Kotler could determine, was that while Kotler owned an impressive flat that occupied the entirety of one floor of his building, Patterson owned an *entire* building, plus the buildings on either side of it. During Kotler's research into the man, he had discovered that Patterson owned large swaths of city landscape all over the world, plus beachfront and mountain estates and tracts of land that included chunks of desert and open plains filled with farms, livestock, windmills and solar panels. All of Patterson's power was produced by sustainable tech—something that impressed Kotler a great deal.

The man was committed to his cause. And that cause, at least on its surface, was humanity's next evolution as citizens of the universe, not just this small part of it.

Kotler and Liz exited the Uber and stood for a moment at the foot of Patterson's building.

"Impressive," Liz said.

"I tried to buy an apartment in this building, when I first came to Manhattan," Kotler said.

"Oh?" Liz looked at him. "It didn't work out?"

"The owner at that time denied my application to the association," Kotler said, looking at her and smiling. "He said I was 'new money,' and they wanted to keep a certain element out of the building."

"Nice," Liz said, smiling and shaking her head. "Where is he now?"

"He died about twelve years ago. Ethan Patterson bought the building from his estate, along with pretty much every other property the family owned in Manhattan and throughout New York State. I don't know for sure where they all went, but they don't live in the city anymore."

"So Patterson... he's the real deal. A billionaire."

"Multi-billionaire," Kotler corrected. "And becoming more multi- all the time. He owns hundreds of businesses worldwide, big and small, and most are aimed at some specific segment of his primary interest. He's known for buying out small tech companies, along with their patents, and turning them into support for Athena Astronautics."

Liz considered this. "Space travel." She shook her head. "It doesn't seem like it could be real."

"Oh, it's real," Kotler smiled. "I couldn't guess at his timeline, but judging from the pattern of acquisitions he's made over the past fifteen years, he's showing signs of being close. His acquisitions are picking up pace, too. Especially in fields like cryogenics and bio-stasis. The *makry ypno* was an important piece in all of this. With it he can create an organic, self-perpetuating stasis system, which will be crucial for getting humans off Earth and out to planets beyond our solar system. It's... well, it's just amazing."

"You sound like a fan," Liz said.

Kotler shrugged. "I guess I am, in a way. The science behind this is fascinating. But beyond that, it's such a grand and ambitious plan, and Ethan is essentially bootstrapping it from the ground up, and without any form of government assistance."

She shook her head. "I just wouldn't have thought you'd be into something like space travel, considering what you do for a living."

Kotler laughed. "Well, don't forget, archaeology isn't my only field of study. I also have a Ph.D. in Quantum Physics. It was a much tougher degree for me, but I..."

He hesitated.

Liz gave him a concerned look. "You what?" she asked.

He glanced at her, hesitated, shook his head briefly. "I... thought it would do my mother proud," he said. "She was a physicist. And my father may have been a geneticist, but he had a thing for archaeology. Sort of a side pursuit."

"Sounds familiar," Liz said gently.

Kotler nodded. "I guess when it comes down to it, we're more the products of our parents' influence than we might expect."

Liz was watching him, and Kotler could read in her expression a note of sympathy and caring. But as he watched, her expression hardened slightly, became wary and guarded.

She's not sure she can trust me, Kotler thought.

And it broke his heart.

But he knew he deserved it. He wasn't entirely sure she could trust him, either.

If there was going to be any hope of repairing the damage he'd done to their relationship, he was going to have to commit to a long, slow road. But even then, Liz might not want to go along. It was possible, Kotler knew, that he'd done too much damage, and there was no going back.

"Should we go up?" Kotler asked, glancing up at Patterson's building, rising above them.

Liz nodded, and the two of them entered the lobby, leaving the conversation and the unasked questions on the sidewalk behind them.

Ethan Patterson was not the only tenant in the building, despite owning the place. There were at least a dozen units, on dozens of floors, owned by tenants who controlled an astonishing amount of wealth. Patterson's personal living quarters occupied the top two floors, and Kotler and Liz were escorted up to these in a private elevator, serving only that suite.

When the doors opened, they were greeted by Stavros, Patterson's personal valet.

"Dr. Kotler," Stavros said, bowing his head slightly. He turned to Liz and bowed again. "And Dr. Ludlum. Mr. Patterson is expecting you both."

Kotler and Liz exchanged glances. "Both?" Kotler asked. "I mean, I know I had an appointment, but I only invited Liz along at the last minute."

"Mr. Patterson tends to be... informed," Stavros said as he turned and bid that they follow.

Again Kotler and Liz looked at each other with questioning glances and then followed Stavros up a set of ornate steps to the second floor of Ethan Patterson's apartments.

Once again, Kotler noted a distinct motif in Patterson's decor—a heavy Ancient Greek influence that spilled over from paintings and tapestries to marble columns and statuary. There were also displays of bronze helmets and weapons, mostly Roman in design, and busts of ancient Greek philosophers.

Of particular note, Kotler observed a bust of Marcus Aurelius, the famed Roman emperor and stoic philosopher.

Kotler suspected Patterson was, himself, a dedicated practitioner of Stoicism. A practice the two of them shared, if it was true. And if that was the case, it could provide a bit of insight to help Kotler get a better read on the man.

Patterson's was as brilliant as he was wealthy, but he eschewed most personal publicity. When he spoke in public, it tended to be focused on his companies and his mission. Interviews with the media invariably centered on whatever the latest innovation was, among his multitude of businesses, and how it furthered the mission to get humanity to other worlds.

He was incredibly open about everything his business was doing. But when it came to his private life, there was little useful information to be found. Patterson kept quiet about nearly every personal detail. Which made him all the more intriguing to the media, and to the population at large. He had attained a sort of cult following as an eccentric futurist.

Though there were many in the media who considered him a crackpot—tilting at the biggest windmill in the universe in a manner that would have made even Don Quixote shake his head in sympathy for the poor fool.

Kotler, however, thought Patterson was no fool at all. In his dealings with the billionaire, he could confirm that the man was, indeed, very eccentric. He certainly had his quirks and his passions. But he was also something unexpected—brilliant to a near-frightening degree. There were very few people in the history of humanity who had as much potential to literally change the fate of the species, but Ethan Patterson was most certainly one of them.

Kotler and Liz were ushered into a large sitting room and offered beverages, which they both accepted. Kotler had learned on his first encounter with Patterson that any beverages on offer were bound to be of the very expensive and rare sort. Well-aged, expensive whiskeys and fine wines were poured as freely as soda from a fountain, and Kotler was absolutely willing to graciously accept.

On offer today was something unidentified but clearly in the "expensive and rare" category. Kotler savored every sip.

It was late afternoon, edging toward evening. Though the windows were closed, there were no shades, and there was still plenty of natural light. This had shifted toward golden-hour hues, casting the apartments in a warm and inviting glow that contrasted nicely with the predominately white marble accoutrement adorning the space.

Patterson seemed to prefer large windows, and lots of light, which Kotler took as a good sign. Those who preferred to practice their craft in shadows and darkness, with the shades pulled so no eyes could see, were often up to no good. And while having large windows and lots of light was no guarantee that Patterson wasn't, himself, a shady character, Kotler still took it as a positive indication that the billionaire was not actively trying to hide something. It was a psychological observation only, with nothing yet to back it up. But Kotler appreciated it all the same.

Once Stavros left them, retreating to attend to things elsewhere, it was only a few minutes before Patterson entered the sitting room and greeted the two of them. He shook Kotler's hand and then turned to Liz, smiling.

"I was hoping to meet and chat with you soon, Dr. Ludlum," he said, shaking her hand.

"Same here," Liz replied, smiling and grasping his hand warmly. "The Oversight meeting was a bit of a whirlwind."

Patterson rolled his eyes. "The only wind in that room was coming from Kendell Young. I thought he'd never get to the point! He's a big fan of himself."

Liz laughed. "I've only known him for a short time, but I think that's true."

Patterson gave her hand one more affectionate shake and released it. "Before we start, call me Ethan."

"Ethan," Liz said, nodding. "And you can call me Liz."

"Excellent," Patterson said.

"Ethan," Kotler said, cautiously, "How did you know Liz was coming with me to this meeting?"

Patterson waved this away and turned, retreating to a wet bar at one corner of the sitting room. He poured something amber into a glass and raised it to his lips. After a sip and a pause of appreciation, he replied, "I'm having everyone on the Historic Crimes staff followed, twenty-four-seven."

"You're... what now?" Kotler asked. "Ethan, is that a good idea?"

"Most of them are aware of it," Patterson said. "Especially the CIA and NSA folks. And I think Kendell knows. But yes, it's a good idea. I don't know most of these people, and if I'm going to be any part of this, I need to understand everyone who was in that room. I'm also having deep background checks done on everyone. I'll provide these to the rest of the Oversight Committee. Everyone agreed to this when they signed the NDAs and contracts," he sipped the contents of his glass. "I made it a condition for me to join this thing."

Kotler nodded at this. It was true, the contracts included a clause that allowed for background checks. So everything about it should have been expected. It was just that it felt somehow unusual for Patterson to be the one conducting them.

Patterson was the sort of man who needed to know everything he could about the people he worked with. Kotler wasn't yet sure what this revealed about the man, but he filed the information away.

"I wouldn't mind seeing the background on Kendell Young," Liz said, suddenly.

Patterson looked at her, then smiled. "Consider it done."

Kotler sipped his beverage, savoring the warmth of the bourbon, then shook his head. "Well, this has certainly gotten off to a different footing than I was expecting. And I don't mind saying, Ethan, I'm not entirely sure how I feel about being followed."

Patterson shrugged. "Not sure what to tell you, Dan. It's happening, regardless of how you or anyone else feels about it. But let's move past it for the moment and get to business. I have the first case for the new and improved Historic Crimes." He turned and motioned for them to follow him as he walked across the sitting room and through a door on the far side.

Dan and Liz glanced at each other and followed.

Through the door they entered a room that would look more at place in a NASA facility than in a Manhattan high-rise apartment. Monitors dominated one entire wall, a bank of large displays forming a grid. Along the walls to the left and right were tables and work surfaces, festooned with equipment both familiar and incomprehensible. Kotler recognized analysis equipment from a wide range of disciplines.

Patterson was, as far as Kotler could tell, the only person accessing this room. Could Patterson really be so brilliant? He'd been rumored to have mastered multiple scientific disciplines, in his pursuit of freeing humanity from isolation upon just one planet. Kotler was seeing hints that the rumors might be true.

"Watch the monitors," Patterson said as he lifted a tablet device from one of the tables. He tapped and swiped at the screen, and suddenly all the monitors came alive, physically moving on the walls, working in tandem to shift from their grid pattern to form one large, seamless screen. The immense display filled with new images, including photos of a dig site, scans of documents, surveillance video, and a number of spectrographs, pulsing as data played through.

It reminded Kotler of the "murder boards" that were popular on police procedurals, on television.

"Three days ago, someone created a distraction at the *Göbekli Tepe* dig site in Turkey," Patterson said. "They had a bunch of local kids set off enough fireworks to put Disney World to shame, and used the chaos as an opportunity to desecrate one of the stone columns within the site, smashing it to pieces with a sledgehammer." A red dot appeared on the screen and wobbled wildly around a photo of a sledgehammer among a small pile of stone rubble.

Kotler felt his heart sink. "They destroyed one of the columns?" he asked. "Do we know why?"

"It gets worse," Patterson said. The photos shuffled on screen, and one came to the foreground. It depicted a body, bloodied and grotesque, its skull caved in. The man was wearing a tactical uniform with the word "SECURITY" stitched in yellow letters on its left breast.

Beside the photo, another image appeared. A human figure, though it was hard to believe this could be true. Whoever it was could only be seen as a silhouette against a sky lit by the multicolored bursts of nighttime fireworks. Spectacular looking enough on its own, but it was the position of the figure that made it impressive. The photo, which appeared to be a still lifted from a security camera, showed the man in the act of leaping over one of the high fences surrounding the site. His body was ramrod straight, and at an angle to the top rail of the fence. The figure had a hand on that rail, holding himself outward and upward, obviously hurtling the fence in an arc and avoiding the rolls of razor wire at its top as if they were not even there.

"The man who did this took an object with him when he escaped," Patterson said. "Something he retrieved from the column."

"Do we know what it was?" Liz asked. She stepped forward, examining the photo of the dead guard. She leaned in, not hesitating to examine the grotesque details. An occupational advantage, Kotler decided. He was used to dead bodies, but they were typically in a state of ancient decay, not quite as fresh as this.

"We're not entirely sure," Patterson replied. "But after it was discovered I had my people do an audit of the entire site. Everything that isn't currently buried for preservation, anyway. They found evidence that someone hacked the servers used by the research team. Not a lot of evidence, however. Whoever did this had the resources to go in clean and leave very little trace. My people are among the best in the world at this, and they almost overlooked it. But there was enough of a trace that we at least know something has been erased."

"Erased?" Kotler asked. "What could anyone possibly want from those servers? It's a team of archaeologists and academics, and all under tight scrutiny from the Turkish government. It's not like there are state secrets kept there."

Patterson nodded. "True. Which is one reason this is so intriguing, isn't it? And alarming, according to the Turkish government. They've requested assistance."

"They have?" Kotler asked. "That doesn't seem like them."

"They were... prompted to request assistance," Patterson said, his expression flat.

"You pulled some strings," Kotler replied. "Why?"

"One of my companies is providing technical support for the dig, as a way to test some next-generation scanning equipment. Those servers that were hacked were *my* servers. And that guard who was murdered... he's a contractor, but the security team was hired by my people, at my request. That makes him one of my people."

Kotler was watching Patterson's face and saw traces of real concern, real outrage.

The more Kotler interacted with Patterson, the more the

billionaire revealed about himself. And it was all adding up to make him even more of an enigma than when Kotler knew nothing about him at all.

"You want Historic Crimes to find who did this," Kotler said.

"Yes," Patterson replied. "And to retrieve whatever it was that this man stole. I also want to recover the data, if we can."

"That's... not exactly my expertise," Kotler replied.

Liz spoke up then. "Historic Crimes has one of the most elite technical teams on the planet, thanks to this reboot." She looked from Kotler to Patterson. "Mostly thanks to you, Ethan. Right?"

Patterson smiled wryly and gave a nod.

Liz nodded. "I'll have them start digging, looking over the logs and anything you're willing to share with us. I also want to see the forensic report on the victim, along with any details captured from the scene."

Patterson nodded. "It's done. You'll have it all when you get back to your office."

He turned to Kotler. "I want you and Agent Denzel in Turkey."

"I'm willing and able," Kotler said. "And happy to go. But if you want Roland, you'll need to go through channels."

"Channels?" Patterson asked.

"Agent Brown," Kotler replied, then nodded to Liz. "And Dr. Ludlum. You may be part of the Oversight Committee, Ethan. But they run the department."

Patterson blinked, nodded, then smiled. He turned to Liz. "Dan makes a good point, and I apologize. I'm overstepping. Will you talk to Agent Brown on my behalf? Let her know what's happening and pass on my... request?"

Liz flicked her eyes to Kotler and then back to Patterson. She smiled. "Of course, Ethan."

Patterson nodded again. "I'll forward the entire case file to you, so you can pass it along to Agent Brown."

They talked for a few more minutes, ironing out details, making arrangements to chat again soon. There were still questions to be asked, Kotler felt, though some might never have answers.

When they left, Kotler and Liz were talking again. Casually. Excitedly.

It wasn't quite 'old times,' but it was close. It was a start. And Kotler was so grateful for it that he refused to analyze it. It was just good to have some common ground with Liz again—something that could to use as a bridge. There was no telling where that bridge would lead them, but Kotler was willing to cross it when they got to it.

Their Uber dropped Liz off first, at Historic Crimes headquarters, and continued on to Kotler's apartment.

He began mentally prepping for a trip to *Göbekli Tepe*.

He couldn't shake the feeling that whatever this mysterious man—the Olympic-grade gymnast with a sledgehammer—had taken from the dig site, it was going to bring more trouble than even the murder and the desecration of the world's oldest temple.

Kotler wasn't sure why, but something within him warned that things were about to escalate.

CHAPTER THREE

SANLIURFA, Turkey

KOTLER AND DENZEL arrived in Turkey via a private jet, courtesy of Kendell Young.

"Is he just showing off or something?" Denzel asked, hoisting a backpack out of the overhead bin and slinging it over his shoulder.

Kotler, too, was pulling his pack from the storage above. "I think so, in a way," he said, "He wants to show that the new Historic Crimes has resources we didn't have before. With part of the Oversight Committee operating from the private sector, we won't have to deal with some of the bureaucratic limitations we had when we were strictly under the wing of the FBI."

Denzel scoffed, and led the way out of the plane, down the steps to the tarmac below.

Kotler smiled, shaking his head and following his friend down and out, making his way to the terminal. They would move through customs quickly, thanks to their FBI credentials. A small perk that, Kotler noticed, Denzel didn't eschew.

Sometimes he wondered if Denzel preferred to be uncomfortable. In the years they'd worked together, the agent had gone out of his way to avoid letting Kotler pop for upgrades, out of pocket, to their flights and hotel. He worried it might read too much like bribery or currying favor.

The man's sense of propriety was strong.

Having access to private jets and other amenities was going to take some getting used to, Kotler suspected.

Kotler himself, however, was perfectly willing to accept some creature comforts. In his career, Kotler had endured more than his fair share of cramped flights on rickety aircraft, depositing him into the middle of God-only-knew-where, so that he could sleep in hovels and yurts, if he was lucky, or on dirt and rocks, fending off snakes and insects and the occasional human who was up to no good.

Kotler endured all of this discomfort and danger just so he could crawl into claustrophobic tombs and spider holes, teeming with all manner of creepy-crawlies and disturbingly macabre things. For this reason, Kotler had decided long ago that any time he had the opportunity to pop for more luxurious accommodations, he would. It was less about luxury or reward and more about establishing balance.

Of course, it helped tremendously that he could afford such luxuries. Most archaeologists could not. But projects he found himself involved in tended to get a few "upgrades" when he came onboard, from which everyone would benefit. Given that he was often on the outs with the archaeological and academic community, providing some creature comforts on site was his way of salving a few wounds. Sometimes it even worked.

They had landed at a private terminal at Sanliurfa Airport, about a fifty-mile drive South to *Göbekli Tepe*. They would have accommodations at the site itself, which was located in a barren plateau, but was conveniently close to several small cities, including Sanliurfa itself. This meant the site was well-stocked with everything they'd need, and not far from civilization, in a pinch.

Quite a switch from most of Kotler's ventures to archaeological sites. Downright comfy, in most respects.

They rented an SUV at the airport and made the drive to *Göbekli Tepe* in just over an hour, winding their way through the barren Turkish landscape between the airport and the dig site. Winter had been particularly harsh on the plateau, but the spring was bringing some promise. Temperatures could become brutal after dark, but in the current season they were tolerable with a light coat. Kotler had made sure that he was prepared in either case, having packed something versatile that could be layered over his clothes, if he needed a bit more insulation.

These trips with Denzel, to remote locations, often ended up with Kotler shivering and severely under-dressed. It had been a tradition since they'd met, nearly five years earlier, when Denzel had purposefully provided Kotler with only a light jacket to fight back the bitter cold of nights in Pueblo, Colorado.

Upon arriving at the perimeter of *Göbekli Tepe,* Kotler and Denzel were greeted by a security contingent. The security team had set up a barricade and fence along the road leading to the site, to prevent anyone from casually wandering in. Security had been tightened more than usual here, since the murder and the theft, which was understandable.

Kotler and Denzel were asked to step out of the SUV and submit to a search before they would be allowed to enter. As the guards were inspecting their vehicle, the two of them stood in the shade of a temporary structure serving as a guard shack.

"Well shave my back and call me slick," a familiar, gruff voice said from behind them.

Kotler and Denzel turned in unison, and Kotler grinned wide as he recognized the immense mass of man approaching them.

"I don't believe it," Denzel said.

"Sarge!" Kotler exclaimed, greeting the man as he approached.

Will "Sarge" Canfield stomped forward, a cigar in his teeth, his actual mouth barely visible under a massive red handlebar mustache. The man was as burly and muscle-bound as Kotler remembered, wearing an olive-green A-frame under-shirt tucked into tightly belted camouflage pants, which were in turn tucked into well-tended combat boots. Sarge had a shock of ginger hair crop-cut close to his scalp, matching his mustache in tone if not volume. Altogether, Sarge's grooming and wardrobe made him look almost like a parody, or like the comic book version of a former jarhead. He could appear almost comical, at times. Especially when unfurling one of his colorful aphorisms.

But Kotler knew from experience, Sarge was no one to take lightly. He was legitimately tough and skilled. He knew his work, knew his men, and knew how to get results. In Kotler's estimate he was one of the best there was at what he did. And what he did tended to involve bullets flying.

"You two boys are like a bad case of jock itch, you just keep comin' back."

The man held out one of his beefy hands, and both Denzel and Kotler endured the rock-crushing grip of a handshake. "Good to see you boys again. I never properly thanked ya for getting me and my boys set up for all them government contracts."

Kotler flexed his fingers to get blood flowing again. "Is this one of those?" he asked, nodding in the general direction of the site.

Sarge shook his head, puffing smoke from his nostrils. "Nah. This one's a private contract. We were brought in by that billionaire fella. One who wants to launch us all into space on rockets." He waved dismissively toward the upper atmosphere.

"Ethan Patterson?" Kotler asked.

Sarge nodded. "That's the one."

That seemed to track, given Patterson's involvement with the site. He would want to hire a team to protect his invest-ment. But it seemed an odd coincidence to Kotler, that Patterson would hire Sarge, of all people.

Kotler had met both Sarge and Denzel at around the same time, five years earlier. Sarge had been hired by another billion-aire technologist then—Mark Cantor, founder of Zelot—to provide security for a dig site in Pueblo. That site had provided evidence of a viking presence in North America, deeper into the interior of the continent than anyone had ever imagined.

Following the theft of the Coelho medallion, and the kidnapping of Dr. Evelyn Horelica, Kotler had become involved and embroiled in an FBI investigation that led to the discovery of a terrorist plot. It had been Kotler's first adventure alongside Agent Denzel, and not something that was easy to forget.

Sarge had resurfaced a few years later, again providing security for another dig site. This time it was a newly discov-ered Mayan tomb, and Kotler was once again assisting the FBI, investigating the murder of a Broadway star who, somehow, had been found sealed in that tomb. Sarge and his men had helped Kotler and Denzel to thwart a plot to unleash a deadly, ancient virus on the modern world.

These were heavy circumstances to meet and befriend

someone under, but Sarge and his merry band of ex-military mercs for hire had proven to be good, reliable men, capable of handling themselves under fire and in tense situations. Because of this, Denzel had arranged for Sarge to become a trusted resource for the FBI and other government agencies, and had set him up to bid on some very lucrative government security projects. It was the least they could do, considering how often Sarge and his people had helped to save both Kotler and Denzel, not to mention the entire world.

Sarge yelled for his men to hurry up with their inspection and ordered them to bring the SUV around when they were done. He then led Kotler and Denzel to a barracks area, where they were shown to a small trailer that would serve as home during their stay.

"You each get your own bedrooms, yer highnesses," Sarge growled, chomping on the cigar.

"Good," Denzel said, clearly relieved. There was a history of people putting Kotler and Denzel in a room together. The *Odd Couple* had a better roommate arrangement.

Kotler nodded. "Great. We can stash our stuff and then get to the site. I'd like to see..."

"No can do, Kotler," Sarge interrupted, crossing his arms and leaning against the door frame.

Kotler blinked. "What do you mean?"

"Site's locked down until morning. Turkish government wants one more look before you muckity-mucks muck it up."

Kotler and Denzel exchanged glances, and Denzel stepped forward. "We were invited here by Ethan Patterson. He said he'd cleared everything with the Turkish government."

Sarge nodded. "Maybe so. But they want one more look, and they get it. Nobody's paying me enough to cross 'em, so I ain't."

"When will we be able to get on the site?" Kotler asked.

"Tomorrow morning," Sarge replied. "First light."

With the air of having given the final word on the subject, Sarge opened the door to the trailer and stepped outside. He leaned back in for a moment and added, "Chow's in an hour. Won't be no more until morning. Miss it and you're eating out of the vending machines tonight, 'less you want to drive back to Sanliurfa. I suggest you don't miss it."

With that he closed the door with a slam, leaving Kotler and Denzel to look at each other in confusion.

"Ok," Denzel said. "I wasn't expecting a delay."

"Neither was I," Kotler frowned.

"Is there anything else we can do, without having access to the site?"

Kotler thought for a moment. "We should visit Ethan's tech team. See if we can learn anything from the surveillance. We might also question some of Sarge's people."

Denzel nodded, and the two of them stashed their things, freshened up a bit, and stepped out of the trailer.

"And chow, of course," Denzel said.

"Oh, absolutely," Kotler replied, his stomach rumbling in agreement.

CHAPTER FOUR

ETHAN PATTERSON SPARED NO EXPENSE.

That was the impression Kotler got as they approached the surveillance trailer. Though it generally resembled the trailer that served as their quarters, in overall shape and design, that was where all similarities ended. Unlike their own quarters, this building was festooned with an array of satellite dishes and antennas, with cables running to it from all directions like kudzu vines, choking off any possibility of sunlight reaching the occupants.

To Kotler it looked like the nest of some bizarre, terrifying technological beast. Or perhaps the remains of a cocoon, from which some techno-horror had erupted. It felt ominous, resting here with a backdrop of Turkish hillside and peeks of the ancient stone structures and pillars of *Göbekli Tepe* in the dig site beyond. Out of place in this, the most ancient site known to man. It was a contrast that made Kotler contemplative.

Ominous or not, though, this was clearly the nerve center of security and communications in the camp. Kotler and Denzel were cleared by a guard at the door and allowed entry.

If the view from outside was tech-macabre, inside the trailer was pure techno porn. Everywhere Kotler looked, there was an orgy of advanced electronics—displays and interface terminals, monitors showing views from all throughout and all around the dig site. Cables inside the trailer were neatly arranged and organized, with lines labeled for the equipment they served.

On a few of the screens there were top-down feeds from satellites, which appeared to be live views. Kotler knew that Ethan Patterson's company, Athena Astronautics, had its own array of satellites orbiting the Earth. And Ethan certainly had the pull to get permission from the Turkish government for an operation such as this.

"Dr. Kotler?"

They turned to see a woman entering the main space from one of the side rooms. She smiled and held a hand out to Kotler. "I am Isoken Edo," she said, her accent a mix of British and, Kotler thought, one of the African dialects, though he couldn't yet place which one. "I am Mr. Patterson's head of security for this site."

Kotler took her hand, giving it a gentle shake and returning her smile. "A pleasure to meet you." He motioned to Denzel. "This is Agent Roland Denzel, from the FBI."

Isoken turned her attention to Denzel and extended her hand. Denzel took it, though Kotler noticed a slight hesitation. Was that a flush in his partner's cheek? He couldn't blame Denzel for finding Isoken attractive. She was a beautiful Nigerian woman, from what Kotler could tell, who exuded confidence and quiet authority. Just the sort of woman Denzel tended to be attracted to.

Kotler smirked, but said nothing.

"This way, please," Isoken said, motioning for them to

follow her to one of the rooms that would normally be used as a bedroom. This one, however, had little space for resting.

If the trailer was the nerve center of the site's security presence, this room was the brain stem. Every surface was obscured by one form of technology or another. A small, utilitarian desk stood in the center of the room, with a chair that could pivot and allow its occupant to take in her domain at a glance. In front of the desk were two folding chairs. Isoken motioned for Kotler and Denzel to sit in these and took her place on the pivoting throne at the center of the room.

"Mr. Patterson has given me instructions to cooperate with you fully, and to give you access to anything you need."

"That's great," Denzel said. "We'd like to start with any footage you have from the night the guard was murdered."

She nodded and turned her attention to the laptop on the desk before her. She tapped a few keys, then motioned for them to look at one of the larger monitors mounted to the wall off to their left.

"We do not have much," she said, in an almost apologetic tone. "Though there were cameras active around the perimeter, none were pointed at that specific location. They appear to have been adjusted to create a blind spot, several weeks before the murder occurred. However, we do have this footage of the man making his escape."

On the screen, a man dressed in dark clothing, including a hoodie pulled over his head, lept deftly up to scale the side of one of the temporary buildings, then catapulted over the fence in a move that would make a professional gymnast weep with envy, before landing on the roof of a truck parked close by. The move was so agile and quick, Isoken had to play it on a loop so they could study it. She slowed this down, and it was still incredible to see.

"So... he's a ninja?" Denzel said, leaning forward to peer at the screen, shaking his head as the man moved like lightning even in slow motion.

"Parkour," Kotler said, watching. "And he's good at it. Those are Olympian-level moves." He turned to Isoken. "That truck looks like one of the security patrols."

She nodded. "The man who was murdered was one of Sarge Canfield's team. Most of the on-site security personnel were dealing with the children setting off fireworks on the Eastern perimeter. Sarge had ordered three of his men to patrol the remaining site. Some parts of the site had no fences or barriers at that time, but this area was secured."

"Why?" Denzel asked.

Isoken sighed. "Unfortunately, I do not know for certain," she replied. "It has been secured by the Turkish government since it was reopened."

"Reopened?" Kotler asked. "What does that mean? Was that part of the site uncovered previously?"

Isoken nodded. "Decades ago, when *Göbekli Tepe* was first being explored. That portion of the dig site was unearthed and cataloged and then reburied."

"Reburied?" Denzel asked.

"Preservation," Kotler said. "Sites such as these have endured for thousands of years because they were buried and protected. Once they're open, exposed to atmospheric conditions and human contact, they can deteriorate quickly. Contaminants can get in and skew test results. In order to preserve sites such as this one for future exploration and study, the easiest and best thing is to simply rebury them."

Denzel consider this and shook his head. "Seems like a lot of duplicate effort."

Kotler smiled. "Redundancy is the purview of scientific exploration," he said.

"And of security," Isoken added. "I prefer to have redundant layers of security. But in this case, those layers failed us, and a man has died. In addition, one of the pillars was destroyed. Though there is some question about that."

"What sort of question?" Kotler asked.

Isoken did something on her laptop again, and the screen changed to show photos of the damaged pillar. There were signs of dried blood on the ground, remnants of the brutal murder that had taken place there. Blood spatter decorated chunks of stone, staining some of the jagged white edges of it.

Jagged white? Kotler thought.

He stood and moved closer, examining the photos for details.

"This isn't stone," he said.

"What?" Denzel replied. "What is it?"

Kotler glanced back to Isoken, who was watching him. "Concrete?"

She nodded. "It was done very well, matching seamlessly with the rest of the pillar. But it is definitely modern concrete, shaped and moulded to fill a void."

"No," Kotler said, shaking his head and raising a finger to hover near the screen. He ran it along the virtual pattern of one jagged edge of the broken concrete. "Not fill. *Create.* Someone made a void in this pillar." He was looking now at the base of the pillar itself, though from this angle he didn't have much of a perspective. "Do you have any shots of the pillar itself?" He asked.

Isoken sighed, and to Kotler it sounded exasperated. "We did. But the Turkish government has taken them. Deleted them from our servers."

"What?" Kotler asked, turning to look at her, his face perplexed.

"Why would they do that?" Denzel asked.

Isoken shook her head. "I do not know. But if these photos

here had not been duplicated for Mr. Patterson, they would be gone as well."

Kotler and Denzel looked at each other. "They've locked down the site until morning," Kotler said.

"They're burying something," Denzel nodded. "But what? And why?"

Kotler turned to Isoken. "What else do you know?"

Isoken leaned forward, her hands interlocking as she rested her elbows on the desk. "Mr. Patterson has a number of contracts with the Turkish government, giving him more or less free rein over this site. But as of this incident," she nodded to the screen, "some of that access has been revoked. Including live satellite coverage."

"But I saw satellite footage as we came in," Kotler said.

"Looped," Isoken said, her face hardening. "As if I would not notice."

"Wait," Denzel said. "You're saying that the Turkish government is *intentionally* looping that footage to fool you?"

She nodded. "Someone is, at least. But our preliminary investigation shows signs that access was granted via the security codes issued to Turkish authorities. There was an attempt to make this so that it couldn't be traced. It is clumsy, however," she said. "As if it was done in a hurry."

"Do you have footage from the days surrounding the murder?" Kotler asked.

She shook her head. "Erased."

Kotler again looked to Denzel. "We have to get onto that site," he said. "And we can't wait for morning."

Denzel exhaled and shook his head. "I have no jurisdiction here, Kotler."

"No," Kotler said. "But we do have permission. From Ethan." He looked at Isoken. "Of course, you're in charge."

"Sarge is in charge of the actual physical security," Isoken said. "But I do have overriding authority, if it's deemed necessary." She thought for a moment. "Mr. Patterson has given me a conflicting order. We are to obey the Turkish government's demands, but I am also supposed to assist you and Agent Denzel in any way you need."

"Did he give you any orders about what to do if such a conflict arose?" Kotler asked.

Isoken smiled, her bright teeth a brilliant contrast against her dark skin. "I believe his words were, 'Use your best judgement.'"

Kotler smiled and looked to Denzel, who was shaking his head.

"I don't think we're getting any chow tonight," Denzel grumbled.

CHAPTER FIVE

RICHARD KOTLER STOOD and stared at the culmination of a lifetime of sacrifice and work. Before him spread an array of secrets and technology that would empower him on the next phase of this plan.

The world was about to change.

Richard felt a presence enter the room from behind. It was eerie and unnerving, how the man moved. He had perfect control over his body, at all times, and could flow like water into a space. Richard knew that the only reason he'd sense the man's presence was because the man wanted it that way.

The man—Travis Bell—was a marvel of physical prowess, and a master of martial arts and gymnastics, and practically every physical skill Richard had ever heard of. A master of Parkour, having won multiple championships, he could move as fluidly through the air as a fish in water. Bell was one of the Jani's finest assets.

Recruiting him to Richard's cause had been both a coup and a challenge.

Travis Bell was a true believer. He operated on behalf of the

Jani, though his cause and his personal mission were entirely of his own design. He operated by a strict personal moral code, was deeply opposed to capitalism, and saw himself as a new-era warrior fighting in defense of American sovereignty.

An odd man, with a frankly bizarre perspective. But highly useful.

If he discovered that Richard had once been the head of the Novensiles, there was no telling what he'd do. So Richard kept Travis Bell in the dark as much as possible.

"You've retrieved the artifact," Richard said without turning.

"I have," Bell replied. He stepped forward and placed the bundle on one of the tables nearby.

Richard moved to it, and forced himself to reach out slowly, his movements measured and controlled. It would not do to openly display his eagerness.

He unwrapped the bundle and stared at its contents.

It was an anachronism in more ways than one—as out of place in this modern, cutting-edge lab as it had been while buried and protected in the base of that pillar in *Göbekli Tepe*, the most ancient site in the world. For its anachronistic nature, however, it still held the potential to shape human destiny.

If its contents survived, it would open the door to a new era for humanity.

"You've done very well, Travis," Richard said, lightly brushing his fingertips over the artifact.

Bell said nothing for a moment, but stepped deeper into the facility. He inspected the rows of large, glowing tubes—chambers filled with a specialized formula of chemicals and nutrients.

"What's in them?" Bell asked, casually.

"You know what's in them," Richard replied.

"I don't mean the bodies. I mean the liquid. The substance you're using."

Richard studied Bell, then nodded. No harm in sharing. "It's a proprietary formula. Something my son invented, though the formula itself has been lost for three decades. There was enough on hand to accomplish this mission, but this is the last of it. We've managed to replicate it to a limited degree, and I have someone working on retrieving a substance that will help. There have been... complications."

"This has to do with the events in the Mojave Desert," Bell said flatly.

Richard was surprised. "How did you..."

"I hear things," Bell said, turning and facing him. "Rumors."

Richard felt a bit of cold dread ease into his spine.

"I know," Bell confirmed. "Who you are. What you're doing."

Richard prepared himself as best he could. He was old. In his nineties, though, his physiology was more akin to that of a man in his fifties, thanks to the work of Vellar-Kotler Genetics Research. His son's company had preserved, even improved Richard, extending his life and keeping him vital.

Richard was in good shape, and he could handle himself in a fight, if it came to it. But he stood no chance against Travis Bell, and both of them knew it.

"I support your cause," Bell said.

It was all Richard could do to keep from sighing audibly in relief. He kept his reaction in check, however. "And what cause is that?" he asked.

Bell motioned toward the chambers, spread in an array across the facility's floor. "The resurrection," he said. "Thirty-six gods, resurrected and placed back into power. They were once part of some global community, but now they are here. *American* gods."

Richard studied him, peering at him. "You do hear things," he said.

"I know a great deal more than most give me credit for," Bell said. "I've known for some time that you were a New God."

Richard winced at the term. "We prefer *Novensiles*. Sounds less pretentious."

"*Novensiles*," Bell nodded. "*Alihat Iadida. Diathan Ùra.* The New Gods. I prefer to call things what they are, in the plainest terms. And in English." He smiled at Richard.

And Richard, hesitating only for an instant, smiled back.

"Well, you haven't killed me yet, so I have to trust your sincerity."

Bell shook his head. "I don't kill unless I have to. And you've given me no reason to. I've looked into you. Currently you're on the outs with both the Novensiles and the Jani. But the work you're doing is aimed at loftier goals than either organization has ever pursued. And it's here, in America. I can see you creating a new world power. A new world order."

"We shy away from describing things in those terms," Richard said, frowning.

"It's what the Jani have preached as part of their mission since the earliest recorded history," Bell said. "But until that mission was brought here, to the United States, to the truly new world, it was an impotent dream. Only you have managed to revive it, with actual, literal life."

Again Richard studied Bell, then laughed and shook his head. "Travis, I must admit, it is refreshing to hear you say this. Welcome to the... team."

"The New Order," Bell said.

Richard shrugged. "Whatever makes you happy."

He turned then, back to the artifact Bell had brought him. "I'll have my people dig into this, but I can't thank you enough for retrieving it."

"What's on it?" Bell asked.

"Everything," Richard said. "All the secrets." He looked up at Bell again. "If you're truly onboard, there are other tasks that would fit your skills."

Bell nodded. "Count me in."

Richard smiled, and then on impulse he clapped Bell on the shoulder. "Son, I think you're exactly who I've been waiting for. And you're right. We're about to raise the dead here. The Novensiles wear the name 'new gods,' but we're actually about to bring the gods themselves back to life."

Travis Bell smiled at this, and Richard felt a sudden form of kinship with the young man. The sort of kinship he'd hoped to have with his grandchildren. But after Daniel and Jeffrey's betrayal, all hope of bringing them into the fold seemed to be lost.

As with most of Richard's life, however, there was a chance to start again.

Travis Bell might be just the surrogate son Richard was looking for. He might be the answer to a lot of Richard's questions.

He again clapped Bell on the shoulder, then picked up the artifact and led the way to the labs where technicians would pry every last secret from the ancient device.

CHAPTER SIX

Sarge hadn't been happy about being overruled on granting them access to the dig site, but he cooperated by arranging for the patrol for that section to be temporarily rerouted. This opened a window that would allow Kotler and Denzel to gain entry to the site, and an hour later they would make their escape.

"One hour," Sarge growled, peering down at them with the cigar strangled in his teeth.

"It's all we need," Kotler assured him.

"It's all you get," Sarge said, pointing one of his beefy fingers at Kotler's face. "And if you get caught in there, me and my boys had nothing to do with it. *Catfish?*"

Kotler blinked. "Do you mean *capeesh?*"

"I say what I mean and I mean what I say," Sarge growled, then turned and left them standing there.

"I've faced down terrorist cells I'd rather piss off more than that guy," Denzel said.

"Let's get moving," Kotler replied. "As soon as that window opens, I want to get in and out as quickly as possible."

They moved then, taking position behind one of the trailers closest to the point where they would make entry. They watched and waited, and sure enough Sarge's men received orders over the radio, calling them away.

The clock was ticking.

Kotler and Denzel sprinted across the path, keeping low and moving quickly. The sun had set, and it was dark enough in the camp that they were able to keep hidden in the shadows. But there were lights all along the patrol route, and for a brief moment they would be visible.

Isoken had assured them that the cameras pointed at this portion of the patrol route would be "malfunctioning" at this time. Kotler hoped she was right. Though he did eye the sky above, wondering if the blackout included the hundreds of micro-satellites above them, on loan to the Turkish government by Ethan Patterson.

They had no choice but to risk the sprint from shadow to shadow. Denzel held up a hand, inspecting the lit path in both directions, then motioned for them to make the run. They both leapt from their darkened hiding space, staying low as they raced to the shadows on the other side.

When they reached the fence, Denzel took out a small set of wire cutters, and made quick work of snipping three of the supporting wires. This opened a gap wide enough for them to each press through, and in moments they were inside.

Kotler had memorized the route to the smashed pillar, and even in the darkness he was able to navigate to it. After only a moment they came to the place and stood, looking at the site of the murder and the destruction.

This was the riskiest part of their plan.

In order to see what he needed to see, Kotler would have to turn on a light. He took out a small flashlight from his pocket and turned it to lantern mode. It was bright, nearly blinding in the darkness of the site, and he shielded it from one side with the cup of his hand.

Denzel took up watch, putting himself between the light and the road in an attempt to further mask it. "Get going," he whispered.

Kotler nodded, then crouched, running the light over the carnage of the site so that he could inspect it.

Except much of the carnage was gone.

"They took the broken stones," Kotler said. "Any trace of the cement. It's all gone. Even the blood has been cleared."

"What about the pillar itself?" Denzel asked.

Kotler turned his attention to the raw and irregular edge of the opening in the pillar.

He couldn't help pausing to admire the pillar itself. It contained reliefs of numerous token animals, including bulls and lions. Most striking, however, was the carving of a human figure with the wings and head of a bird.

Avian human hybrids were a common motif in nearly all ancient cultures, occurring even among those that would historically have had nothing to do with each other. In fact, separated by oceans and continents, the bird-man motif appeared simultaneously in not only Asian, African, and European cultures but also in Meso American sites. It was a curious and intriguing indication of the existence of some former civilization that predated known history.

Kotler was an avid student of comparative culture and mythology, and would love nothing more than to dig into the revelations of *Göbekli Tepe*. But their time here was short, and they needed answers.

He refocused and turned his attention to the jagged remnants of a small void in the base of the column.

This was certainly not concrete. The column was carved from the same soft limestone that composed the majority of structures in the site and across the region. It was as ancient as anything here. It appeared that the opening had been the result of some ancient damage, perhaps something impacting the column and creating a gap. This was later exploited by someone who went to great pains to match a concrete patch to the existing limestone.

The question was, who would have gone to this trouble? And why?

Kotler stooped, shining the light into the small opening, peering inside.

There was something there, tucked into a half-buried corner of the gap.

He reached in, brushing at the spot with his fingers, then pulled the object out and into the open. It was a piece of paper.

Kotler felt a shock, but recovered quickly. This could easily be some piece of trash, blown into the opening while no one was paying attention. It was probably nothing.

But when he examined it, he felt a chill go through him.

It was the scrap of a note. Most of the message was lost, and what was left was barely more than random words. But the note started with a greeting—a name.

Kotler shook his head, blinking, clearing his eyes. It could not be what he thought it was.

"Berrett," he said aloud.

"What?" Denzel asked.

"It's... it was my father's name," Kotler said, looking up at his partner.

Denzel shook his head. "What's your father's name doing on a piece of paper in an ancient pillar?"

Kotler wasn't sure. And he didn't have time to ponder it. Not yet. He tucked the scrap of paper into his pocket. He'd inspect it later.

For now, he stooped again, and this time took out his phone.

He turned on the camera and aimed it at the inner walls of the small chamber. He placed the flashlight on the ground, illuminating the inside of the stone void, and then felt around with his fingers. He watched the screen of his phone, using it to guide him, like a miniature periscope.

He saw flecks on the inside of the column. Grey splotches that looked familiar. He picked at one of these with his fingers, and was able to pull it away like a little grey scab, flaking off from the inside of the void.

"Got it," he said, holding up a blotch of dried cement. "Someone hid something here and used concrete to make it look like the pillar was complete. It must have been a gap in the base when they found it, back in the 90s. They would have known it was going to be buried, so it was a perfect hiding place for... something. Something small."

"Any idea what?" Denzel asked.

Kotler shook his head. "No. Not yet. But I think we have all we're going to get here."

Denzel nodded. "Kill the light. It's time to move."

THEY HAD RETURNED to their trailer, where Kotler placed the slip of paper and the remnant of cement onto a little table that served as a desk. A lamp illuminated the objects, and Kotler took photos of both. Given that the Turkish government seemed to be actively eliminating evidence from the scene, Kotler made sure that anything he documented was immediately replicated somewhere offsite and safe.

Having photographed both sides of the torn slip of paper, along with closeup details, Kotler now examined the note itself.

It was handwritten, penned in a looped cursive that Kotler was stunned to find familiar.

"This is my mother's handwriting," he said.

"Are you sure?" Denzel asked.

Kotler nodded, bending to look closer. "I've studied their journals, their letters, everything they've ever written. The vault at Vellar-Kotler had thousands of documents. It was all I had left of them. I'd know it anywhere."

"Can you make out what the note says?"

Kotler inhaled slowly and read the message aloud.

BERRETT,

It's done. "Manticore." This one goes to the potbelly hill. Please be careful.

"THAT'S IT," Kotler said. "That's as far as it goes."

"What does it mean?" Denzel asked.

Kotler shook his head. He studied it, turning it over. "Nothing on the reverse side. But it seems like instructions. Basically 'hide this in *Göbekli Tepe.*'"

Denzel shook his head. "How did you get to that?"

"My mother referenced 'the potbelly hill,'" Kotler said. "That's an English translation of *Göbekli Tepe.*"

"What does 'manticore' mean?"

Kotler inhaled and let the breath out slowly. "Well, mythologically a manticore was a beast that had the body of a lion and the head of a man, with a scorpion's tail for good measure."

"Sort of like the bird guy on that column?" Denzel asked.

Kotler thought for a moment. "Yes and no. These are two disparate mythologies. As far as I know, there's nothing resembling a manticore at this site or in local mythology. But the concept—the idea of a human-animal hybrid—that's similar enough to make me pause."

He studied the note a bit longer, then shook his head. "There just isn't enough here. I can't figure it out."

"It's fine," Denzel said, taking the note and the bit of cement and placing them in plastic evidence bags. He sealed these, writing the date and other pertinent information on them, and then stowed them in the bottom of his backpack. "Let's keep this to ourselves for now."

Kotler nodded. "I think we can trust Isoken Edo. And Sarge. Verdict is still out on Ethan Patterson."

"I'm going to play it safe and trust no one for now," Denzel said. "Something about this isn't sitting well with me."

"So, what now?" Kotler asked. "They're letting us visit the site tomorrow. We should probably go through the motions."

"Yeah," Denzel said. "We'll let them give us their story, and we'll pretend to go along with it. For now, I think we'd better grab some shuteye. We'll work this in the light of day. I want to track someone down who can give us answers about why the Turkish government swept in to cover this up." He huffed, then stretched, and Kotler heard a couple of pops from his neck and back. Then there was the sound of a gurgle from Denzel's stomach. "But first," he said. "I have to find those vending machines."

CHAPTER SEVEN

LIZ LUDLUM WAS STILL GETTING USED to her new duties as second-in-command for Historic Crimes.

So far, those duties had been similar enough to her prior role with the FBI. She was still in charge of the forensic lab, though now it was being reorganized to focus entirely on Historic Crimes cases. Liz had insisted, however, that it remain an overflow lab for FBI work, and for the NYPD. This was out of loyalty to her brothers and sisters in law enforcement, but it also served a more practical purpose—during times when Historic Crimes work was light, she could keep a robust staff engaged, occupied, and sharp. And, no small bonus, she and her department could continue to bring justice for people who had been victims of a crime.

That was the point of it all.

She more or less had the forensic lab and its staff set up as a self-regulating system. The rest of her job... that was more of a challenge.

She wasn't used to politics, and this new role had politics grafted into it, right down to its DNA.

For a start, there was a lot of back and forth that had to be managed between the various government law enforcement agencies. For departments and organizations that all purported to work for the same team and the same goals, there was a surprising lack of cooperation, communication, or even trust between them. Information, resources, and assets were often held close to the vest, and in tight fists, shared only in the most grudging fashion. Sometimes it was withheld altogether until someone higher up in the chain of command dropped the hammer.

It was a war of red tape and bureaucracy that Liz had never had to fight before and frankly found distasteful and tedious. She kind of hated it.

Dani, of course, had it worse.

As head of Historic Crimes, Agent Brown was on the front line. Liz got the ripples, but Dani dealt with the tidal waves. And so Liz had determined that one of her chief responsibilities, as second in command, was to take any pressure she could off of the shoulders of her boss and her friend. She would make Dani's job easier in every way possible.

Now, Liz just wished she could find someone to do the same for her.

She reminded herself that all of this was still pretty new. Historic Crimes had gotten a reformat, and an expanded charter, with new resources and new allies. Of course there would be some growing pains. But things would level out, eventually.

They had to.

Liz prayed to God that her optimism wasn't delusion.

She had just left her desk, after another round of phone calls with the CIA and NSA liaisons, and was ready for a break. Or to break something. Either would do.

As she exited the glass doors that segregated the forensic lab from the rest of the Historic Crimes offices, she paused for a moment to appreciate the bustle outside the doors of her comparatively docile domain.

The cubicle farm comprising the "ground floor" of Historic Crimes had been a bit empty and depressing for several months now. The FBI had shut down the department and reallocated its personnel and resources, following the events surrounding the abduction of several Senators and their staff. Historic Crimes had been instrumental in finding and returning the Senators to safety, but in the process some facts regarding Dan Kotler had surfaced.

Somehow, Vellar-Kotler Genetic Research—the company founded by Dan Kotler's own father—had become embroiled in these events. Worse, Dan's grandfather, Richard Kotler, had played a role. This had thrown suspicion on Dan, but it had also brought Historic Crimes into the crosshairs. Inquiries and investigations had ensued.

And then... they had stopped. Or, Liz reconsidered, they'd been swept away. Blind eyes were turned. Kendell Young had somehow gotten involved and had rebooted the program with new leadership and a new charter.

Now, with that new charter and the resources provided by the Oversight Committee, there were agents and operatives everywhere again. Some were FBI, but there were representatives from all the US law enforcement agencies in this mix. There were also civilian consultants of every description.

It was a menagerie of highly trained and resourceful people. An immense support network working to solve global problems and eliminate global threats that emerged from history like snakes from the underbrush.

When Historic Crimes was simply a fledgling division of the FBI, their scope was limited primarily to the things that fell within the Bureau's purview—white-collar crimes, mostly, such as the theft of artifacts and historical documents, but also the occasional murder and terrorist plot. It was a humble sort of beginning, but from those roots the division had achieved some remarkable wins. The bad guys—some *very* bad—had been thwarted. The world had been saved, more than once.

With the new charter, however, the scope of Historic Crimes was exponentially expanded. What had initially been a byproduct of the limited scope of one small division of the FBI was now the full-time focus of an enhanced, self-directed organization. There were now initiatives to track the movement of terrorist cells and bands of guerrillas hiding in tombs, temples, and pyramids worldwide. One team was tasked with tracking patterns of forgery for paintings and documents, on the hunt for a black market that might fund any number of despicable operations globally. Another team was actively tracking smugglers and pirates who were raiding archeologically significant sites, stealing from shipwrecks and other treasure-bearing locations.

Funds generated by such acts as tomb-raiding and art forgery had been funding terrorist organizations worldwide for decades. Historic Crimes was the first organization of its kind—created specifically to focus on and specialize in these sorts of actions, to stop and even prevent them before they could impact the world in negative or even horrific ways.

Liz's own forensic team had a directive to provide support in investigations tied to historical locations, artifacts, or events, especially murder investigations. Though the department wasn't limited to that. They had recently taken on new staff, trained in pathology and disease vectors, and the containment thereof, and had enhanced their technical forensics capabilities, thanks in large part to Ethan Patterson. Forensics was the heart of Historic Crimes, as far as Liz was concerned.

Historic Crimes, itself, was the first of its kind—a ludicrously empowered interagency initiative with nearly unlimited resources, both governmental and private, all aimed at scouring the world for historically linked threats and crimes, and eliminating them.

Liz felt the crushing weight of the responsibility of it all. And she knew that Dani did, too.

Liz wandered up the steel steps that swooped in a parabola to the second floor. The offices running along the catwalk were glass and chrome, with windows overlooking the Manhattan skyline and doors and blinds for privacy. There were conference rooms on this level as well, and it was in one of these that Liz found Agent Dani Brown, the new head of Historic Crimes, seated at a large conference table that was absolutely covered in folders, documents, digital tablets, and of course, Dani's laptop.

Liz knocked on the glass wall of the conference room, and as Dani looked up Liz asked, "Busy?"

"Always," Dani said, huffing. "I came in here so I could have more room to spread out." She waved a hand over the seeming chaos on the conference table.

Liz took it all in, then nodded. "So, coffee?"

Dani glanced back to the pile. "God, yes."

Dani locked the conference room and gave her assistant some instructions as they left, then she and Liz rode the elevator down to the ground floor of FBI headquarters. They chatted amicably, mostly about how busy they were, how many reports they'd read, just today, how many phone calls and video conferences and emails they'd had to ingest and respond to. Casual talk, but still tainted with work.

As they exited the ground-floor lobby, out onto the sidewalk, Liz paused just long enough to take in the sights, sounds, and smells of Manhattan.

She was a transplant here, but after more than a decade of living in the city, it all felt like home. She couldn't imagine leaving. Not anymore. But she still had that little small-town girl inside her who occasionally had to marvel at how *big* everything was here. How *busy*. Manhattan was a living, breathing organism that spread over an entire island, and it still amazed her sometimes that she was a part of it.

They wandered along, chatting about nothing in particular, until they came to the coffee shop. It was mid-afternoon, on a pleasant Spring-like day, but the shop only had a few patrons lingering out on its outdoor patio. Liz and Dani got their coffees and took a seat outside. Dani adjusted the umbrella overhead to block the direct sunlight, and they sat, sipping, letting what passed for silence in Manhattan wash over them like warm bathwater.

Liz felt a little numb. It was the sort of feeling she'd always gotten after a long day, her senses bombarded by noise and activity, and then suddenly met with stillness and quiet as she shut the door to her apartment and slumped to her sofa. This was a similar experience, though she could hear the sounds of traffic from the street, people chatting as they moved by on the sidewalk, music from the speakers mounted overhead. The white noise of Manhattan was comforting and healing in its own way.

The numbness was a tingle in her veins. She sipped her coffee, closed her eyes, and sighed.

"Busy," Dani said.

"Busy," Liz nodded, looking up at her. "I'm hoping it will slow down soon."

"It will," Dani said. "It has to." She shook her head, sipped her coffee, and looked at Liz. "You getting settled in?"

"Mostly," Liz replied. "There's bickering among the various liaisons, but I'm dealing with it. My department is running almost on autopilot, at least. I check in to make sure there's nothing to deal with, but my team takes care of everything."

"You'll get there with the rest, too," Dani said. "You'll build a process and a system."

"I hope so," Liz said. She shook her head. "I'm just not sure I'm cut out for this. Heading Forensics was in my wheelhouse. This?" She sighed.

"I know," Dani said. "But I also know you. And you have this."

Liz looked to her, and could see she meant it. This was encouraging. Not so long ago there was a question of trust between them. Both Liz and Dani had each suspected the other of potentially being on the wrong side. Things had changed, however. Amends had been made. Trials of fire had been endured. And at this point, they were each the only person the other thought they could trust.

"I got an email from Agent Denzel," Dani said. "He and Kotler are working the case in Turkey, but they're short on leads. The Turkish government has been interfering."

Liz squinted. "The government? Why? Isn't it mostly a murder investigation?"

"No idea yet," Dani said, shaking her head. "Denzel said they locked down the site and wouldn't let our people in until the following morning. By then, the Turkish police had removed all the evidence from the scene."

Liz considered this. "Maybe it's a professional jealousy thing? Dan and Agent Denzel are only there because Ethan Patterson requested it. Maybe they resent the intrusion?"

Dani shrugged. "It's anyone's guess, so far."

Liz nodded. "Anything we can do to help?"

"I've already pinged the Oversight Committee, updating them on the status and asking if there are any strings that can be pulled. I'm waiting."

Again, Liz nodded, then sipped her coffee. She peered out at the street, watching traffic move by. People were going about their day, moving from place to place, driving or walking as if they were totally unaware of things such as Turkish police and ancient temples and disrupted crime scenes.

She felt her phone vibrate in her pocket.

She fished the phone out and looked to see that she'd received a text message. "It's Senator Acosta," she said, glancing up at Dani. "She's asking if we can meet her at the 'usual place.'"

Dani frowned. "When?"

"Tonight," Liz said, holding up the phone.

"Tonight," Dani repeated. She sighed and sipped her coffee. "I was really hoping for a night off."

HEMINGWAY'S HAD A HEAVIER crowd than usual, but Liz was still able to snag their preferred table. It helped that she and Dani had cut a deal with the owner—a deal that mostly hinged on having some goodwill with law enforcement. The owner's father was a retired cop, which gave him a soft spot for the badge. But having a couple of FBI agents in your corner was never a bad deal to make, regardless.

When Liz and Dani arrived, they found that Senator Acosta was already sitting at their table, tucked into a corner and wearing large sunglasses and a scarf to hide her features. She couldn't have looked more like someone in disguise if she tried, but Liz figured there was little else she could do. Just getting here, without her usual escorts, was challenging enough.

Liz and Dani took their seats, scooting close enough that from any casual observer it looked like a "gals night out." This also had the advantage of allowing them to keep their conversation low, masked by the ambient crowd noise.

"Senator Acosta," Dani said. "Is everything alright?"

Acosta took off the sunglasses. Her eyes were dark and hollow. She looked as if she hadn't slept much recently, which Liz figured was likely true.

Senator Acosta was currently being "handled" by her own team, and at the request of Kendell Young. Acosta was a member of the Oversight Committee for Historic Crimes, and it was clear that this was part of some grand plan on the part of Kendell Young. The influencer's involvement with the Novensiles was something that fretted both Liz and Dani, but it was a constant, haunting nightmare hanging over Acosta.

"I had to get out," Acosta said. She looked nervous. There was a glass with something amber and dark on the table in front of her, and when she reached for it Liz could see that her hand was shaking. She raised the glass to her lips and drew a long sip before placing the glass back on the table.

"What happened?" Liz asked.

Acosta gave a quick bark of a laugh. "Cameron," she said, shaking her head.

Liz and Dani exchanged glances. Cameron Michaels was Acosta's chief aid, but he was also her handler. And, publicly at least, her boyfriend. Though the two of them hadn't had an actual romantic relationship for several months.

Dani squinted, leaning in toward Acosta. "Did he do something to you? Hurt you?"

Acosta looked up, her expression seeming almost shocked. "No! Sorry, no, nothing like that. He... he came by this afternoon. To my DC office. He was all stressed out and weird. Weirder than usual. There was someone with him. Someone I didn't know. He was... *huge*. Like a mountain with legs."

"Did he have a name?" Dani asked.

Acosta shook her head. "He told Cameron to leave, and when we were alone, he gave me something." She reached to her side and withdrew an envelope from her bag, placing it on the table in front of Dani.

Dani opened it and took out the contents—a series of photographs.

Some were of Acosta herself and appeared to be taken within her apartment. There were shots of her in the various rooms of her home, from high angles, indicating that these were hidden cameras. There were also photos of her from both her DC and New York offices, and in the back seat of a car. Generally, the message seemed to be that she was being watched everywhere. A warning.

Liz was looking at the photos as Dani placed them on the table and felt an icy dread in her stomach. If this stranger was sending her a message, it might mean things were about to get ugly.

Then Dani placed another set of photos on the table—an older couple, a man and a woman, with Hispanic features. They appeared to be in a grocery store, pushing a cart side-by-side.

Dani looked up at Acosta.

"My parents," she said.

There were more photos. A younger woman, who bore a striking resemblance to Acosta, was stooped and kissing a young boy on the cheek.

"My sister and my nephew," Acosta said.

Dani slid the photos back into the envelope and handed them back to Acosta. "What did he say to you?"

The Senator shook her head and put the envelope back in her bag. "He said he just wanted to remind me what was at stake."

Liz leaned back with a huff. She reached to the table to take her own drink and tilt it to her lips. The warmth of the whiskey was soothing, and she felt her nerves go. Something about all of this didn't gel. She ran through all of it in her mind, clicking details into place, seeing the hazy outline of some larger picture.

When she placed the glass back on the table, she shook her head. "This doesn't make sense."

"What?" Dani asked.

"The photos," Liz replied, motioning toward the envelope. She looked at Acosta. "This man—a stranger—he just gave these to you? Just like this?"

Acosta nodded.

Liz looked to Dani. "*Physical* photos? That's like something out of an old spy movie. Who would do that these days? He wants to send her a message, but he leaves her with evidence? Something she can take with her and show to the authorities?"

Dani scowled and shook her head. "Or to us," she said.

She stood from the table, looking around at the bar. Liz followed her gaze, and as they watched a man across the bar turned and walked out of the door.

Dani cursed and nodded toward Acosta. "Get her out of here!"

She rushed away from the table, her hand reaching to her side, where Liz knew there was a weapon holstered.

Liz also cursed. She patted the pocket of her jacket and found her FBI credentials. No weapons, but there might be some other way to help. She turned to Acosta. "We have to get you out of here. You can't go back to DC. Not yet. We need to find you someplace safe."

Acosta's eyes were wide, and she looked pale. "What's happening?"

"I think you and Cameron were being used to set us up," Liz said. "Come on!"

She slid out of the booth and held a hand out to Acosta, who took it.

Dani had followed the man through the front door, so Liz thought it might be a good idea to take another exit. Their arrangement with the owner gave them free access to the kitchen and back door. A quick nod to the bartender and there was no resistance as Liz dragged Acosta out that way now, through the kitchen and into the alley behind the bar.

From there they clung to the wall as they moved, keeping low, taking cover as they neared the sidewalk. Liz put a hand on Acosta's shoulder, holding her back before stepping forward and peering out into the darkened street.

There was no sign of Dani or the man she'd chased. There were people moving about on the sidewalk, but none seemed particularly interested in Hemingway's or anyone going in or coming out. Liz brought Acosta closer, and as a group of three people moved past the alley entrance, the two women joined close behind. Acosta was wearing the sunglasses again, though Liz thought that might seem conspicuous on the street at night. Still, Liz was wishing for some sort of disguise of her own at the moment.

They moved along, eventually splitting from the group they were using as cover and turning onto the street where FBI headquarters was located. They were a few blocks away, but at the moment Liz couldn't think of any safer place to go.

She paused for a moment, dragging Acosta into a small bodega, the two of them lingering near the door while Liz took out her phone and sent Dani a text. She wanted to make sure Agent Brown was updated on their destination.

She had just sent the text and was nudging Acosta to follow her when a man entered the bodega.

Liz's eyes widened when she saw that he was drawing a gun from inside his coat.

"Down!" Liz shouted, leaping to tackle Acosta. The two of them went to the floor just as shots were fired. The rounds struck the shelves of items just above the two women, raining debris down on them.

"We have to move!" Liz shouted, and she and Acosta crawled quickly around the shelves, crouched to their feet, and sprinted for the back of the bodega.

Another shot was fired, though to Liz it sounded different. More shots, and some shouting.

Liz realized that whoever was manning the sales counter had started firing back at the man. She worried about the clerk's safety, but for the moment she needed this cover. They took advantage of the chaos to get to the rear of the store, to push through into the backroom, and to find the rear exit.

They were close to HQ, but to get there they would have to run out in the open.

There wasn't much for it. Liz yanked Acosta along behind her, and the two sprinted at full tilt, passing startled civilians on the street.

Liz fumbled with her phone as she ran, managing to dial 911. "Shots fired!" she shouted into the phone. She identified herself and gave their location. "Be advised, there is an armed FBI agent in pursuit of one suspect, whereabouts unknown!"

The operator started to ask questions and give instructions in a calm voice, but Liz couldn't hear any of it. They were rushing desperately across the street, dodging cars, keeping low.

"Wait!" Acosta said as they reached the sidewalk on the other side. She pulled her hand away from Liz and then stopped with a hand on one knee. She held her side with the other hand, and when she took it away Liz could see it was coated in blood.

"Were you shot?" Liz asked, immediately reaching out, probing, looking to tend to Acosta's wounds.

Acosta shook her head. "When I went down, I banged against one of the metal shelves," she said. "It think it's a cut, but my side feels like it's on fire. It's... hard to breathe." She huffed, wincing.

"You may have a broken rib," Liz said. She looked around, frantically. "We're just a couple of blocks from the FBI," she said. She looked back at Acosta. "Can you make it?"

Acosta took a long breath and nodded. The two of them started moving again, racing as quickly as they could.

They hadn't made it a full block before a van suddenly drove up onto the sidewalk in front of them.

Liz immediately halted, stepping in front of Acosta. She held her hands out to her sides, but then quickly reached back into her pocket and took out her FBI credentials. She held these up, shouting. "FBI! Don't come any closer!"

There were still people on the sidewalk around them, but most were looking for places to hide. Liz stood with Acosta behind her, the ID raised high. It felt pathetic, but it was the last move. The only thing Liz had left.

Four men, dressed in black and wearing what looked like SWAT gear, had erupted out of the van, rifles raised..

"Call the FBI!" Liz shouted to anyone nearby. "My name is Liz Ludlum! This is Senator Acosta! Call—"

Shots rang out from behind them, and Liz and Acosta ducked to the ground as the armed men addressed the threat. Round after round was fired over Liz's head, causing her ears to ring.

In the next moment she was yanked to her feet and thrown into the van.

She thought she could hear screaming, possibly from Senator Acosta. More shots were fired, and in a moment Acosta was tossed inside the van alongside Liz. The door was slammed, and the van rocketed away from the scene.

Liz and Acosta huddled close, trying to push to the furthest corner of the van's interior.

From the front a huge and imposing figure turned and moved from his seat, crouching and edging toward the back of the van. His face was exposed. No mask. No attempt to hide his identity.

"Dr. Ludlum," the man said. "My name is Granger. I'm a... *friend* of Dr. Kotler."

Liz recognized the name immediately. "You're not his friend," she said, positioning herself between the Jani operative and Senator Acosta.

"He doesn't seem to think so lately," Granger nodded. "But right now, I'm certainly the only friend *you* have." He turned once again and settled back into the front seat of the van as they rumbled down the darkened Manhattan avenues. "That will have to be enough."

CHAPTER EIGHT

In the light of day, without the fear that they might be caught, the site took on an almost mundane vibe. Kotler and Denzel made a show of inspecting everything, comparing crime scene photos with what they were seeing, asking questions to clarify details. A Turkish police official accompanied them, along with Sarge and Isoken.

The scene was such an obvious mismatch to the crime scene photos, Kotler and Denzel were forced to remark upon it. Though neither of them mentioned the concrete, and they had asked Isoken to keep that part quiet as well.

"This site has been disturbed," Denzel said.

The Turkish official, Deputy Commissioner Eyman Polat, was quick to step in with an explanation. "Out of respect for the murdered man," he said, "and to safeguard certain Turkish interests."

"While I can appreciate the respect for the dead," Denzel said, some edge to his voice, "This crime scene was the entire reason we came here. You've removed evidence. What Turkish interests could you be safeguarding?"

Polat sniffed and replied, "Obviously, Agent Denzel, if I were to tell a foreign operative, those interests would be compromised."

Kotler was watching Polat throughout this exchange, getting a read on his body language.

It was clear the man knew a lot more than he was saying. His demeanor practically screamed "I have a secret." There was also something there—worry and anxiety of some sort. Guilt.

What wasn't clear was whether that secret Polat was protecting was official Turkish business, or was perhaps something more personal. Kotler was beginning to suspect the latter.

Polat's demeanor was at times officious, but from moment to moment Kotler could see signs of paranoia in the way the man behaved. He was watching Denzel like a hawk, that much was certain. He saw Denzel, or perhaps Denzel's badge, as a threat.

The bright side to all of that, however, was that Polat seemed to pay virtually no attention to Kotler, which left Kotler free to observe.

Denzel stooped and used a pen to prod through the remaining rock and rubble at the base of the column. He peered into the opening, then looked up at Polat and the others. "Was something taken from this site? I mean, *before* you and your people took everything?"

Polat ignored the jibe. "We can't say for certain. But given that there was a space there, in the base of the pillar, we believe so. The murderer smashed this with the sledgehammer, took something from within, and then killed the guard before leaving."

"And you have no idea what that something from within might have been?" Denzel asked, standing and brushing his hands on his pants.

Polat shook his head. "None of the security footage can even confirm that he took anything at all."

Denzel nodded and glanced at Kotler, who gave a slight nod of his own.

"Ok," Denzel said. "It's pretty clear we're not going to find anything here. Deputy Commissioner, would the Turkish government be willing to share anything they've found? During their... respectful cleanup?"

Polat nodded briefly. "Of course. Any relevant information we have is yours, as long as it does not conflict with Turkish interests."

Denzel smiled. "Well, who could ask for better reassurance than that?"

The group wandered away from the site then. Isokan and Sarge paused briefly at the gate in the security fence, speaking with some of the archaeologists and support staff. They were giving permission for the research to continue, now that the site had been cleared.

Kotler and Denzel accompanied Polat to the Jeep that was waiting for him. One of his men was driving, and as Polat climbed into the passenger seat he said, "Please, Agent Denzel, feel free to contact me with any further questions. I will make sure that we share anything we have."

"Of course," Denzel said.

Polat nodded, and the Jeep revved its engine as it sped away, leaving a cloud of dust in its wake.

Denzel waved the dust away from his face, annoyed and shaking his head. "Prick," he said.

"He's hiding something, for sure," Kotler said. "More than just government over-caution."

"Yeah," Denzel said. "I picked up on that. I was already a little skeptical, though, when he showed up. Why would the Deputy Commissioner come to a scene like this, personally?

Especially after the Turkish Police had just scrubbed the site clean the day before?"

"What do you think it means?" Kotler asked.

Denzel shrugged. "No idea. Yet. Which is frustrating, because we're now short on any actual leads."

"Not... entirely," Kotler said.

Denzel eyed him. "You've thought of something?"

Kotler sighed and shook his head. "Not something I particularly want to explore. But our only lead is that note. It isn't much, but it's something. And if my folks really were involved with this site, there may be a record of it."

Denzel studied him, then nodded. "Ok, I get it. There's only one person who still has access to all of your parents' old records."

Kotler inhaled, squared his shoulders, and nodded. "It's time to call my brother."

JEFFREY KOTLER's face appeared on screen, a little too close to the camera. From Kotler and Denzel's perspective, he was looking directly at them, squinting and peering closer as if they were bugs.

"Dad," a voice said from offscreen—Kotler's nephew, Alex. "Dad! Lean back, they're on the screen!"

Jeffrey leaned back and settled into his office chair with a slight creak. Kotler could now see his brother's full upper torso. But more, just off to Jeffrey's left he could see his nephew.

"Alex!" Kotler said. "You've grown!"

"Hi Uncle Dan!" Alex said, waving. It was hard to tell exactly, from the video, but he seemed a full foot taller, by Kotler's estimate. He was nearly twelve-years-old now, Kotler realized, so the growth spurt made sense.

Had it really been so long since he'd spent time with his nephew? Other than emails and text messages, they really hadn't had much contact since... well, since Jeffrey had been kidnapped in a revenge plot against Kotler.

Some things were not yet water under the bridge.

Jeffrey leaned back and looked up at his son, telling him to go outside. "No listening at the door. Promise?"

Alex huffed and rolled his eyes. "I promise," he said, and left the little office, closing the door behind him.

"He's grown so much," Kotler said, smiling.

"Boys tend to do that," Jeffrey said.

Kotler nodded. It was going to be like this, then. No real surprise. It had been chilly between the two of them for years now, but the events of the past couple of years were making it tough to reconcile.

It didn't help that Jeffrey kept finding himself embroiled in his brother's messes.

Most recently, Jeffrey had helped Liz Ludlum and Agent Brown to gain access to Vellar-Kotler Genetic Research. He'd given Liz access to their parents files, stored in a vault on site. Since Vellar-Kotler had been seized and shut down by the government, after the discovery of an illegal cloning operation, the contents of the vault had been scanned and scrutinized, but eventually turned back over to Jeffrey.

It had been an odd thing, by Kotler's estimate. And Denzel and Agent Brown agreed. For all intents and purposes, every scrap of information in that building was part of an ongoing investigation. Releasing any of it—personal or otherwise—into the care of a civilian who also happened to have his name on the building that was raided, seemed almost bizarre in its connotations. Kotler suspected there was someone else at work, behind the decision. He shivered to think who that might be. But there are a number of possibilities.

"What do you need, Dan?" Jeffrey asked.

Kotler nodded. "You have mom and dad's files now," he said. "We've... come to a turn in our investigation that might be explained by something in that database."

Jeffrey was looking at the screen, so still and quiet that for a second Kotler thought the signal must have dropped and the image was frozen. He was about to say something about this when Jeffery spoke. "I have them," he said. "I've built something. A place to store their files and journals, and... all the other stuff."

"Other stuff?" Kotler asked. Then it clicked. "Oh," he said, quietly. "The wreckage."

Kotler had used his sway at Vellar-Kotler to create an exhibit. A sort of homage to his parents. Everything related to their deaths had been placed in a room within the Vellar-Kotler building, including news footage and even pieces of the aircraft and other wreckage from the crash site. It was a bit macabre, Kotler knew. But it was something he'd had trouble letting go. It was his last connection to his mother and father.

"You kept all of it?" Kotler asked.

"I recreated the exhibit," Jeffrey said. "And I've added to it. I made it about their lives as much as their deaths. I had plenty to put on display. Things I had in the old house."

"The old house?" Kotler asked. "You moved? You didn't tell me."

"We moved," Jeffrey nodded, as if to say, *here's your notice.* "New place. New town. New... new start."

"New start," Kotler said, quietly, nodding. "I... understand. And I don't blame you."

Jeffrey's features registered no emotion at all at Kotler's words, which was worrisome all on its own. Kotler's brother had always been tough to read, however. Ironic, considering Kotler had worked so hard to master reading body language. It was as if Jeffrey was naturally immune to Kotler's one super-power. Or maybe Kotler was too biased to be able to read him, knowing Jeffrey's obsession with privacy. Kotler could be subconsciously ignoring the tells and signs that would give him insight into his brother's thoughts, out of a reflexive respect for him.

Or maybe Jeffrey really was just that good at masking his thoughts.

Either way, there was no real way of knowing what Jeffrey was thinking.

Kotler couldn't blame his brother for pulling up stakes. He had lived close enough to Vellar-Kotler that the name meant something in his home town. Lots of jobs had ended. Lots of rumors had started.

Jeffrey had spent his life living under the radar when it came to his wealth. He had worked in remodeling, taking pains to appear to be just like his neighbors. A nice, normal, blue collar sort of life. And that would have been entirely shredded with the news that he was, after all, one of "*the* Kotlers" in Vellar-Kotler.

"Jeffrey," Kotler said. "Can you search the library and send me anything Mom or Dad may have mentioned about the word 'manticore?'"

"Manticore?" Jeffrey asked. He jotted the word down on a notepad to his side. "I'll check. Is this... is this more trouble? Is it about Grandfather?"

Kotler still wasn't used to the idea that their grandfather was still alive. But suddenly the idea of Jeffrey moving his entire family to a new town made even more sense. He wasn't just escaping the scrutiny of gossiping neighbors, he was attempting to add a layer of safety and security to his family's daily lives.

"It's not about Grandfather," Kotler assured him. "At least,

I don't think so. There's been no hint of that, so far. But Mom and Dad came up during this investigation, here at *Göbekli Tepe*. I want you to look for references to that, too. Anything to do with this site, with the Turkish government, and with the word 'manticore.' In fact, if you find anything about human-animal hybrids, let me know."

Jeffrey looked up from his work. "My God, Dan... are you saying...."

"No!" Kotler replied, realizing the implications of what he'd said. "No, there's nothing about human and animal cloning in this. It's fine."

Jeffrey's gaze lingered for a moment, then he turned back to the note pad and jotted everything down. "I'll look," he said. "There's a lot of material. But luckily it was all digitized during the investigation. Alex put it all in a database that I can log into without having to go to the exhibit."

"Wait," Kotler said, shaking his head. "It's on a remote server? If that's true, can't I just access them from here?"

Jeffrey paused, blinking, then turned away from the camera, looking toward the door of his office. "Alex," he said, his voice a normal tone. "Can Uncle Dan access those records from where he is?"

There was another pause, then Alex's guilty-sounding voice spoke through the door. "Yes sir."

Jeffrey looked back to the screen. "Ok," he said. "You heard him?"

Kotler was smiling over the exchange and nodded. "I heard him. Ok, have Alex send me the details."

Jeffrey nodded, and Kotler could tell his brother was about to attempt logging off. Before he could do so, Kotler said, "Jeffrey, thank you. I'm... sorry that you had to move."

Jeffrey sighed. "I know," he said. "It's fine. Christina was excited about the change. She's already taken over some local historic restoration groups and is heading the restoration of a landmark hotel nearby."

Kotler nodded. "And you?"

Jeffrey shrugged. "I opened a resale shop that does furniture restoration."

Kotler's eyes opened with delighted surprise. "Really! I think that's right up your alley."

Jeffrey shrugged again, and for the first time Kotler saw a sign of something positive in his features. "It gives me something to do. I enjoy it. Quiet. Solitary. Working with my hands."

Kotler nodded again. "Perfect for you," he said. He paused briefly, then added, "Can we catch up later? I've... I've missed you. And Alex and Christina. Maybe I can come see your new place? Tour the shop?"

Jeffrey also nodded. "Yes, that would be fine."

Kotler smiled. It was a flat sort of reply, but coming from Jeffrey it was practically exuberance. "I'll reach out once we're done here in Turkey."

Again Jeffrey nodded, then he reached toward the laptop. In an instant, he was gone.

It was the most productive and heartfelt conversation Kotler and his brother had engaged in since Jeffrey's abduction, a couple of years earlier. Their relationship had always been a little strained, but after that incident things had gotten downright icy. So any sign of a thaw was welcome.

There was a ping from Kotler's email. A note from Alex, telling him how to access the database.

And a surprise—Jeffrey had called the exhibit, "The Kotler Memorial Library."

Kotler couldn't imagine the place would have that much business. But then, that wasn't what it was for. Jeffrey certainly didn't need it as a revenue source. In fact, in Kotler's experience Jeffrey didn't care much about keeping the exhibit active in the first place. He didn't like to revisit the pain of his past.

So why was he going to such lengths to preserve it?

The only answer Kotler could think of, and the one that gave him a warmth of hope, was that Jeffrey was preserving it for his brother's sake. There may have been some measure of keeping family records safe, keeping the memory of their parents alive in some way. But the wreckage? The news footage? Jeffrey would have just as soon destroyed all that than keep it around as a reminder.

So this was a gesture. This was for Kotler.

It was encouraging. And Kotler was determined not to waste the olive branch. The first opportunity he had, he would visit his brother and the library. He would help build the bridge between them and meet Jeffrey halfway.

For now, however, he had a job to do.

Using the login credentials Alex had sent, Kotler gained access to the library's database.

In addition to the digital records that had already been available, someone—likely investigators involved in the case—had done an exquisitely thorough job of scanning and cataloging all the letters, journals, and other written records of Berrett and Alexandria Kotler. Optical character recognition had been applied to all of it, and artificial intelligence had been used to create a context web, linking ideas so that an organic search was much easier and produced much better results.

This was impressive stuff. With this system, Kotler was able to do intuitive searches and bring up not just exact-word matches but also contextually relevant passages. It made it far easier and faster to make intuitive leaps during the research.

It also raised some questions.

Primarily, why had investigators simply handed this information back to Jeffrey Kotler, just months after the Vellar-

Kotler operation was shut down? Wasn't this all part of the ongoing investigation?

It was strange. But then Kotler wondered about the technology itself.

AI wasn't exactly new or rare at this point. But the AI used to create the contextual database for this was something Kotler had only seen at the government level. It was slowly trickling down to academia, but the closest Kotler had seen to this so far was government databases, usually via his FBI credentials.

Letting that sort of technology out into the wild was a strange lapse in the infamous paranoia of government law enforcement.

Kotler paused his research for a moment and now focused on looking at the workings of the database itself. He started looking at the metadata, peeking at the code of the thing to see what he could discover. He wasn't an expert at this sort of work, but he knew enough to make some progress.

In a moment, he spotted something familiar.

Aether Technologies.

It rang some bells, for a number of reasons. Not the least of which was that *Aether* was the name of one of the primordial Greek gods—the god of air, light, and the heavens.

Space, in other words.

Greek gods and space. That definitely sounded familiar.

Ethan Patterson.

Kotler did a quick search online and found confirmation in seconds. Aether Technologies was one of Ethan Patterson's businesses—a sister company to Athena Astronautics. And its primary mission was the development of artificial intelligence to assist in the creation of contextual databases. The software emerging from Aether Technologies was revolutionizing everything from medical and law enforcement databases to online search engines. Rumor had it that Patterson had struck a deal with Google for licensing the tech in the next generation of search.

It was a rumor with a price tag in the multiple billions. Serious stuff.

Ethan Patterson. Again.

It seemed that Patterson was making appearances in Kotler's life at strangely opportune times, and with increasing frequency.

Kotler wasn't yet sure what that meant, or how he felt about it. At the moment, however, it was a bit of good fortune, at least. He wrenched his attention away from the mouth of this particular gift horse and focused instead on his manticore hunt.

There would be time enough, in the near future, for Kotler to ask Ethan Patterson some very pointed questions.

CHAPTER NINE

Liz concentrated on keeping Acosta comfortable, but she was aware that the van had slowed down. And she could see, from her limited vantage point, some hints of the surrounding area.

Once they had reached—wherever they were—the van turned and pulled into a warehouse. A large, metal rolling door was lowered behind the van, effectively sealing them off from the outside world.

Liz had tried to keep track of where they were, catching glimpses of their location through the windshield of the van as they bounced along. They crossed at least one bridge, though Liz couldn't identify which one.

Her attention had been split between trying to track their progress and tending to Senator Acosta.

The young Senator definitely had a broken rib. Liz had asked for and received a med kit from the van's other occupants —though it was hardly more than a collection of bandages and Neosporin—and had used this to treat Acosta as best she could, wrapping her ribs and stabilizing her as much as possible.

There had been dried blood on her side, from the cut, but this was washed clean with water from a plastic bottle. Once bandaged, it was fine.

There could be more internal injuries, by Liz's estimate, but until she could get Acosta to a hospital, there was no way to be sure.

She mentioned this to Granger.

"We have medical personnel," he responded. "We'll take care of her when we get there."

True to his word, once the van was sealed inside the large warehouse space and its side doors were slid open, a team of people rushed to retrieve both Liz and Acosta. They placed Acosta on a stretcher and rolled her out of sight before Liz could say a word.

Granger excised himself from the front seat of the van like some immense beast emerging from a winter barrow. The van literally tilted and rocked with the shift of his weight, and as he stood to his full height, Liz felt slightly cowered by his presence. He had to be close to seven foot tall, and likely weighed in at around 300 pounds, seemingly all muscle. He was a massive figure.

"Our people will take good care of her," Granger said to Liz.

"It's good to know you treat your prisoners well," Liz replied, her tone icy.

Granger smiled and nodded. "That we do. This way."

He walked ahead of her, and Liz was nudged by the men—and, to her surprise, a couple of women—dressed in SWAT-like gear. They held rifles at the ready, aimed at the ceiling instead of at Liz, which was a relief. But the message was clear: Follow Granger. Not optional.

Liz followed Granger.

They moved deeper into the facility, which appeared to be

a new-build space. Everything was clean to the point of being immaculate. Lights engaged, clicking on one by one as they walked down the long corridor. Liz saw that the walls here were made of corrugated metal. The floor was bare concrete, which meant their every step echoed through the corridor. They occasionally passed sets of orange roll-up metal doors.

"Is this a storage facility?" Liz asked.

"Just built last month," Granger said over his shoulder. "We bought it from the original owner before it had even seen its first client. I like to find places like this early, before people move in. Dealing with the clientele for places like this can get messy."

"People are such a nuisance," Liz said.

Granger laughed. "Well, yes. But so are rats and cockroaches. Which tend to gravitate to places like this when they're full of old clothes and cardboard boxes and the detritus of modern life."

Liz shook her head, listening to Granger speak. He was such an immense man, but he appeared to be in no way a stereotype. He seemed sharp, even amicable. He moved with a great deal of grace as well, as if he'd practiced fluid movement to compensate for his size, so that he might not play in to those stereotypes. He was graceful, not lumbering.

Liz shook her head again. She was letting his charm fool her, and that was dangerous. Dan had told her about Granger, about his role in the Knights of Jani, and about their first meeting. Granger had kidnapped Dan and forced him to help retrieve a cache of ancient treasures buried in Cheyenne Mountain.

And since then, Granger had tried to recruit Dan into the Jani, on multiple occasions. Usually, these recruitment opportunities came as the result of Dan being placed in immense danger. One such instance was the events surrounding a satchel of Spanish papers from the World War II era, leading to the discovery of an ancient trove of treasures that became a battleground between the Jani and the Novensiles. Dan and Agent Denzel were both nearly killed in those events, and Granger had used them as leverage to try to convince Dan to join the ranks of the Jani.

Granger might be charming and intriguing, but that made him more dangerous, not less.

They came to an open storage bay at the end of the corridor. This had been converted into an office, with a facade built to provide some privacy, along with a door that Granger could close behind the two of them. The roll-up metal door was still in place above the facade, perhaps as a means of camouflaging the office, if need be.

Or maybe as a way to lock someone inside, Liz thought.

Granger ushered Liz into the office, told his people to return to their regular duties, and then closed the door. They were now completely alone, but it was still clear that Liz had no hope of escape.

"Can I offer you something to drink?" Granger asked. He moved to a small electric refrigerator that was serving double duty as a side table for his desk. He took out two small bottles of water, and Liz accepted one of them.

The events of the evening had left her parched and frazzled. The cool water was refreshing, even if the circumstances in which she drank it were bizarre.

"Granger," she said, after taking a sip and swallowing. "What the hell are we doing here?"

Granger studied her, then nodded and took a seat behind the desk. He leaned forward, placing his elbows on the table top. This caused the wood to creak slightly under his weight.

"Things aren't what they seem," he said.

"No?" Liz asked, sipping again from her water and eyeing

him sternly.

"You believe you've been abducted," he said.

Liz considered this. "Yes, I do." She looked around at the room, pointedly.

"In fact, you've been rescued."

Liz stared at him and shook her head. "Your people chased us down. They shot at us."

"No," Granger said. "Someone shot at you. But it wasn't our people. I believe it was Kendell Young's people."

"Kendell?" Liz asked, her expression shifting to confused disbelief. "Why would Kendell Young try to have us killed? He's had plenty of opportunities. He wouldn't have to threaten Senator Acosta or hunt us down at Hemingway's."

Granger nodded. "True. That was us. We compromised Cameron Michaels and gave those photos to Acosta. Though I have to admit, I didn't realize she'd bring them to you. That surprised me."

"Why?" Liz asked.

"I thought for certain her contact was Dr. Kotler or Agent Denzel," Granger said.

Liz's eyebrows shot up. "Because they're the guys?"

Granger chuckled at this. "No sexism implied. It's just that the last time I spoke to Dr. Kotler, he was trying very hard to keep you insulated from the Jani and the Novensiles."

Liz accepted this. Dan had only recently opened up to her with details about his encounters with the Jani, and he had said essentially the same thing. He had kept things from her in an effort to protect her.

It was annoying.

"So if you thought Acosta was working with Dan, why bother with this setup?"

Granger shrugged. "I had to be certain. I also hoped it would flush out any Novensile operatives. Which it did."

"The people who shot at us," Liz responded.

Granger nodded.

"You could have gotten us killed," she said.

"This is true," Granger replied. "This sometimes happens."

"Great," Liz said. "You're a sociopath."

"Merely a pragmatist," Granger shrugged. "The Jani have a more accepting view of death than most."

"How cozy for them," Liz replied. "Not so convenient for the rest of us."

Granger smiled. "It's easy to see why Dr. Kotler is so drawn to you. But let's bury the hatchet, at least a little. I had you and the Senator brought here for your protection. Let's consider that an act of good faith, in the interest of progress. We also have Agent Brown, though she was a lot more trouble. She ran down one of my people, which is impressive. But then there was another firefight in the streets. It's a messy business, and we'll have to pull some strings to downplay it in the media."

"Bummer?" Liz offered.

Again Granger chuckled. "Well, let's get to it. Now that we know you are Acosta's contact, I have a proposition for you."

"And what's that?"

"I want your assistance in taking down Kendell Young."

Liz blinked and felt her heart thump. "Take... take him down how?"

"Eliminate him from play, we'll say," Granger said. "He's insulated and protected, and has the resources of the Novensiles behind him. But I think you and Agent Brown, as well as Senator Acosta, represent a vulnerability for him."

Liz shook her head. "I think you're wrong," she said. "Kendell is effectively our boss at Historic Crimes. Dani and I know that he's leading the Novensiles. But we've been working on ways to bring him down from within for a while now. He's too protected. Too much influence."

"I'm sure you've done an admirable job," Granger nodded, "considering the resources you have. But I can offer you more resources. I can help you, if you help me."

"To murder Kendell Young?" She shook her head. "You know we can't do that."

"I never said anything about murdering him. Though, I'll confess, that isn't off the table if it comes to it. But no, I think we can work out something less lethal. If you cooperate."

"So," Liz said, "if we help you, Kendell can be taken down without being taken out."

"Yes," Granger replied.

"But if we don't help you…" she let the implication hang.

Granger only stared at her, saying nothing.

"Ok," Liz said. "Dani will ultimately be the one to make this decision, but I think I can put my support behind it. But haven't we blown this already? With all the shooting tonight?"

Granger smiled. "We've… contained Young's people. He'll get his usual updates and reports, they just won't come from anyone involved in tonight's events. Once we'd managed to compromise Cameron Michaels, we were able to infiltrate Young's organization to a certain degree. You, Agent Brown, and Senator Acosta can help with the rest."

"Where is Dani?" Liz asked.

"In this facility," Granger replied. "In another room. I'm letting her cool down. She's a bit volatile."

Liz could only imagine Dani's reaction to being taken into custody by Granger's people. It was probably best that she be allowed to cool off in some storage unit for a while. But Liz wasn't entirely sold on Granger and the Jani being benevolent benefactors.

"Ok," she said. "I'll need to know the plan. All of it."

Granger studied her and nodded. Then he started to outline exactly what he and the Jani had in mind.

CHAPTER TEN

COMBING through his parent's old files and records was a surreal enough experience that Kotler found himself taking frequent breaks. He stepped away, sipped coffee, stretched and moved around the trailer.

Procrastination born of reluctance, perhaps. He was having a tough time with this.

But the job had to be done, and if his parents were, somehow, tied to this murder, Kotler needed to know exactly how, and exactly why.

He sat back down, rolled his head on his shoulders, tried to ease the tension in his neck, and dove back in.

He had narrowed his search to key terms that he felt related to their present circumstances, including *manticore* and several similar phrases. This had produced some interesting results, but so far nothing altogether useful. For the next few hours Kotler followed trails that opened up myriad possibilities, but he was having trouble finding a thread that would bring him all the way to present day Turkey.

Finally he took a break to wander to the commons, where

he could grab a bite to eat and, more importantly, refill the large thermos of coffee he'd come to rely on.

As he was retreating with a paper bag filled with lunch and a thermos filled with coffee, Agent Denzel appeared, looking somehow somber and angry at the same time.

"Progress, then?" Kotler asked, with a quirky smile.

"I did some digging into Deputy Commissioner Polat," Denzel said. He glanced around. "Let's go back to our trailer."

They marched back to the trailer serving as home for their stay, and once inside Kotler unpacked his lunch and ate while Denzel described what he'd found.

"Polat used to run security here, back in the 80s and 90s. Actually, he ran security for a bunch of sites like this, but during the early 90s he was mostly stationed here, at Gobble key tiki."

"*Göbekli Tepe*," Kotler corrected, around a mouthful of sandwich. He shook his head, swallowing. "You're kidding. Let me guess... he was running things here during the period that column was exposed for the first time?"

"Exactly that time," Denzel replied. "I think we can guess what the scenario is here, now."

"He's covering up his involvement with whatever was put in there," Kotler said.

Denzel nodded. "I think so. I don't have a lot of friends in the Turkish government, but I was able to pull a few favors from some buddies I have at Interpol. They told me that Polat was running security for the entire site at that time, and that once he left and started his career with the police force, he maintained a special interest with this place. He was a regular here, over the next decade. Did a lot of off-hours volunteer guard duty."

"Interesting," Kotler replied.

"And this isn't the only site he's had an interest in," Denzel replied. "I have him at dozens of archaeological sites across the country, in one capacity or another. Once he rose in the ranks of the police force, he used his influence to gain access for one reason or another, and at that point the official records started getting a little hazy. My contacts were only able to track him down via scanned sign-in sheets and other records. There may be a lot of gaps in that."

Kotler consider this. "So what do we think he was doing at these sites? Actually, what do we know about him? What's his interest in archaeology? Does he have any sort of background in it?"

"Other than working security for some of these sites, there's nothing I've been able to uncover," Denzel replied, shaking his head.

Kotler huffed and took another bite of his sandwich. Polat's ties to *Göbekli Tepe* hinted at something, but without more information Kotler was stuck.

"Wait," Kotler said. He dropped the sandwich on the small table and retreated to his room for his laptop. He brought this out, shoved aside his lunch and put the computer on the table. He sat and typed in a new search query: *Eymen Polat*.

Immediately there were a number of hits.

Kotler felt his heart pounding, though he wasn't sure if he was glad about this or disturbed by it.

Denzel was leaning over his shoulder. "Your parents had a connection to Deputy Commissioner Polat?"

"It looks that way," Kotler replied quietly.

He started opening files, scanning and reading through them as quickly as possible. In a moment he found a notation that twisted his guts. "Here," he said, pointing.

Denzel peered at the screen. "GT?"

"It's a notation," Kotler said. "*Göbekli Tepe*. It's a log entry."

He read the entry aloud.

"*Eymen has gotten us access to GT. We leave for Turkey tomorrow. The first packet will be sealed into a spot he's scouted for us ahead of time. Reference #626842673. Alexandria's encryption is in place.*"

Kotler looked up at Denzel. "It fits. Polat was helping my parents to bury something at this site, thirty years ago."

Denzel shook his head. "And no idea what it was? Anything else in here about it?"

"I'll see what I can run down from this reference number," Kotler said

"What about this number?" Denzel said, pointing at a string of alphanumeric characters following the excerpt.

"That's a log number," Kotler replied. "Part of the filing and archival system for Vellar-Kotler. It's modern, like within the past five years. Part of a system overhaul to update security."

"You don't think it might bring up something else we can use?" Denzel asked.

Kotler shrugged. "I was keeping my search aimed at things from the era, but now… I'm not sure. Let me run this."

He opened another window and copied and pasted the log number into the search field. In a moment it brought up a dozen or so files in a zipped directory—a directory that had more or less been hidden from earlier searches. Kotler unzipped the directory to reveal a collection of video clips, scattered among various other directories in the database, rather than gathered in one place. If not for the log number, Kotler surmised, these files would be hidden in dozens of different folders, never appearing together. There would be no way to connect them with each other.

"It looks like there's a series of videos here from the '90s," Kotler said quietly. "Digitized at some point and stored on the server." He glanced up at Denzel and sighed. "I'm not ashamed to admit, Roland, I'm a little afraid of what we're going to find here."

"Do you want me to get someone else to run through these first?" Denzel replied.

Kotler considered then, but shook his head. "No. This is on me. I need to see this."

Denzel nodded. "Ok," he said. "I'm going to grab a bite to eat and come back here. We can go through these together."

Kotler nodded and, as Denzel left, he slumped back in the chair, staring at the screen, filled with videos from three decades past.

It was clear that his parents had gone to great lengths to bury a secret. That was concerning enough. But now, here at the *Göbekli Tepe* site itself, three decades in the future—Kotler wasn't sure of what he and Denzel were about to discover, or what it would mean. He steeled himself for the worst.

Denzel returned several minutes later, lunch in hand, and the two of them settled in to watch history—Kotler's history—unfold.

CHAPTER ELEVEN

THIRTY YEARS AGO | *Vellar-Kotler Genetic Research, Upstate New York*

IT WAS LATE, and the lab was lit primarily by desk lamps and the green glow of computer monitors, all of which were sheathed in microbe-resistant plastic. Though that precaution may have been overkill, considering the air in this place was pumped in from the outside, filtered three times before passing through a wall of UV light, before seeping into the lab itself through yet another carbon filter. From there it would be breathed by precisely no-one—used only for keeping machinery and the bulky, beige computer CPUs cool and operational before being recycled and run through the entire process all over again.

One could, hypothetically, breathe in this room. It just wasn't allowed.

There were no windows here, no way to know day from night other than the presence or absence of other people, or a quick glance at the clock hanging just outside of the chamber door. There was no light in the room that was not artificial and meticulously tuned for color and intensity, so that it would not impact the specimens kept and studied here.

It had to be this way: The work done in this room had to be isolated from the rest of the world down to the tiniest particle. Errant sunlight was as bad as stray particles of dust or a misplaced eyelash, in an environment as tightly controlled as this one.

Despite all these precautions, all this prevention of outside contamination, everything in this room was routinely cleaned and sterilized both by hand and by automated jets, issuing disinfectant spray over every surface, further removing any chance of bacterial or microbial contact. Everything here was, literally, as clean as something could possibly be.

Including its current and sole occupant.

Dr. Berrett Kotler—Chief Researcher and, not incidentally, Co-Founder of Vellar-Kotler Genetics Research—stood from his chair and stretched as much as the containment suit would allow. He had an itch on his nose, and he'd been ignoring it for the better part of two hours. But now, as his bladder also began to demand his attention, and his focus was finally drifting.

He needed a break.

It was time, anyway.

Berrett made a few notes on the computer, clacking away on the bulky, plastic-covered beige keyboard with his two index fingers. He had never learned to touch-type, as Alexandria had. He'd always considered it to be a "woman's skill," right through grade school and even University. How was he to know both a "sexual revolution" and a "computer revolution" would take place? It seemed like overnight, the world had gone from women working in steno pools and computers filling rooms the size of warehouses to women running corporations and micro devices that could be placed on a desktop, taking up only the space needed for the monitor and the CPU.

All of it was just incredible. A marvel and a testament to humanity's ingenuity.

Even more incredible, Berrett had heard recently that the people over at CERN, particularly Dr. Berners-Lee, were working on something that would build on ARPANET—the interconnected network of computers worldwide that was used almost exclusively by government agencies and academic institutions.

CERN, it was rumored, was building something that would make this network accessible to everyday people, even *outside* of government and academia.

Impressive stuff. But Berrett wasn't certain that the general population would have any real, productive use for an interconnected global network. Berrett's experience with this "internet" was so far dry and, at times, tedious, scanning through line after line of text and code, written in the blocky, green system font such networks relied upon. In this era of Nintendos and music videos and special effects in movies, who among the general public would possibly be interested in the *internet?*

But for businesses such as Vellar-Kotler, it might represent an evolutionary leap in the power of shared data.

Simply having the ability to connect and communicate with colleagues across the globe, without the cost of long-distance calls or airfare, was an exciting prospect! Sharing data across time zones and continents could make their pursuits here much easier, and much more profitable. Results could come quicker. Tests could be run offsite, and data shared with colleagues around the globe, instantly. Research results and papers could be shared among disparate groups, allowing for the cross-pollination of ideas. It could certainly revolutionize scientific research.

He would just have to watch and see what happened next. But he doubted, very seriously, that the internet would ever come to anything useful for the layman. Everyday people simply had no real or practical use for computers.

Berrett passed through decontamination, shrugged off the containment suit, and hung it from the peg just inside the door. Once he passed through the outer door the decon mode kicked in, hosing down everything in the chamber with antibacterial spray, then hitting it with ultraviolet light and negative ionized airflow. Upon re-entering and waiting to go back into the lab, this exact process would happen again. Anyone not wearing a containment suit at that point would be in for a pretty nasty and stinging experience.

The whole process took several minutes and effectively barred anyone from entering or exiting until it was complete.

This was a minor delay, but it could stack up, with people entering and exiting with any sort of frequency. Each time Berrett stepped into that chamber he had to suit up and endure the decon process before proceeding. Which was why, once he was inside, he tended to endure any physical discomfort or biological need for as long as possible before exiting, attempting to minimize the impact on his time.

The downside, of course, was that once he was outside of the clean room, he was usually in a rush for the men's room, where he could relieve his bladder and scratch his nose or his ears or his scalp or his body in general, as much as he needed. He did this now, and laughed at himself as he realized what a spectacle he must make, standing before a urinal and scratching his head and upper body for a long stretch.

A consequence of his long hours working without food or drink was that Berrett was thin. Too thin, according to Alexandria. Which was why, with regularity, she appeared morning, noon, and night with containers of food. Absolute mounds of it.

And typically heavy on the calories, not to mention nutrients and fiber.

Tonight was no exception. As Berrett exited, the men's room and made his way into the general offices, he noticed the aroma of something spicy and Italian wafting from his office.

He wandered in to find that Alexandria had created a spread on the little round table that Berrett used for meetings. Alexandria had brought in placemats, silverware, wine glasses, and a basket brimming with covered dishes. She glanced up at him as he entered. She was radiant as always, still wearing the smart blouse and pants she'd been wearing when they'd left home for the office that morning.

That had been over fifteen hours earlier, Berrett realized, glancing at the clock on the wall.

"You're running late," Alexandria said, disapproving.

Berrett looked contrite and shook his head. "I've made some progress. I got carried away."

"How surprising," Alexandra replied, giving him a stern look before smiling. She waved him to a seat and joined him from across the table.

Berrett looked down at a plate of chicken Parmesan and felt his stomach grumble. "I guess it really was a longer stretch than usual," he said, placing a napkin on his lap. He looked up at Alexandria. "Have you seen the boys?"

She nodded as she sipped from a glass of wine. "I left here a few hours ago and checked in on them at home. Daniel has discovered the novels of Michael Crichton. He's reading one now titled *Jurassic Park*. You'd find it interesting. It's about an archaeologist who becomes involved with a program that clones dinosaurs from ancient DNA, recovered from a mosquito preserved in amber."

Berrett was in mid-bite and stopped, fork near his lips, blinking. "That *does* sound fascinating!"

Alexandria smiled. "I thought you'd like it. And Jeffery is building something from LEGOs. I'm not sure what it's meant to be, but it's a massively large project, and he absolutely refuses to discuss it until it's complete. It's taking up about a quarter of the den at the moment."

Berrett smiled at this. "Not hard to see what our two boys are interested in." He shook his head. "They're so *different* from each other. Are they still fighting?"

"Always and often," Alexandria said. "Or so the nanny tells me." She shook her head lightly, and became thoughtful, the smile still playing on her lips but a touch of something else in her eyes that he thought he recognized.

Regret, he thought.

"We don't spend enough time with them," Berrett said, putting a voice to what he knew she was feeling.

She glanced up at him. "I was just thinking that."

He smiled again. "We've been married for eighteen years. I'm a scientist. I was bound to observe you in that time. At least a little. I know how to read your body language, at least."

She cocked an eyebrow. "And in all those years of observation, what have you learned?"

He winced and chuckled. "That some questions are best left unanswered."

She smirked and nodded. "Well, I *was* thinking we don't spend enough time with them. Not lately. It might be time for us to take a family trip. Since I started working with you and Cristoff here, you and I have only taken two full vacations. For the past year we haven't even stuck to our weekend rule."

Berrett nodded. The "weekend rule" had been their promise to each other, and to the boys, that though they would be very busy during the week, they would always clear the weekend for family time. It hadn't quite worked out that way, of course. Something they both felt guilty over.

"I know," Berrett said. "I was thinking the same. It just... it got tough. I was so close to figuring this out. And now..." He hesitated, glancing at her, a twinkle of excitement in his eyes.

"And now?" Alexandria asked. "You mentioned you've made some progress."

He sipped his wine and smirked. "I have. And I have you to thank for it."

"Me?" she asked.

"Your equations, for a start. Plus, the work you did on comparing patterns in evolutionary genome drift to kinetic particle theory. Just brilliant."

Alexandria smiled. "That? It was a pet project, Berrett. A thought experiment. What's a physicist to do? Woman does not live by equations alone."

"We've come to rely on you for your mathematical prowess, my love," Berrett said, smiling. "But your theoretical work may have just opened the door to a whole new future for humanity."

Alexandra, a little surprised, squinted at him. "Sounds like it would make an impressive credit on the CV," she said.

He laughed. "It will change everything. Once we patent it, of course."

"And what is this revolution in genetic research that I have inadvertently contributed to?" Alexandra asked, taking a bite of chicken parm.

"You know my work—my passion project. I've been studying the evolution of the human genome, comparing modern DNA to samples from corpses found in ancient sites. I was looking for markers that might indicate the various leaps we've made as a species."

"It's all you talk about, sweetie," Alexandria said, rolling her eyes, her tone tolerant but loving.

He smiled and waved this off. "Aside from the mainstay work we do here, this is something I feel has some very real potential for altering the genetic destiny of humanity as a species," Berrett said. "The thing that has slowed down my progress is that I couldn't spot any particular pattern among the samples I have. I've looked at nearly a thousand samples from archaeological sites worldwide. Most were not entirely viable. Some held a great deal of promise. But I really made very little progress until the human genome project started."

"The project Robert Sinsheimer invited you into?" Alexandria asked.

Berrett nodded. "He held that workshop in Santa Cruz, but his idea has evolved since then. Charles DeLisi and David Smith, from the Office of Health and Environmental Research, have received funding to sequence the *entire human genome!* Charles knows our work here at Vellar-Kotler. He invited me to participate. I've been giving them access to our facilities and equipment and running some tests myself."

"Sounds like the sort of thing that you'd be brilliant at, as a contributor," Alexandria smiled.

Berrett nodded his thanks. "They're still decades away from completely mapping it, so I'm essentially working with incomplete data. But just having the ability to share and discuss the data we *do* have—that has changed everything! Suddenly my little passion project has a purpose beyond my own interests."

"So you've cracked it?" she asked. "The human genome?"

Berrett's eyes widened a bit, and he shook his head, laughing lightly. "Not even close. I've been sharing everything I've learned, and so have they. I think we're making some headway, but the goal is still a distant horizon. However, I may have uncovered something else. A way to not only predict genetic evolution, but to..." He hesitated. "To *initiate it.*"

There was a pause. Alexandria was staring at him, waiting, watching.

Berrett was smiling, then shook his head. "I know it sounds crazy."

"I'm not sure about that," Alexandria replied. "I'm not actually sure what you mean."

He became excited, even agitated, not rising from his seat but flailing his hands in complex patterns in the air as he talked. "Alright, let's relate this to your ideas on kinetic particle theory. You explained the idea that the distinction between the various states of matter—solid, liquid, gas—this distinction comes from the strength of the bond between atoms. Solids have the strongest bond, gas the weakest. Heat a substance in any of these states and you can see kinetic particle theory play out. Heat energy is converted to kinetic energy, and the rate of expansion is determined by..."

"Berrett," Alexandria said, holding up a hand. "I'm a physicist. I know how this works."

Berrett nodded. "Right. Sorry. But in your research you were comparing this to genetic diversity and evolution. You made some leaps, for sure. And I'm aware a lot of it is theoretical, even hypothetical. But it got me thinking of the genome in a new way. I started thinking of it in terms of particle expansion."

"So genetics as a state of matter?" Alexandria asked, squinting and shaking her head.

"Metaphorically, at least, yes," Berrett nodded. "It started as a thought experiment. A framework. But we know that physical systems often have characteristics that repeat at both the macro and micro scale. They act like fractal patterns. Every part tends to be a reflection of the whole. Pull out or push in, and the patterns repeat into infinity. That was one of the things that nudged me toward a breakthrough. I started thinking that, perhaps, these same patterns replicate on a meta level as well."

"I'm still not following," Alexandria said.

"Macro to micro," Berrett replied, moving his hands from spread apart to close together. "From big picture to small picture. We're starting to study the human genome. We're mapping base pairs, studying how they fit. That's the macro view. I decided to take what patterns we know and see if I could find them on a smaller scale. I asked the question: What if the larger pattern translates downward? Could we figure out more of the larger pattern, by looking at the smaller one?"

He was smiling at her, staring, waiting.

She immediately got it. "You found it. You know the pattern."

"Better," he replied. "I can *predict* the pattern. And in fact, using just the technology we have here—technology you helped to build—I can not only predict the pattern of evolution, I can *induce* it! *Influence* it!"

She blinked, and after a long moment she picked up her wine, sipped, and placed the glass back on the table.

When she next spoke, it was quiet, cautious. "You can influence evolution?"

He nodded, smiling. "Do you realize what this means? It's an end to disease. An end to aging. An end to all human frailty, maybe even an end to death itself!"

Alexandria, wide-eyed, was shaking her head. "This is..." She drifted, leaving the statement unfinished.

"It's *astounding!*" Berrett supplied, rising from his chair a bit before settling back. "It changes who we are as a species! Can you picture it? I can't even begin to express how profound this is!"

"No, it's certainly profound," she agreed. "But it's also..." she hesitated.

Berrett's expression shifted from exuberance toward curiosity. He was still smiling, but he peered at her. "Also what?"

She took a breath, let it out in a huff, and said, "It's... dangerous."

Berrett blinked and leaned back, studying her. "Dangerous?"

She shook her head, leaning forward. "You don't see it? You just told me that you have the ability to *influence human genetics*. You can jumpstart human evolution, possibly even direct it into whatever path you choose. You... don't see the danger in that?"

After a long moment, his expression sobered. She watched his features drop, becoming contemplative. He settled back in his chair, and picked up the fork from his plate, using it to nudge a severed cube of chicken parm. A moment later he dropped the fork to his plate, resting his hands on the table as he inhaled and exhaled, and shook his head.

"You're right," he said, shrugging. "I wasn't thinking about that, but you're right. I hadn't considered the *consequences* of this sort of leap. I was so busy wondering if I *could* do it..." he drifted.

"You didn't stop to consider if you *should*," Alexandria said quietly.

He looked up at her and nodded.

"This could be used for more than just advancing humanity," he said. "It could become..." he struggled for a term. "It could become designer genetics. Parents could choose their child's eye color, or predispose them toward a higher IQ. But that just means that people in power could do the same, or more. Or worse. Having this capability could give someone the means to create their own preferred species." He picked up his wine and drained the glass. "A master race." He shook himself. "My God, I wasn't even thinking about that." He put the emptied glass back on the table and tilted his chin to his chest.

Alexandria reached out across the table and touched his

hand. "No, you were thinking only about the *good* it could do. Because that's the kind of man you are." She smiled at him. "But you're also brilliant and responsible. You couldn't imagine anyone abusing this science because that just isn't who you are. Which is exactly why I can't think of anyone more qualified than you to make decisions about how to proceed from here, with what you've learned."

He looked up at her and turned his hand so that their palms met. He nodded. "Thank you. I think I needed that. *This,*" he said, nodding to the dinner, though it was clear he meant so much more.

He needed to be grounded, to have the influence of his family to remind him that science, for the sake of science, could lead down dark paths, even with the best intentions.

"Until this moment, I hadn't considered this, which is disturbing. I lecture our staff about considering the consequences of our work all the time, almost daily. And here I barged ahead without even a thought."

Alexandria shook her head. "You were caught up in the moment, sweetie. You would have come down from that in time."

"But you brought me around quicker," he smiled, raising her hand to his lips. "I think I married you so I could siphon your brilliance when I need it."

She laughed. "Alright, that's flattering. But what now? You've made this discovery. What will you do with it?"

He thought for a moment, then replied. "Fragment it," he said.

She shook her head. "I'm sorry? What do you mean?"

"I'll break the research apart. There are aspects of it that will help with other research we're doing, and the things we're developing. I don't want to lose that. I can push Vellar-Kotler ahead on the curve in a number of silos, all of which will help humanity. I can think of at least twelve patents that could come out of this. None of which, taken individually, could give anyone the key to the whole."

"But taken as a whole?" Alexandria asked.

"It'll be hidden in plain sight," Berrett said. "A secret that I know, and no one else will see. I can manipulate project notes, use encoding to essentially keep records right out in the open. The only way anyone would know the whole truth is if they broke that code. And they won't be able to do that."

"And what makes you so confident of that?" Alexandria asked.

"Because my brilliant wife is one of the world's foremost mathematicians and physicists," he replied, reaching out for the bottle of wine and refilling both of their glasses. "And she is going to create an encryption that no one will ever be able to break."

Alexandria considered this. "Ok," she said. "I can do that. But may I suggest a further step?"

Barrett raised his eyebrows. "Certainly."

"You have access to a number of outside projects," she said. "Things that no one else at Vellar-Kotler would have access to."

Barrett nodded enthusiastically. "You're right. I can bury bits and pieces of this among hundreds of outside projects, as part of my contributions. That's brilliant."

She smiled. "So, do you have some projects in mind?"

Barrett grinned and nodded. "If you're going to bury something, what better place than an archaeological site?"

He turned and rose from his chair, then went to his desk. The surface was covered in folders and paperwork, and he riffled through this until he found what he was looking for. He brought a colorful pamphlet back to the table, dropping it in front of Alexandria as he settled back into his chair.

"This came across my desk a few weeks ago, and I've been

offering my assistance, here and there. *Göbekli Tepe* is a newly discovered site in Turkey. They've been uncovering bits and pieces of it for the better part of a year now. What they're finding there... it's simply astounding. The sort of discovery that will rewrite history books!"

Alexandria had picked up the pamphlet and was reading through it, nodding and glancing at her husband as he explained his plan.

"They're reburying each section as they go. It's how they'll continue to preserve it," Berrett said.

"Interesting," Alexandria said, nodding. "So anything that's exposed now will be reburied."

"For decades to come," Berrett said, grinning.

Alexandria smiled. "Well, I'd have to say, that does seem just about perfect. How will you gain access to it?"

"I have an invitation to fly there, to get a guided tour," he said. He thought for a moment. "You know I have some... contacts. People of influence."

Alexandria glanced around out of instinct. "Your father."

"The people he works with have a lot of reach," Berrett said, nodding.

"Berrett, dear... I don't know about this. Those people... they seem to be as dangerous as this thing you're trying to hide. I've never been comfortable with all of that."

"Which is why I've worked so hard to stay out of it," Berrett agreed. "But I don't have to join them to use their network. I can call a few people, get something set up. But I think this would be the perfect place to start. I can hide the research there, keep it out of sight for good, if need be."

Alexandria's first instinct was to ask why Berrett didn't simply destroy the research, but she kept that question to herself. She already knew the answer. Her husband—an ardent pursuer of knowledge and discovery—could no more destroy this research than he could burn the Mona Lisa. This was more than just idle discovery, it was something that resonated to the heart of humanity in Berrett's eyes.

He could never destroy it. She knew that about him as much as she knew anything in her life. Burying it and abandoning the research would be challenging enough for him. It was all anyone could really ask of him.

She would protect this secret for him. She would create an encryption so tight that it would take millions of years to crack. That would be how she protected her husband and his discovery. How she would protect their family, and maybe even humanity itself.

She raised her glass and after only a moment Barrett followed suit, tipping his own glass toward her. "To secrets hidden in plain sight, then," Alexandria said.

They clinked their glasses and each took a drink.

Berrett dabbed his mouth with his napkin and stood. "Let's clean this up and go home," he said.

"Home?" Alexandria asked, checking her watch. "This early?"

"It's nearly 9 pm," he shrugged. "The boys are still awake, I'm sure. And suddenly I want to see them more than I want anything else in the world."

Alexandria smiled and nodded, then rose from her chair. They packed up the remains of dinner and left the offices within minutes. They took Alexandria's car, driving from the executive garage out onto the street, winding their way home. It was a short drive, and they'd be there in less than twenty minutes.

It would be a rare and wonderful night, with all four Kotlers enjoying each other's company for once. A happy moment of family, and one that Berrett and Alexandria would want to freeze in time. A night that little Daniel and Jeffrey

Kotler would think back to often, as they grew to adulthood. One of the few memories they could cling to, when their lives changed forever, when the happy family moments were all part of the past, and all that was left was a struggling bond between brothers, and a secret buried in plain sight.

CHAPTER TWELVE

KOTLER SAT BACK from the laptop. Denzel had stood and was just behind Kotler, sipping coffee as he watched the clips play out.

It had taken time to piece the various clips together, in the proper order, weaving it into a piecemeal story that brought a startling clarity to their situation. But that story impacted Kotler on every level. Seeing his parents, alive and exactly how he remembered them, was an emotional punch all its own. But learning about his father's discovery...

"My God," Kotler said, finally.

"I can't believe those clips are just out in the open," Denzel replied. "No one at the FBI put this together?"

"Look at the file structure," Kotler said, pointing. "We found this sequence, in this order, only because we used this specific log number. Those files are scattered all over the database, otherwise."

"Meaning someone knew what they added up to," Denzel said, "and hid them in plain sight."

"It's becoming a common theme," Kotler replied, shaking his head. He thought for a moment. "Cristoff," he said, finally.

"Crisotff..." Denzel said. "Vellar? Your... what, adopted father?"

"Just our guardian," Kotler replied, shaking his head. "But yes."

"You think Vellar was the one who put this together and hid it on the server?"

"I believe so, yes," Kotler nodded. "Think about it, Roland. He would have been one of the few people to have the sort of access it would take, as well as the knowledge of my father's research."

"But wasn't Vellar working with your grandfather? Part of the whole illegal cloning operation?" Denzel asked.

"Coerced," Kotler said.

Denzel nodded at this, pragmatically. "Sure."

"I know things look pretty bad for him," Kotler said. "But I've always believed Cristoff was a good man, doing everything he could to protect me and Jeffrey. I believe he loved our parents, and me and Jeffrey, like family. And I think my grandfather has used that love to manipulate Cristoff for decades."

"No offense, Kotler, but your grandfather seems to be a real dick."

Kotler let out a bark of laughter at the rare obscenity from his partner and shook his head. "A little crude, but I agree."

Denzel nodded. "Ok, then. Now what? Your folks hid the mother of all secrets here at *Göbekli Tepe*, but it's been stolen, and we have no idea who did it."

"We do have leads, though," Kotler said. "Eymen Polat."

"And now that I know the connection, I can press him a little," Denzel nodded. "But he's got heavy connections here. There's only so much I'll be able to do. It would help a lot if we knew exactly what was taken from that site."

"I think I know," Kotler said. "I'm not a hundred percent on the particulars and specifics, but somehow my father managed to hide data from his research here. My mother created an encryption for it—that implies some kind of technology."

"Memory chip?" Denzel asked.

Kotler shook his head. "It was the early '90s," he said. "The technology existed, but it wasn't common yet, and it was still very limited in terms of capacity and long-term stability. No, I think it's something more basic than that. A hard drive, I think."

"A hard drive?" Denzel asked, dubious. "Buried under all of that dirt for thirty years?"

"*Protected*," Kotler said. "Sealed in a vault of cement in an arid climate, surrounded by mounds of soil that kept air and moisture out. The same process that has preserved these ruins for almost thirteen thousand years would theoretically preserve that device as well."

Denzel considered this, sighed, and shrugged. "Ok. This is making some kind of sense. But Polat's interference... that feels like a butt-covering exercise to me. He's trying to make sure he doesn't get implicated in this murder."

"Exactly. If Polat was part of hiding a hard drive or anything else here," Kotler said, "he might worry that he could lose his position, if it ever came out. I do think he's covering for himself, though, and not the person who took the hard drive."

"Do you think he knows it was a hard drive that was hidden in there?" Denzel asked.

Kotler shrugged. "I'm not even 100% sure of that myself, but I think the odds favor it, yes."

Denzel nodded. "Ok. I think that could give me the leverage I need. I think it's time we talk to Deputy Commissioner Polat."

Kotler nodded and leaned back in his chair as Denzel went to his room, getting ready for the trip to see Polat. Kotler needed to get a few things ready himself, but for the moment he could only sit where he was, a feeling of being stunned still clinging to him.

Seeing his parents, hearing their voices, even by way of grainy security footage—it hit hard. Kotler had long ago learned to live with the loss of his parents, but the pain was still there. Of course it was. It was a hurt that had driven Kotler to become exactly who he was today, pushing him to learn, to doggedly pursue multiple PhDs, to maintain total independence. Maybe too much independence, considering the string of relationships he'd seen come and go in his life.

The death of his parents informed everything about who Kotler was. Seeing them alive, even if it was just thirty-year-old security footage, hit him like a bolt of lightning.

At the moment it felt raw, like an exposed nerve. He kept going back to it, kept picturing them, kept hearing their voices. He kept thinking about the fact that they had left work "early" for once, specifically to come home and spend time with their sons. With little Daniel and Jeffrey—so different from each other, but still their parents' boys.

He couldn't remember the specifics of that night, and that bothered him. There should be something significant about a moment like that, when it led to all of this. Try as he might, however, Kotler could only conjure up vague, non-specific memories of times spent with his parents and his younger brother.

Perhaps not exactly the night they returned home, after discovering they had the power to reshape humanity as a species. But Kotler eventually remembered to be grateful he had those memories at all.

He thought about the astonishing discovery his father had made. The implications of it... mind boggling.

Kotler's mother had been right to point out the inherent

danger of it. And his father had been right to realize and accept that danger, despite his passion for what he'd discovered. It showed that both were good and responsible people, and this made Kotler proud.

It felt good to feel proud of his family for once. His grandfather had tainted everything Kotler's parents had built, and it had started to feel like that corruption went to the core of the Kotler family. But seeing this video gave Kotler hope.

"Kotler," Denzel said quietly, from the doorway to his room.

Kotler looked up to see his friend watching him, concerned. "You good?"

Kotler nodded, slapped his knees and rose. "Good. Sorry. I'm ready."

Denzel's concerned expression remained, but he nodded, and the two of them left the trailer, climbed into the rental car, and made their way to Polat's offices.

CHAPTER THIRTEEN

JUST AS LIZ PREDICTED, Agent Dani Brown was having none of it.

"You've abducted two Federal Agents," Dani said, her voice tight and controlled.

"I understand your annoyance," Granger said.

"Annoyance? You're under arrest."

"And how do you propose to exert your authority at this moment?" Granger asked.

"Give me my gun," Dani replied.

Granger chuckled.

"Dani," Liz said, "I've heard his plan. I agree, they probably should be arrested. But they're offering us a way to take down Kendell Young."

Dani looked to Liz, her expression sharp. It softened, just a tiny bit, and she nodded. "I get that," she said, then turned to Granger. She stepped forward, closer to the giant, looking up at him defiantly. "You don't get to get away with this."

"I believe I do," Granger said. "But let's just put a pin in that, for the moment. You are free to bring the full power of the FBI down on me and my people once we have Kendell Young."

"You'll turn yourselves in?" Dani asked.

Granger smiled. "You should learn to be content with the gifts you're given, Agent Brown."

Liz stepped closer to Dani, putting a hand on her arm. "Dani..."

Dani nodded, stepping back, breaking her glare.

Granger nodded as well. "I believe with the three of you onboard, we can lure Kendell Young into complacency, and the Jani can penetrate his organization."

"The three of us?" Dani asked.

"The two of you and Senator Acosta," Granger replied, nodding toward the Senator.

Acosta was sitting on a chair off to one side of the makeshift office. She had an arm pressed to her side, protectively. She'd been given a clean bill of health—as well as painkillers—from Granger's people, which was a relief to Liz. But she was oddly quiet. Liz wasn't sure if she was withdrawing from all of this, on some level, or if maybe she was relieved to have some sort of intervention, to help break the hold Kendell Young had over her.

"Haven't you already gained access to Young's organization?" Liz asked. "You have Cameron Michaels, and you've taken out the Novensiles who were working with him." She glanced at Acosta, at the mention of Cameron's name, but it didn't appear to register with the young Senator.

"I need deeper access to his network," Granger said. "Since the Chairman left the organization, Young has filled the void and implemented new measures of security."

The Chairman, Liz knew, was actually Richard Kotler—Dan's grandfather. She would hardly say he "left the organization." He had been the target of some master plan orchestrated by Kendell Young, aimed at accelerating Young's takeover of the Novensiles, cementing the influencer's power within the rogue faction.

She wasn't sure how much of this Granger knew, however. And she had no intention of sharing intel unless it was absolutely necessary.

Granger continued. "He's been busy, recruiting people from the deepest levels of government, both here and abroad. Until today, I believed he had recruited the three of you, as well. I'm still not convinced about the Senator."

Acosta looked up, and Liz saw something pass over her features. Anger?

"What do you need from us?" Dani asked.

Granger nodded. "I've explained the plan in detail to Dr. Ludlum, but the short version is that I want you to return to duty and continue to build trust with Young. And to do that, the first thing I want is for you to alert him to the presence of my people."

Dani blinked. "Wait... what? You... *want* us to turn on you?"

"I have specific people in mind," Granger said. "Volunteers."

"So the idea would be to build trust with Young by exposing your people, in a controlled way," Liz said.

Granger nodded.

"Won't this endanger your people?" Dani asked.

"They've volunteered, knowing the risks."

Dani made a disgusted noise, shaking her head. "No way. Young's people will kill them."

"I don't believe that will be the outcome," Granger said. "He will want to know how deeply we've penetrated his organization, so he will keep them alive."

"While he tortures them," Dani replied.

Granger said nothing.

"The Jani have a different view of death than most people," Liz said, sarcastically.

"You should know that I have other plays in motion," Granger replied. "Whether you do this or not, I have people voluntarily putting their lives on the line for this. The Novensiles are a cancer within the Jani. We have worked for more than a century to root them out. With the Chairman's departure, we have our opportunity."

"What's kept you from getting to them so far?" Liz asked. "It seems like you know a lot about them."

"The Jani are a secret order," Granger replied. "As such, it can often be difficult to tell what motives are in play."

"In other words," Dani said, her tone sharp, "your super secret order is so super secret, you don't even know who you can trust."

Granger shrugged. "Within the Jani there are cells. We operate by objectives, guided by ancient rites and rules. It isn't always necessary to trust who you work with, to get the job done. But for the sake of moving forward, let's say that the Novensiles are still Jani. They know the secrets of the order, they know how to hide, and they know how to operate in a clandestine way, even out in the open. They look and behave just like any Jani, making it difficult to find and remove them. But recent events have opened a window of opportunity. For the first time, we know exactly who is leading the Novensiles, while this person is still in power. We can track his movements, and map out those he's in contact with. He's very public, which makes this easier. But he's also surrounded by layer upon layer of protection, which makes things exponentially more difficult. His public persona is both a weakness and a strength."

"Because exposing him could also expose the Jani," Dani said.

Granger shrugged.

"Ok," a voice said from behind them.

Liz and Dani turned, joining Granger's gaze toward Senator Acosta.

She was still sitting, arm against her side, but as they turned, she got to her feet, wincing slightly but standing straight. Liz could see she was mustering strength from within. She was determined. "Ok," she said again. "I'm in."

Granger nodded and looked to Liz and Dani.

Liz glanced at Dani as well, who hesitated, then nodded, though somewhat reluctantly.

"Ok," Liz said. "We're in, too. So... what next?"

"Next, you escape," Granger said. "And bring down this facility and everyone in it."

Dani looked at Liz, then back to Granger, surprised.

"You... *want* us to bring this place down?"

"It will show Young that you aren't compromised," Granger said. "It will also provide some cover for my people to get Senator Acosta back under Young's control."

"I am *not* under Young's control," Acosta said, her voice acid.

"I'm afraid you are," Granger said. "Or you were. But don't worry. Now is your chance to fight back, with the full power of the Jani behind you. It's the most empowered you've ever been," Granger smiled.

Acosta said nothing, but stared angrily at Granger's desk.

Granger turned and opened a drawer in the desk, raising a handgun and a badge from within. He handed these to Dani. "Agent Brown, your people have been alerted, using your mobile phone. They'll arrive any minute to help you take this place and everyone left inside."

"Just like that?" Brown asked, taking the gun and the badge. "What's preventing me from arresting you right now."

With a speed that Liz could barely comprehend, Granger's hand shot out, seizing Dani's wrist. She cried out in alarm, but was on the floor before she could react. Granger held the gun and the badge up, showing her.

He stepped to the door and tossed the items back to Agent Brown before exiting and closing the door behind him.

"I hate that guy," Dani said, rubbing her wrist and retrieving her badge and gun from the floor.

Liz helped her stand. "He seems to like you, though," she joked. Dani didn't seem to appreciate it. "We'll deal with him later," Liz said. "For now, let's get out there and start arresting Jani."

CHAPTER FOURTEEN

THE OFFICES of Deputy Commissioner Polat, located in SanliUrfa, were in a squat, multi-story building that looked to have been built in the '80s. The facility was surrounded by temporary fencing, as a response to recent violent activity in the region. The curved front entrance, with its columns on either side of the walkway, was the only distinct architectural feature Kotler could observe, and seemed an odd contrast—its modern design felt almost welcoming, even against the backdrop of such a heavy military presence.

The facility was guarded by men wearing black riot gear and balaclavas, presenting automatic rifles that they seemed overly ready to put to use at any instant. They were an intimidating force. The fact that Polat was barricaded beyond them did nothing to raise Kotler's confidence.

Denzel seemed more or less at ease, however, as they passed through the security checkpoint and were escorted into Polat's private offices.

"You seem unusually chill," Kotler said to him, quietly, as they were escorted through the building by armed guards.

"Chill?"

"Calm," Kotler said, "considering." He nodded to the armed and imposing guards.

"I'm always chill," Denzel replied.

"Right," Kotler said, smiling.

"Besides, this might be the safest place on the planet for us, right now," Denzel said. "Everyone back in New York knows where we are. So do my contacts at Interpol. And if Polat really is trying to keep his involvement with burying something at that site a secret, he's going to mind his P's and Q's on a whole different level. Especially once we let him know what we know."

Kotler considered this and nodded. "Ok," he said. "That makes me feel a little better."

"Of course, he could just have us shot and make up a story to cover it up, after the fact," Denzel shrugged.

"Roland..." Kotler started, but their conversation was cut short as their escorts opened a set of large, oaken doors and ushered them inside.

"Agent Denzel," Polat said, rising from his desk as they entered the room. "Dr. Kotler," he continued. "Have you made progress in your investigation?" He extended a hand to each of them in turn.

Denzel shook the man's hand, then nodded. "We have, yes," he said. They all took their seats around Polat's desk, with Denzel and Kotler sitting in front of the desk in two cushioned guest chairs.

"And what have you concluded?" Polat asked.

Kotler admired the man's confidence. His tone, his body language and demeanor, everything about him indicated that he had nothing to worry about. He was a man used to being able to rely on the power of his position, and on the people who worked under him. He demanded absolute loyalty and competence, and he got it. And here, in this office and surrounded by armed police, he was at the absolute pinnacle of his power.

They were on his turf.

"We've concluded that you hid something at *Göbekli Tepe*, in the base of that column, about 30 years ago," Denzel said, casually.

There was a long, stunned silence as Polat looked to each of them, surprised. "You cannot be serious," he said.

"I am," Denzel replied. "We have evidence that you were paid by Berrett and Alexandria Kotler to use your position as head of security, during the first excavation of that site. You gave them access to the pillar, so they could hide something there before it was reburied."

Polat glanced at Kotler, with the mention of his parents' names, then leaned back, folding his hands over his stomach. He was shaking his head throughout Denzel's speech. "No," he said. "No, not at all."

"We can prove it," Denzel said. "We have records that show your involvement."

This, Kotler knew, was at least a partial bluff. They didn't have much specifically linking Polat to any of this, but they did have a paper trail and enough evidence to give Polat a black eye with his superiors, if it came to that. Given the lengths to which the man was willing to go, to protect his reputation and career, even at the expense of letting a murderer go free—Kotler guessed Polat would be more cooperative, under threat of exposure.

Polat was looking around the office, glancing at the door, ensuring they were not being listened to.

He stared at Denzel, waiting.

"We have no intention of causing you any trouble over this," Denzel said. "I'm not even sure it would be considered a crime. It was thirty years ago, after all. And as far as I can tell, all you did was let Berrett Kotler bury something at that site. For all anyone knows, it could have been a time capsule, or some sort of experiment he wanted to run off the books. You'd really have no way to know. But it's going to look pretty suspicious all the same, isn't it? You helping Berrett Kotler bury something at the site, where thirty years later someone was murdered for what he put there?"

Polat looked from Denzel to Kotler "Your... father?"

Kotler nodded. "You must have known."

Polat hesitated for a moment, then sighed, leaning forward, placing his elbows on his desk. "I suspected it was not a coincidence."

"Then you admit you were involved," Denzel said.

Polat glanced at him and nodded. "You must understand," he said, his voice pleading. "My position here would be threatened, if anyone learned the truth. I... had no choice."

"That's debatable," Denzel said. "But the fact is, I don't care about your involvement with burying something there, three decades ago. What I care about is the death of that security guard, and the implications of whatever was stolen from that site. You erased evidence I could use in my investigation."

Polat nodded. "I am aware," he said, dejected. He sighed then. "I had my people thoroughly document the scene. I will have them turn everything over to you."

Denzel nodded. "A good start. But I'm hoping you can help me further. Do you have any idea what the contents of that void were? The object that this person stole before killing the guard?"

Polat again sighed. "I was not supposed to know, officially, but yes. Dr. Kotler—the *senior* Kotler—buried a device there. A computer hard drive."

Kotler felt his pulse quicken. He'd been right. "Do you know what was on it? Why my father hid it there?"

Polat shook his head. "No, I never knew. I was just the head of security for the site. He... bribed me to give him access. I thought perhaps he was going to steal an artifact."

"And that was ok with you," Denzel said, flatly.

Polat looked at Denzel, and Kotler could see something haunting the man's expression. "I'm... afraid that at that point in my life, it was common."

Kotler was stunned. "You're admitting you took bribes? To let people steal from these historical sites?"

Polat nodded, his expression pained. "It was a difficult time for me. A different time. I had a family. My son... he was sick. He needed medicine and treatment. I couldn't afford it on my salary. And so... I took bribes. I am ashamed." He tilted his head downward, his chin resting on his chest.

"But eventually you joined law enforcement," Denzel said. "Did you continue to accept bribes?"

Polat shook his head, adamant. "Never. Not once in my entire career. Not... precisely."

Kotler almost wanted to groan. It was clear that Polat wanted to think of himself as an honorable man, but it was equally clear that he had done things that tarnished that honor. Everyone was the hero of their own story. Polat's identity had some cognitive dissonance, but that wasn't uncommon.

But Kotler was riding Polat's body language, and could see something in the way the man hesitated and hedged.

"Someone approached you," Kotler said. "Recently."

Polat shot him a surprised glance, then nodded. "He... knew things. He knew about the bribe I'd taken from Dr. Kotler... your father. He knew that something was buried in that site. And in other sites, where I worked with security. He wanted the specifics, and he threatened to expose me if I didn't cooperate. But he also offered me money. A great deal of money."

"To keep you under control," Denzel said, shaking his head. "He paid you so that he could have even more leverage over you."

Polat looked back to Denzel, then nodded, his eyes brimmed red, his expression ashamed.

"I'm guessing you don't have a sick son to use as an excuse this time," Denzel said.

Polat said nothing, but leaned back his chair, raising a hand to his brow.

"I need you to tell me everything you can about this man," Denzel said.

Polat looked back to Denzel again, nodded, and began to speak.

The details started to sound familiar, and as Kotler glanced at Denzel from time to time, the agent taking careful note of the conversation, Denzel occasionally glanced up to acknowledge that he was getting the same picture.

The man Polat was describing, who knew all the secret details of Polat's relationship with the Kotlers, who could so casually offer such a vast amount of cash, could be only one person...

Richard Kotler.

Kotler's grandfather had access to all the Kotler family records and journals, as well as all the files from Vellar-Kotler Genetic Research, for decades. It was a sure bet that he still had copies. He did, after all, have Cristoff Vellar himself. He also had a more complete picture of things than Kotler and Denzel currently had.

Richard was ahead of them on this. Kotler realized he was the one who had orchestrated the theft of the device from *Göbekli Tepe.* And by extension, the murder of the guard.

They wrapped up the conversation with Polat. Denzel assured him that he was safe, for the time being, but warned him that this wasn't yet over. "You participated in a cover up that might keep us from finding this man's killer," Denzel said. "If that turns out to be true, there are going to be consequences."

Polat visibly winced at this, shaking his head, denying the reality of it to himself.

"We'll be in touch," Denzel said, and he and Kotler left the same way they'd come in.

Driving away from the offices, winding their way back to *Göbekli Tepe*, Denzel broke the silence after a long stretch. "Your grandfather."

"And my father. And my mother," Kotler said, quietly. "The whole Kotler family. Just one secret after another. But I think we now know what the plan was."

"We do?" Denzel asked, shooting him a glance.

"Thirty-six," Kotler said.

Denzel shook his head. "I'm not tracking."

"That's how many genetic samples Richard forced me to hand over to him," Kotler said. "From that crypt in the Cheyenne Mountain facility. Thirty-six figures from history. *Gods and men of great influence*," he intoned, quoting his grandfather. Kotler shook his head, looking out at the Turkish countryside as they passed through.

"My grandfather is about to perform a resurrection," Kotler said.

"Unless we stop him first," Denzel replied, grimly.

CHAPTER FIFTEEN

Travis Bell watched the flow of activity in the facility as things ramped up. The Chairman orchestrated everything, standing on the elevated platform that gave him and Bell a view of the entire lab and workspace.

There were *thirty-eight* cylinders on the floor, Bell realized. Two more than he'd been told. It was a curious thing for the Chairman to lie about.

It didn't matter. Lies were sometimes necessary, especially within the Order. And here, at the fringes of that Order and everything it purportedly stood for, secrets and lies became a vital part of daily life.

Bell could live with lies.

Lies didn't matter, as long as they were in service of a greater goal. And from what he had learned of the Chairman and his operation here, this was certainly a great and worthy goal.

New gods. *Actual* gods, and men who had influenced the lives of billions throughout history. The Chairman was performing the work of the Creator here. He was granting new life to these thirty-six gods, who would then go on to do his bidding, to reshape and remake the world. A new era of power and prosperity. And it would start right here, in America. The greatest of nations in the history of the world.

"I have something I need your help with, Travis," the Chairman said. His tone was authoritative but kind. Bell felt there was some sort of affection there. He and the Chairman shared some sort of bond.

The Chairman was a good man. Strong. Intelligent. He was well into his 90s and yet was as strong and vital as Bell himself.

Well... perhaps not. But certainly more vital than his years should have warranted.

"What do you need?" Bell asked, ready to do anything the Chairman asked of him.

The Chairman smiled. "I need you to overcome my weakness," he said. "My people have been unable to unlock the secrets buried within the hard drive you recovered for me. It seems my daughter-in-law's reputation was well earned. The encryption she created has proven impossible to circumvent. The only way I will be able to get to the information I need, to complete this work," he nodded to the thirty-eight canisters, glowing with a soft green light, "is if I can learn the key used to lock it. And I only know one person in the world who has any hope of uncovering that key."

"Who?" Bell asked.

The Chairman sighed. "My grandson. Daniel Kotler."

Bell nodded. "Is he an expert in this sort of encryption?"

The Chairman chuckled. "He's essentially an expert in everything. Just ask him." He laughed again, lightly and regretfully. Bell saw real pain there. Perhaps the pain of a lost relationship. "But no, he's not an expert in this, specifically. However, he is an expert regarding his mother and father. And he has a mind... oh, Travis, such a mind. It makes me regret the rift that has grown between us."

Bell understood. He was estranged from his own family, for a variety of reasons; corporate greed being chief among them. Beyond that, however, Bell's family had never understood him or his passions. And his mother...

She tended to understand him the least, and to take the most extreme means of letting him know how little he pleased her.

He still had the scars.

He treasured them, traced them with his fingers each night. Almost a meditation. His mother, he felt, had been the single biggest driving force in making him who he was. His hatred for her and for the corporation she ran, for the single-minded dedication she had to conquering the world through greed. It drove him to make himself a perfect specimen of *real* American virtue. He was strong because he had the force of his mother's will to push against his entire life.

"What do you need me to do?" Bell asked.

"I need you to bring Daniel to me. And then I need you to make sure he's cooperative."

The Chairman said this last with a touch of regret, and Bell understood how much strength this man truly had. He was willing to sacrifice anything, *everything*, in the service of this goal. He would bring the gods back to this world, and nothing, not even his own blood, would stop him.

Bell's father was a weak and worthless man, satisfied to live an existence that was little more than clinging to his wife's robes. Bell had chosen to turn to stronger examples of humanity. He'd chosen his new name—Travis Bell—based on American men he respected and admired. And he sought out men of great strength so that he could serve them, to make their objectives a reality.

The Chairman was one of those men.

"I will bring him here," Bell swore, nodding. "He'll give you what you want."

The Chairman studied him for a moment, and then nodded, his eyes a bit haunted, his shoulders a little slumped.

Bell wanted to tell him not to worry. His grandson, brilliant as he may be, had proven to be unworthy of the Chairman's loyalty and affection.

But Bell would not.

CHAPTER SIXTEEN

IN TOTAL, Agent Brown and the FBI reinforcements made twenty-seven arrests over a six-hour period.

The storage facility had proven to be a formidable stronghold, and not at all easy to clear. Every bay had steel, roll-down doors that had to be tested, opened cautiously, covered from all sides. Progress was extremely hampered by the metal walls of the storage units, which blocked both thermal scanning and the Range-R units—handheld radar scanners that the FBI used to "see through walls."

There was no seeing through these walls. Every breach was as dangerous and time-consuming as the last, with agents going in practically blind. It was grueling, bit-by-bit work that took precision and patience.

Liz was impressed, however, at the efficiency of the SWAT team, and marveled at the way the operation was run. Agents swept through the facility at a steady pace, taking down enemy cells and rounding up the members of the Jani with remarkable skill.

Granger, of course, was not among any of those who were captured.

"Six hours," Dani huffed, shaking her head and drinking from a plastic water bottle.

They were outside of the storage facility, in a zone taped off and enforced by local PD. There was some attention gathering —reporters looking for a scoop, as well as locals wondering what new threat the world was facing today.

"Granger's people couldn't make it look easy," Liz replied. "It had to look like a real firefight."

"It *was* a real firefight," Dani replied. "Six of our people were shot and injured. Mostly minor gunshot wounds, if there is such a thing."

"Was anyone killed?" Liz asked, afraid to hear the answer.

Dani took another swig and shook her head. "Everyone is alive and mostly well. Eight of the Jani were injured. The rest fought back but were ultimately pinned in place with no choice but to surrender. Our team is celebrating the win." She shook her head again, her expression mildly disgusted. "They have no idea that this was all just handed to them."

"Not exactly *handed* to them. They fought for it and earned it just as much as if it *was* real," Liz said. "They're every bit the heroes they seem to be. They've earned it."

Dani considered this and nodded, grudgingly. "Now we start grilling them for intel. That should be fun. If they're this dedicated to faking a takedown, they're going to give us hell in interrogations."

Liz was thinking about this when a couple of agents came over to debrief with Agent Brown. Dani spoke with them quietly, just out of earshot, as Liz wandered away.

It was the intel that was the most important thing, Liz agreed. Granger would have ordered his people to make this as real as possible, to cover for their cooperation and the setup being orchestrated for taking down Kendell Young. Realism would be crucial.

But the other side of that coin would be timing. If it took too long to crack the Jani that were taken into custody, to get the information they needed to move forward, that could put the whole plan in jeopardy as well.

Granger would know that.

Granger seemed to know a lot of things in advance.

Liz couldn't shake the thought that there was something they were missing.

All of this had gone down so quickly and so suddenly—and so violently—that it all felt spontaneous. But that wasn't true, was it? The fact was, from the moment SWAT had arrived on scene, right up until the last Jani operative was detained, this had all been an elaborate show.

But what if that show had started even earlier?

Granger had put assets in place to drive Acosta out of the brush. He'd had an operative in the bar, waiting to ID Acosta's contacts. Granger *himself* had been waiting, with some of his team, to nab both Liz and Acosta, during the firefight on the street.

Was *any* of that real?

Looking around, seeing the lengths that the Jani were willing to go to with this subterfuge, suddenly Liz questioned everything that had happened over the past twenty-four hours. If the Jani were willing to engage in a six-hour firefight just to keep their cover, they'd be equally willing to put the same effort into the appearance of rushing in to save the day, out on the streets.

Liz glanced back at the storage facility. Dani and the others were circled up, discussing next steps. There were FBI vans full of Jani prisoners, rolling out one by one, on their way to secure locations. The interrogations would start almost the moment the first batch of prisoners were processed.

That was the plan.

But Liz now realized that her timeline was off.

The *real* plan had been set in motion much earlier. This— the raid, the takedown, the shuffle of Jani into FBI custody— was just the most obvious and evident part of it.

Granger had this set up from the beginning, right down to purchasing this storage facility. And what was so important about this place? It had never even opened to the public.

Liz moved away, looking for some of the FBI agents she knew personally. A lot of the Historic Crimes team was here, including some of the operatives from other agencies. Liz spotted the familiar yellow FBI logo emblazoned on jackets and vests and body armor, and she made her way to a few agents who were carrying boxes of bagged evidence.

She showed her credentials and asked, "Did you find any computers or other devices in there? Any paperwork?"

"Several laptops," one of the agents replied. He placed the box he was carrying into the trunk of a car, then rifled through the other contents of the trunk until he lifted out a box. This one had half a dozen laptops slotted neatly between foam inserts. Each contained in marked and taped evidence bags.

Liz started lifting them out of the box, one at a time, inspecting them without opening the evidence seals.

They were all identical. Same brand, same model, same operating system. All the same.

Except one.

While the rest of the laptops were clean and unmarked, with nothing to differentiate them, this one had a sticker on the lid. Liz could make it out through the plastic—a logo for a campground in New Hampshire.

Liz recognized it immediately.

The campground was close to Cathedral Ledge—where Liz and Dan Kotler had spent a weekend rock climbing and camping. That trip was supposed to give them both a break from their work at Historic Crimes, and a chance to deepen their bond.

But it had been interrupted when a group of senators, including Senator Acosta, and their personnel were abducted straight from the Senate floor, in broad daylight, on live TV. That had stirred a global reaction, and it was enough to pull Liz and Dan out of their romantic getaway and set them both to work on finding and recovering the abductees.

It had also marked the end of Liz's romantic relationship with Dan, for reasons Liz was still piecing together.

Dan's encounter with his grandfather—long thought deceased but revealed to be one of the Jani, and the leader of the Novensiles—had set a series of events into motion. The casualties of which included their relationship.

That trip to Cathedral Ledge had been their last good moment together.

Liz saw this for what it was—a message. A note from Granger, telling her where to focus her attention. "This laptop gets scanned first," she said to the agent. "Have the tech team dismantle it down to the screws and tell me everything they find. I want a mirror of every folder and every file sent straight to me. Every detail, no matter what it is."

The agent nodded, reaching to take the laptop back, but Liz hesitated.

She looked again at the sticker, peering closer.

Something was wrong.

The web address. It wasn't the right domain, she realized.

Liz had booked their trip to Cathedral Ledge, and in her way, she'd been meticulous about it. She'd done her research, found recommendations for the best spots, and the best services. This campground had gotten not only rave reviews from past campers, it had the best presentation of amenities, among all the other campgrounds she'd researched. Their website was well done, and easy to navigate, especially considering the hundreds of others she'd had to pick through.

Essentially, she had every reason to remember the site. And this wasn't it.

The URL was similar, but not quite exact. The top-level domain for the site she'd used was a .COM. But this URL, otherwise identical, ended in .INFO.

She made a mental note of it and handed the laptop over to the agent, then retreated to a quiet spot and took out her phone. She opened a browser and entered the URL from the laptop.

The browser automatically inserted the ".COM," since she'd visited this site before. She deleted this and typed in .INFO, and hit "go."

The page that loaded was familiar. It was identical to the .COM version of the site, in every way that Liz could determine. It was so identical, in fact, that she started to doubt herself.

She shook her head.

Granger was a sharp strategist. That much was obvious. In an operation such as this, any equipment his team used would be as generic as possible. Nothing distinguishing about it. So the fact that this one laptop had something making it unique *had* to be a message. It simply *had to*.

What was it that Granger wanted her to find here? Was she on the wrong track? Maybe this was just a "near miss" URL—a second domain name pointing at the same website. That was common enough, though Liz couldn't think of why a near-miss domain name would be used on the campground's logo. People tended to think of the web in terms of "dot-com," so putting "dot-info" on a sticker made little sense.

No, there was a reason for this. She inhaled and exhaled, rotating her neck a bit, relaxed, and focused.

She went over the entire web page, inspecting every element. She was not an expert in digital forensics, but she knew enough to look for certain things. She was able to view the source code for the page and scanned through this looking for anything that might pop out at her. So far there was nothing of any particular import. Nothing that seemed like a hidden message.

Maybe that was diving too deep?

Hiding something in the source code would keep it away from the eyes of most people, but it wouldn't keep the FBI's technical team from finding it. If Liz was able to inspect the code, that was nothing compared to the scans her team would run on it.

So whatever message Granger had hidden here—if there even was such a message—would be something only Liz would catch onto. It had to be. Because this campground was something personal to her and to Dan Kotler.

This message was meant for Liz, so only Liz would be able to find it.

She went back to basics. She opened a second browser tab and brought up the .COM version of the site, comparing it to the .INFO version.

This proved fruitless. Every pixel of the two sites seemed identical, as far as Liz could determine. Every word was replicated between the two. Every image was the same. Logos, icons, colors, fonts... all the same.

They were identical. In every way, they were identical.

She huffed, frustrated. She couldn't be wrong about this. It would just be too bizarre, that someone among Granger's team not only broke protocol and personalized their laptop, but did so with something that would just *coincidentally* align with Liz's own life?

But here she was, with a thread that lead, apparently, to nowhere. The sites were the same.

At least, as far as all the public-facing pages went...

In the upper right corner of the home page she saw the login button. She hadn't logged in, hadn't checked anything beyond the home page and any other pages that were right out in the open. Was it possible that what she was looking for was on the other side of that login?

She clicked the link, and when the little pop-up appeared she entered her username and password.

Suddenly she was no longer looking at the same website.

The colorful photos of mountain vistas and New Hampshire foliage and happy hikers and campers were replaced by an all-black screen with white font. A message informed her that everything she needed was contained in the file linked below. She tapped this and the file opened, revealing its contents.

It was a database of dossiers and profiles for people within Young's upper echelon. It included the names of numerous high-ranking US government officials, CEOs of major international corporations, military leaders, and even members of foreign governments. Each entry was tagged with details that Liz knew the FBI could use to track down everything needed to bring each individual down if need be. Or, at the very least, to compromise them to a degree that would give the FBI—and the Jani, Liz was sure—an inroad into Young's organization.

And there was more. Photos. Videos. Forensic files that seemed to have been otherwise excised from official records. The file was a trail leading not only to Kendell Young, but to everyone he relied on or had dirt on or otherwise needed to keep his empire of influence running.

It was the evidence they would need to take down Young and start dismantling his network.

She downloaded the file, moving it to a password-locked folder in the cloud that she knew would sync with multiple devices. That would help to protect it, but for good measure she saved a copy to an obscure and well-hidden corner of her sister's Dropbox account.

If it was discovered, Liz would say she'd accidentally saved it there, and to leave it alone until she had time to move it. But Liz knew her sister would likely never notice it, and would certainly not open it, even if she knew the password.

Liz knew that Dan would have a hundred different ways to protect and preserve that file, but she felt she'd done a good enough job of it for now. She'd look into something else later.

For the moment, she knew what she had to do.

It wouldn't work to just start going down the list and making arrests. That would start sending out shock waves. Before they could get to Young, he'd get spooked and take precautions. What they needed was to build a case, to set the trap, and to spring it when Young least expected it.

Knowing who was in Young's inner circle helped them to avoid talking to the wrong people. Now they just had to find the right ones.

Liz tucked her phone into her pocket and made her way back to Dani. She'd pull Dani aside at the first opportunity, to explain what was happening and keep her looped in.

Until then, all of this would stay Liz's secret.

Granger had handed her the keys to take down Kendell Young and, maybe, the Novensiles. It was an incredible stroke of luck.

Liz just wondered what it was going to cost them.

CHAPTER SEVENTEEN

THE DRIVE back to *Göbekli Tepe* had given Kotler and Denzel time to plan their next steps. Now that they knew Polat's role in covering his own culpability in hiding a hard drive at the site, he was effectively eliminated as a suspect in both the guard's murder and the theft.

That still left a lot of holes to fill, however.

Once back at their quarters, on site, Kotler was pleased to see that Polat had been true to his word. All the excised files and evidence were waiting for them, on Denzel's account. There was a note assuring them that the physical evidence, properly bagged and cataloged, was on its way as well.

It seemed that once Polat realized he was caught, he wanted to make amends, being as forthcoming as he could. Admirable, Kotler thought, though it may be too little too late.

"I'm not sure how useful any of that is going to be," Denzel said with a huff, waving toward the index of files on Kotler's laptop.

Kotler shook his head. "Neither am I. But these files may

give us something to work from, at least. Otherwise, I don't know that we have any real leads."

Included among the digital trove released to them by Polat was the satellite and security footage from the night of the murder.

There wasn't much of use on the satellite imagery. Denzel had hoped they might be able to identify and track any vehicles the killer might have used to escape. But between the multiple bursts of fireworks over the area and the cover provided by the terrain, they lost sight of the figure almost the instant he left the scene.

And to Denzel's frustration, there were dozens of vehicles moving to and from the area at the time. Any one of them could have had their killer onboard. It would take weeks to trace them all out.

The security video also showed practically nothing of value, since at some point the cameras had been adjusted to create a blind spot for that particular part of the site. Backing up through the days and weeks prior to the murder, Denzel and Kotler were able to pinpoint exactly when that adjustment had been made.

A man—a local, judging by his appearance—could be seen timidly and cautiously walking into frame, then using a small, folding step stool to boost himself up and toward the camera. One full frame of the footage showed his face in great detail, and Denzel captured this, forwarding it on to both Sarge and Isoken Edo.

"I figure this guy is going to turn out to be nobody," Denzel said.

Kotler agreed. The man had the look of someone who wasn't entirely certain about what he was doing. His body language screamed hesitation and nervousness, and he showed a real lack of understanding that this glass eye he was staring into, at the time, was making a perfect recording of his features.

Kotler's guess was that he was a local who might have access to the site as some sort of service provider, perhaps someone who made deliveries or restocked the mess and vending machines with food. Kotler felt a little bad for him, if that was the case. This could lead to a lot of trouble, and it seemed likely that he had been bribed and possibly even threatened into adjusting the camera.

But it could pan out into a lead, and at the moment they sorely needed one.

Sometimes people—even people who otherwise were innocent or even victims themselves—had to be held responsible for their role in things. Justice, as the adage went, really was blind.

They played the rest of the footage, and watched as the camera was turned just so, no more than a few centimeters, physically. But the effect was to create a gap of a few feet in the coverage of that spot, giving the assailant a way in without being discovered.

"How did no one see this happening?" Kotler asked.

Denzel shrugged. "It's possible it was just overlooked. But my money is on an inside man."

"You think one of Isoken's team covered for this?"

"Or one of Polat's people," Denzel said. "Isoken and Sarge both told us that the Turkish officials have been interfering, sending orders from above, dropping in for surprise inspections, generally making things difficult. Turns out, those officials were mostly Polat and his people."

Kotler nodded. It made the most sense. "Polat's being very forthcoming, but maybe someone else in his organization isn't."

"So they're compromised," Denzel said.

"I'd put money on the Novensiles. Or..." he hesitated,

double-checking how he felt about what he was about to say next. He sighed.

"Or maybe it was my grandfather."

Denzel studied him. "You think Richard Kotler has someone inside the Turkish government?"

"He was the head of the Novensiles," Kotler shrugged. "He's shown that he has tendrils in governments and businesses all over the world. We know he had a hand in the founding of Historic Crimes, which shows he has some reach within the US government, at a minimum."

Denzel nodded. "So, not such a stretch. Ok. But he's had a break with the Novensiles, right? Would they continue to work for him?"

"They may not realize he's not the Chairman anymore," Kotler said. "It's a very insular organization. Lies, deceptions, plans with multiple moving parts—like playing 4-D chess. Richard knows the ins and outs of the Jani and the Novensiles better than practically anyone. He'd have no trouble keeping his network alive for his own use."

Denzel thought for a moment. "Ok. So even though Polat's sharing now, we still might not have everything we need."

Kotler shook his head and turned back to the footage. He raced it forward to the night of the murder. There was nothing to even differentiate it from every other night, beyond the flashes of fireworks in the air, occasionally illuminating darkened objects within the camera's view.

He checked his notes, getting a timeline for the murder. He brought up the footage and photos they already had, showing their assailant springing over the fence and making his escape like some sort of ninja, disappearing into the shadows.

In the recovered footage, Kotler watched the same timeframe, letting it play out in real time first, then backing it up and reviewing it frame by frame.

There was a flash from the fireworks, illuminating the entire landscape.

Kotler saw the murderer, in that instant, in plain sight. He had stopped, and was looking up at the show above, as if admiring the spectacle of it. This was someone who had just killed a man in one of the most brutal and gruesome ways possible, and here he stood, like a beguiled teenager, watching the show overhead as if he were standing in front of the castle at Disney's Magic Kingdom.

By the next flash, however, he was gone. Kotler backed up and held that one frame, looking at it closely, trying to discern any details he could. Try to read the man before him, to study and learn everything he could about him.

The figure had dark hair, close-cropped but styled. He held himself the way highly trained special forces operatives do—his body relaxed but taught. His stance loose, but ready to spring into action at any instance. Kotler could see by his silhouette, even while he was wearing a loose-fitting hoodie, that the man was incredibly fit. The muscles of his neck were visible in the cast of light from the fireworks, and stood like cords against the contrast of shadows.

There was no real way to identify him. As clear as the footage was, he was still standing a good distance away, barely lit by the fireworks. His face was visible, and vaguely recognizable, but likely not enough to run him through a database and find a positive match.

The FBI's digital forensics team might be able to enhance this image a great deal, but Kotler doubted there'd be anything useful in it. No identity, no clue to where he went next. Nothing.

"Travis Bell," Denzel said quietly, looking over Kotler's shoulder.

Kotler looked up, surprised. "You know him?"

Denzel shook his head. "Not personally. I've seen him in competition."

"Competition?" Kotler asked.

"Parkour," Denzel said, seeming a bit sheepish. "I... watch it. Sometimes. ESPN."

"You're telling me that this guy is famous?"

Denzel shrugged. "Maybe *famous* is a little strong. But he's a champion. He never allows interviews, and he disappears without collecting his winnings. So of course, there's some legend built up around him. Mysterious guy who can move like Spider-man? He's got a lot of fans."

Kotler shook his head, dumbfounded. "You have to be kidding me," he said. "Of all the dumb luck... our murderer turns out to be a sports figure?"

Denzel had already straightened and was tapping something into his phone. A few minutes later, he nodded. "We got him on a commercial flight out of Turkey," Denzel said. "The night of the murder."

"Where to?" Kotler asked.

Denzel smiled. "Utah," he replied. "Salt Lake City."

Kotler huffed, then laughed lightly. "Ok then," he said. "It looks like we're going to Salt Lake."

Denzel looked as if he were about to say something to that when a voice spoke up from the doorway of Kotler's room.

"I will save you a trip, my friends."

Kotler and Denzel both looked to the doorway, startled.

Travis Bell stood, hands splayed out to his side, looking at them. His eyes sparkled with what Kotler could only describe as *zeal*, and he had a slight smirk on his face that hinted at utter confidence. He stepped forward, hands still out to his side, but certain in his movements.

He did not see either Kotler or Denzel as a threat. In fact,

Kotler could read by his stance that he welcomed any resistance.

He wants this fight, Kotler thought. *To prove himself.*

Denzel drew his weapon. "Stay right there! Hands on the back of your head! Get down on your knees, now!"

Kotler watched Bell, and saw just the slightest twitch—a tiny movement in the rope-like muscles of his neck that instantly translated into an explosion of movement, at a speed that was almost incomprehensible. From one instant to the next, Bell's body accelerated, moving with such speed and such force that Kotler almost wasn't certain the man could be real. In less than an instant he had Denzel's weapon, which was promptly dismantled and dropped to the floor in a clatter.

An instant after that, Denzel took hits to the sternum, the throat, and his right temple, and then was suddenly airborne, crashing through the door of his own room before landing in a heap on the other side.

Kotler leapt to his feet, and wasted no time grabbing Bell's right wrist, turning it quickly up and over, at an odd and painful angle, before swinging to punch Bell in the throat. Kotler had the fingers of his hand curled back, striking with his palm, in a move that could crush Bell's windpipe... if it landed.

Bell made no attempt to break free of Kotler's grip. Instead, he used the momentum of Kotler's attack as direction.

Bell did a back flip in place, landing in a slight crouch and reaching up with his left hand to seize Kotler's own wrist. He turned then, spinning on his heels and yanking Kotler down, rolling him over his back.

Kotler landed with a heavy thud that knocked the wind out of him. Dazed, colorful spots dancing at the edge of his vision, he tried to roll onto his hands and knees, to spring back to his feet.

Before Kotler could complete the roll, Bell punched him in

the solar plexus, followed by a jab to the throat—the same jab Kotler had tried to land.

Kotler gasped, pain shooting through his body, but a numbness quickly following. He was having trouble breathing, and Bell took advantage of this. He yanked Kotler upward and pressed his carotid artery in an iron grip between Bell's bicep and forearm.

Kotler struggled, but in almost no time his vision darkened, then faded to black as he slumped.

His last thought was of Liz.

He'd meant to call her.

He'd meant to make things right.

He'd meant to be better at this.

No thought followed that, however, as the darkness flooded over him, and all thought and emotion and sensation was gone.

CHAPTER EIGHTEEN

"How sure?" Dani asked.

Liz exhaled audibly. Debriefing Dani about the cache of intel that Granger had given them had been a long and uncomfortable conversation. "About the veracity of this?" she asked. "Or about whether we can trust it?"

"Either," Dani replied, then threw her hands up. "Both."

They were sitting in the glass conference room at Historic Crimes headquarters. Dani was once again barricaded behind a mountain range of files and papers, empty and half-empty paper cups of coffee, and more than one laptop and smart pad. Much of this was left over from the previous few days' workload, but the pile had grown exponentially since the last time Liz had dropped by.

Liz had a pile of her own, though much of it was digital.

Her email inbox was brimming with forensic results from the raid, as well as reports from various field agents. Nothing useful seemed to be coming out of the recovered laptops, beyond a few low-level contacts and names they could look into.

All of that was to be expected, Liz figured. If they were able to get seriously actionable intelligence from a bunch of Jani laptops, it would look very suspicious. It would likely alert the Novensiles, and Kendell Young's people specifically, that something wasn't right.

"I'm a hundred percent certain it's factually accurate," Liz said. "Maybe... ninety percent that we can trust it. I definitely think we're being manipulated."

"What was your first clue?" Dani asked, perturbed.

"Hey, don't shoot the messenger. I'm with you. Granger set all this up from the start, so he's definitely got a play in motion. The thing is, he's too smart to think we wouldn't figure it out."

Dani considered this. "So figuring it out is part of the plan," she said.

"Or doesn't matter to him," Liz replied. "In a way, it's kind of like a gesture of good faith. He didn't bother trying to actually fool us. He left us plenty of clues to figure it out. Sort of a chronic liar's way of telling the truth."

"Super reassuring," Dani said. "I don't like games like this. I have a duty to fulfill here. I can't allow this to turn into some kind of Jani-led operation." She thought for a moment. "Granger is a source. I could contact the DOJ. See about maybe making him a confidential informant."

Liz laughed, then shook her head. "I can't claim to know Granger well, but I do know him enough to say he's never going to reveal his actual identity. The DOJ is going to demand that."

"Among other things," Dani admitted. "It wouldn't work, anyway. CI, source, witness, whatever we choose to call him, there's no way I'm going to be able to keep his involvement secret, if I move through official channels. And there's no way anyone is going to approve it anyway, since I'd have to report it through the chain of command."

"Meaning that just by trying to stick to official procedure," Liz said, "we'd be tipping off Kendell Young."

Liz slumped back, miserably, in the rolling conference chair. They were in a precarious scenario here, having this large cache of intelligence that they would never be able to explain. Not without putting themselves in jeopardy and nixing any shot at taking down Kendell Young.

Suddenly she had an inspiration.

"What about the Jani we're questioning?" Liz asked.

"So far they aren't giving up much," Dani replied, her expression sour.

Liz thought about this for a moment. "Maybe that's because they don't have much to give up?"

Dani shook her head. "I'm not tracking."

Liz leaned forward. "Granger delivered this intel to me via that phony website. Only I would have been able to get to it. The Jani... they're so insular, so siloed. I'm sure they keep certain information on a need-to-know basis, if for no other reason than to make sure the Novensiles don't have access to it. There could be Novensile plants among the people we brought in from that facility, for all we know."

"So they keep key information a secret from the people in the field," Dani said, thinking.

"And deliver it to us, while we're busy arresting everyone left in the facility," Liz added.

"So these foot soldiers have nothing to tell us."

"Not yet," Liz replied. "Not until we give it to them to say."

Dani looked at her, sharply. "You're talking about feeding information to a suspect? Tampering with their testimony?"

"I'm talking about giving the intel the Jani have given us to the delivery system they provided us," Liz said. "We supply the answers we already have to a bunch of mouthpieces, who give it back to us in chunks. That's why Granger wanted us to arrest so many of his people. He knew we'd isolate them, so that none of them could know the full story. They'll only know their piece. Whatever pieces we give them."

Dani shook her head, leaning back and crossing her arms over her stomach. "This is walking a very thin line," she said. Then she leaned forward slightly. "Why not just give his people the bits and pieces himself? Why have us do it?"

Liz shrugged. "I can think of a few reasons, but I'm betting it's mostly about expediency. We have the full story already. We can start putting things into motion now, being careful about how we move. But if we can feed information to the Jani, they can start sharing it with our interrogating agents. The story will start to unfold, and we'll have a paper trail. But we can start moving pieces now, to speed things along. We just have to be careful about it."

Liz paused for a second, then added, "This also gives us a better chance to catch Kendell Young unprepared. And to root out any moles we have in our own organization."

"How so?"

"It's a fair bet that Young and his people will be closely monitoring anything coming out of those interrogations. And they'll likely suppress any intel they don't want us to follow up on. We have the whole puzzle, but no one will know that. We can monitor and track which pieces we share, with whom, and which we get back. We can see where the walls go up, and we'll know where the intel stopped."

Liz continued. "And beyond that, we'll be able to orchestrate an action we take based on the whole cache of intel, even while Young and his people think we're missing key pieces. We have a chance to misdirect them, and flush them out."

Dani was staring down at the stacks of folders on the table before her, thinking and nodding along as Liz spoke. She looked up, a strange expression on her face, then sighed and shook her head. "You're starting to get good at this sort of thing."

Liz blew out another breath, one she hadn't known she'd been holding. "Yeah," she said, an odd and darkly exhilarated feeling sweeping through her. "That's what scares me."

CHAPTER NINETEEN

Denzel awoke to a searing pain in his shoulder. One he recognized.

Out of socket, his mind supplied, but only after he'd clumsily gotten to his feet and felt the rage of the offended shoulder reminding him that it would prefer not to be moved.

His right arm hung uselessly at his side, pain radiating from the shoulder in waves. He didn't have to see it to know. He'd had this sort of injury before. College football had given him a whole raft of interesting ailments, but the ability to dislocate his shoulder, against his will, was an old standby.

He scanned about, looking frantically at the living quarters. There was no sign of either Travis Bell or Kotler. There were plenty of signs of a ruckus, but no blood or severed body parts. That was good, at least.

Denzel turned, facing the door frame of his room. The door itself was a splintered wreck, but the frame seemed solid enough. It would have to do.

He lined himself up, took a few deep breaths, in and out, and then counted.

On three, he rammed his shoulder against the door frame while pulling hard against it with his left hand.

There was a sickening pop, followed by excruciating pain, slight nausea, and a blue streak of profanity that would have made a Tarantino film blush.

His right hand tingled and burned with the return of blood flow, and his neck and shoulders protested their former state of misalignment by pulsing and throbbing in rhythm with the migraine he felt coming on. He took several deep, controlled breaths, and then fished his phone out his pocket, pawing at it numbly with his right hand. Dexterity was returning, and the fine movements helped.

His first call was to Kotler.

Predictably, he heard Kotler's phone ring from the table where they'd been sitting and reviewing footage. So that wasn't good.

There was no more dangerous place on Earth than the space between Kotler and his phone. He would never have left it voluntarily.

The next call was to Sarge. Denzel ordered him to scramble his people, check security footage, find any trace of what happened after Denzel was knocked unconscious and Kotler was taken.

Sarge would alert Isoken Edo, and he swore to Denzel, in profoundly colorful language, that they'd find the assailant.

Denzel didn't doubt Sarge's sincerity, but it seemed unlikely that Bell and Kotler would be anywhere near this place.

At any rate, now came the more challenging phone call.

Denzel punched up the number for the Historic Crimes offices, and when the receptionist answered he asked to be put through to Agent Brown.

Brown and Ludlum, he was told, had left the offices a few

hours earlier. There was an operation in progress, and they were leading a team. She couldn't give him specific details, of course, but she offered to transfer him to Agent Brown's mobile line.

It rang through, and he was redirected straight to her voicemail. He left a message and hung up.

He considered calling Ludlum, but decided against it. Brown could tell her the news. If she needed to talk to Denzel, she'd call. But for now, he couldn't waste anymore time on this. He needed to get moving.

Gingerly, easing into it, he stooped and picked up the pieces of his weapon from the floor.

Bell had dismantled the piece in seconds—faster by far than Denzel could have done on his best day, even when he was still in Special Forces, daily stripping his weapons to clean sand and other debris out of them. It was impressive.

It was frightening.

A man with that level of skill, in hand-to-hand and weapons, was dangerous to an immeasurable degree.

What had he wanted with Kotler?

Because it was pretty obvious, at this point, that Kotler *was* the target. Since Bell didn't kill him outright, it likely meant that Kotler was being snagged at the request of someone else. And Denzel figured the most likely suspect was Kotler's grandfather, Richard Kotler himself.

Bell, Denzel decided, had stolen the hard drive for Richard. And in doing so, he'd killed the security guard. It was probably an improvisation, when the original plan had gone pear shaped. That didn't make it any less appalling—that Bell would kill so willingly, so casually, just to keep to his schedule.

So, a couple of mysteries solved, at least.

And it meant that Kotler had been right. Richard really was

trying to use his son's research to clone and resurrect people from history. Gods and kings, as Kotler had said.

And that explained why Richard would want Kotler brought to him, as well.

If anyone on Earth had any shot at breaking Alexandria Kotler's encryption, it would be her eldest son. Not only did Kotler know his parents better than anyone, he was one of the best riddle-solvers and code breakers Denzel had ever met. No one was more qualified to do this.

Of course, what Richard would do with his grandson, after that code was cracked, was anyone's guess. He was a man obsessed. A man with a plan for world domination that, somehow, *might actually work.*

His grandson was a foil to that plan, and might be more trouble than familial bonds could justify keeping around.

If Denzel couldn't find Kotler within the next 48 hours, he knew what the odds favored.

Kotler might never be seen or heard from again.

Denzel glanced at the disassembled firearm laid out on the table. He started piecing it back together—a process that was a bit slower than usual, thanks to his tender shoulder. But the minute and controlled movement was helping him recover, his manual dexterity was slowly returning, and soon he lifted the weapon, inspecting it. He picked up the clip and locked it into place, then racked the slide to put a round in the chamber.

Back to right.

And now it was time to find Travis Bell, and Richard Kotler, and bring this whole thing down in a rain of hell on both their heads.

CHAPTER TWENTY

KOTLER HAD a few vague flashes of memory that, he assumed, were moments of consciousness and semi-lucidity interspersed with what was likely a drug-induced stupor, as he was being transported out of Turkey.

He had no real memory of how Bell had accomplished getting him out of the country, but it likely involved a private plane. A jet, by Kotler's estimate. There was a fuzzy memory of being buckled into a seat, in what felt like a comfortably posh interior, and occasionally awaking to the white noise of jet engines rather than the rumble of a prop plane or the rise and fall of a boat.

That meant this could be the following day... or possibly a couple of days later. It also meant he could be anywhere in the world by now.

He lifted his head to find himself laid out on a hospital bed, in a room that was decidedly *not* a hospital. In fact, it was barely a room, as any modern human would think of it.

The walls appeared to be natural stone, with signs of

tooling to indicate that at least part of the space had been hewn by hand. But it was done remarkably well, with great precision.

This was no abandoned mine or hastily enhanced cave network. Someone had meticulously planned this space, right down to running ventilation and power through conduits that zig-zagged along the line of the ceiling. A set of LED panels lit the room from above.

Modern work. Or updated relatively recently, at the very least. But from what Kotler could tell, all the fixtures appeared to be new.

Someone had gone to a lot of trouble.

"Hello, Daniel."

Kotler felt a sickening thrill in his stomach, at the sound of the familiar voice.

"Hello, Grandfather."

"You've been out for nearly two days, if you're wondering."

"That tracks," Kotler said, sitting up and stretching, rubbing his eyes.

He was still dressed in the clothes he'd been wearing when Bell had taken him.

But they were clean. Freshly washed from the smell of them. He held the front of his shirt with two fingers and looked to Richard, questioning.

"I had them clean you up. I hope you don't mind."

"Thank you," Kotler said.

This was all very strange. All very... well, not *normal*, exactly, considering where they were and their relationship with each other. They were being formal in how they interacted, but there was still something less formal hovering there. The casual familiarity of family, even if neither of them cared much for the other.

"So," Kotler said, swinging his feet off of the bed and

standing slowly. "You have me. Let's go take a look at that hard drive."

Richard laughed and shook his head. "I should have known," he said. "Of course you'd figure things out. You always were very bright. Though, I sometimes wonder if Jeffrey might be smarter. He's certainly more sensible. Less prone to rush into danger."

Kotler nodded. "I'm willing to accept that he's smarter than I am," he said. "He has a family, a home, work that doesn't get him shot at. Most of the time. I envy him."

For an instant, Kotler thought he saw something pass over his grandfather's features, even partially hidden as they were by the shadows of the room. Kotler saw hints of an emotion that he had assumed Richard no longer felt. Something nostalgic and regretful.

"I do too, I think," Richard said.

Then the expression was gone, along with the moment, and whatever it may have meant.

"Well, you're smart, and you've figured out why you're here, at least. Let's not waste anymore time. How about a quick tour?"

Richard stood from the chair he'd been using in one darkened corner of the room. He left the room through the open door, without even bothering to look back.

Where was Kotler going to run to, if he tried to escape? He was trapped, and they both knew it.

He sighed and followed Richard out of the room, down the hall, and into an elevator. From there they rode slowly downward, deeper into the stone surrounding them.

A *marvel of engineering*, Kotler determined, taking in the overall space in these tiny slices that hinted at so much more. The Jani certainly liked their underground facilities.

This particular underground facility was an elaborate

complex of hand-hewn spaces coupled with a natural network of tunnels and caverns. To Kotler—perhaps because of his recent travels—it brought to mind Turkey's famous underground city, Derinkuyu. A city carved into the bedrock of the region, lying hidden for thousands of years until someone discovered by accident, while renovating their basement.

There were some parallels in them and construction, at least. Though this space was decidedly more modern.

What sort of resources did it take to pull off a feat such as this?

Money, of course. But there wouldn't be enough money in the world to not only build this but keep it so completely off the radar.

Power, then. A level of power and influence that rivaled nations. Power that had been amassed and accumulated over multiple millennia. Maybe even since the time of Derinkuyu itself.

And that same power was now being brought to bear on resurrecting ancient beings. People of tremendous historic and mythological influence. Gods and kings.

It was mind-boggling, Kotler thought, to realize how entrenched his family line was in all of this.

Kotler, who had dedicated his life to studying and understanding science and history and human culture, was learning that his own bloodline was deeply intertwined with the influence of all three. A secret he'd never even considered, and one that impacted his perspective on everything he'd ever known or believed.

And if this was what the Jani were capable of? Even if it was just a small hint of their reach, it was beyond anything Kotler would have imagined.

It explained why he'd made practically no headway in his quest to bring the Novensiles down. The Jani, the root of

Novensile history, had a level of power that was frightening. The fact that they had not so much as attempted to conquer the world before now was shocking.

Which raised a number of questions.

If the Jani had this much power, and resources at this level, and did not use them... were they a threat, after all?

Perhaps it was better to have such power in the hands of an organization that had proven itself over millennia, than to try to wrest it away from them out of a sense of fear they might abuse it some day.

That was an intriguing thought, but Kotler still erred on the side of "too much power means too much of a threat."

The Novensiles were proof that such influence and reach could have disastrous side effects. If they gained control of that full power, they'd use the resources of the Jani to rule. Humanity's destiny would be changed forever. A new, dark era was only a few heartbeats away.

And yet...

It was absurd to think that something like this had never happened before, wasn't it? Thousands of years of this secret order, operating just off camera, just out of sight, and not once, prior to the past hundred years or so, had anyone thought to abuse such power?

Kotler was starting to see that he'd been naïve. The Jani had things under much tighter control than he'd assumed. And he and Denzel might just be better off leaving things as they were. They might be opposing something that was necessary to the continued survival of humanity, when it came down to it. Like hunting wolves to near extinction before realizing they kept the population of other species in balance.

It was a strange and even chilling thought, but one that was gaining traction, the more Kotler considered it.

The elevator finally stopped, and as the doors opened

Richard stepped forward, walking out and away without a word or a glance. Kotler followed, in the same way.

For the moment, there was nothing to do but play along. If he had any chance of surviving this, he needed more intel. More resources. More information. More opportunities.

At the moment, all he had was the thin slice of insight that told him what his grandfather needed from him. That would only protect him so far, Kotler was aware.

Richard led him into a large, gaping space, possibly a reshaped natural cavern that was now festooned with modern accoutrements. Conduits for climate control, power, water, and natural gas all ran along the walls and ceiling in neat and orderly lines. If Kotler had suffered from OCD, the site would be downright soothing. As it was, it felt aesthetically comforting, as if the organization of it hinted that someone was in control, that things were safe because someone had taken such care.

A psychological delusion, of course, but one that had its advantages. As dangerous as this situation was for Kotler, he needed to keep his mind clear of anxiety, in order to best notice opportunities as they arose. He'd take any cues he could find to help keep himself on an even keel.

From their vantage point, they now stood on a metal catwalk that continued on to encircle the entire room, hovering perhaps thirty feet above the floor below. Stretching before them, in a grid along the floor, Kotler could see dozens of chambers, standing vertically like columns, glowing and pulsing a soft green.

He recognized them. He'd seen something like these before, at Vellar-Kotler Genetic Research.

Maturation chambers.

Though these were several magnitudes larger than those he'd seen in the labs. The smaller chambers were used by

Vellar-Kotler to cultivate cells in small batches, to aid in study and research.

The content of each of these larger chambers, Kotler knew, was the end result of the genetic samples he had been forced to retrieve for his grandfather.

Gods and kings.

"As you can see, things have been progressing. I can't thank you enough for helping me unlock the samples."

"My pleasure," Kotler said dryly.

Richard laughed. "Ok, I can see we're going to be ironic about it all. But don't you think that this, alone, is a remarkable achievement? Look at it, Daniel! This! The culmination of not only my work, but that of your father, and your mother!"

Kotler turned on him then, sharp and sudden, closing the gap between them in an instant. "Do not invoke my parents in this," Kotler said, squaring off only inches from Richard, their eyes aligned. "You dishonor their memory with every breath you take."

His words were cold, quiet, but not without emotion. There was something icy and dangerous there that Kotler himself wasn't sure he recognized.

He watched Richard's face. His grandfather's eyes flashed for an instant, though it could have been either anger or fear. Perhaps it was a mingling of both.

And then his glance darted past Kotler. Richard gave a slight shake of his head, and Kotler knew, instantly, that Travis Bell was near.

"If Travis touches me again, I'll die before I'll help you in any way."

Richard was studying Kotler now, sizing him up. He pressed his lips together and nodded, impressed. "Alright. I believe you. Travis, stand down."

Kotler spared a glance behind him and saw that Bell had

been close. Within reach, for sure. He'd managed to move so quickly and silently that Kotler was almost certain he'd have been dead before he could lay a finger on Richard.

Bell was going to be a problem, Kotler knew. He was the biggest threat in the room. The biggest *immediate* threat, at any rate.

Kotler stepped past his grandfather and leaned, placing his hands on the rail of the catwalk, surveying the chambers below. He did a quick count, multiplying columns and rows to get the number of chambers.

There had been 36 genetic samples in the sarcophagus that Kotler had unlocked for Richard, all retrieved by the Jani from archaeological sites around the world, over a span of decades.

But there were 38 chambers on the floor below.

He turned to face Richard, and noted that Bell had retreated a few steps back, lingering in the doorway.

"Who do you have in the other two chambers?" Kotler asked.

Richard said nothing for a moment, then shrugged. "Does it matter?"

"It does to me."

Richard smiled. "Well, then, I'd say it doesn't matter."

Kotler turned back to the array of chambers, thinking.

Richard had been using this technology to keep himself vital, even into his 90s. So it seemed likely that at least one of the chambers contained his clone—a grotesque source of spare organs and genetic material that would be used to keep Richard alive and vital for years to come.

That left one more chamber, with one more clone, and Kotler couldn't decide who that could be. There were myriad possibilities. No one, horrible possibility trumped the others, however.

"It's time you help me with the next phase," Richard said.

Kotler turned again. "And what is that? I'm no geneticist. I can't do anything to help you."

Richard smiled, and shook his head. "No, you're not a geneticist. But you do have a particular knack for solving puzzles. And I have one for you."

Kotler nodded. "You want me to crack the encryption on the hard drive. My mother's code."

Richard nodded as well. "You are every bit as smart as I tell the other grandpas."

Kotler let the absurdity of that idea pass without remark.

Richard turned and left the room, again with the implication that Kotler should follow. Kotler did so.

As he stepped through the doorway, he passed perilously close to Travis Bell.

The temptation to try for a rematch was strong, but Kotler decided it was too foolish. He was clearly outmatched. Bell's physical prowess could overcome anything Kotler threw at him.

He'd find another way to even the score with Travis Bell.

Later.

First, he had to find a way out of this place.

CHAPTER TWENTY-ONE

Liz was watching Kendell Young's office windows from the street below.

She and Dani were parked in Dani's company car, a black sedan with government plates. They were close enough that they could watch the building but far enough back to keep anyone from noticing and becoming suspicious.

The past two days had been grueling and exhausting, as the two of them worked long hours, alone, to find the best way to feed pieces of intel to Granger's people.

In the end, they had landed on getting Liz into each captive's cell under the guise of taking DNA samples.

It was pushing things a little. Each prisoner had been subjected to cheek swabs as they were processed, and there was no legitimate reason to repeat the procedure. Which meant they would have to *invent* a reason.

Liz had gone into their records and made some changes that would, she hoped, introduce the idea that a mistake had been made. The easiest and least suspicious change, she decided, was to swap the results for two of the prisoners, and then flag it as something she'd discovered upon closer inspection.

She made sure that any record of who had taken the initial swabs was deleted from both the current record and the backup, and included her own name among those who had done the work. She didn't want any of her people taking the fall for this—she'd fall on her own sword, if it came to it. But the error gave her the chance to claim that she'd prefer to handle a do-over herself, to ensure the results were accurate.

It would read to some like she was covering her own butt, which was part of what she intended. She had a solid reputation, and there was little chance of an official reprimand, considering her boss was in on the plan. She could take the scrutiny and the ding.

At any rate, the plan worked. One by one, Liz had interacted with each prisoner, taking his or her DNA, and leaving them with a predetermined piece of intel that they would share with interrogators later.

Each Jani operative had nodded, silently memorizing their parts. And over the next few days, all the Jani became much more forthcoming and cooperative with the interrogators, who dutifully wrote and submitted reports of their findings. The intel was now pouring in.

The greater challenge had been planning and tracking which pieces of intel were being shared, and with whom, as well as which pieces were being modified or not shared at all.

This part was key and had to be done precisely and with great discretion—the point of paranoia. Any resources that flowed through the system within Historic Crimes headquarters would be subject to scrutiny by the oversight committee. And thus by Kendell Young.

Liz created a spreadsheet using a cloud-based service, under a hastily created new username, and with a laptop she purchased second hand from a pawn shop. She had sat in a coffee shop she'd never before visited, using their WIFI to create the spreadsheet and encode the intel, the Jani operative, and the Historic Crimes operative with separate identifiers.

In this way, Liz and Dani were able to track the progress of the intel, and see where any divergence took place. The data was kept away from anything that Young's people might be able to trace, and was disguised in such a way as to be inscrutable, even if Young somehow gained access to it.

With the information tagged and encoded, Liz started seeding it among their captives, testing by Jani and Historic Crimes personnel.

To their dismay, they did find that certain key pieces of intel were blocked. Not enough to completely stymie the operation, but it indicated where the leaks were.

Dani noted who, within their organization and among the Jani captives, was turning out to be a mole. They'd be dealt with, eventually. For now, however, it helped to know who they could and could not trust.

This operation, with Liz and Dani on the street and a dozen hand-selected operatives preparing to make a breach, would be a lynchpin move in taking Young down.

At least, that was the hope.

Dani's phone chirped, alerting her to a new voicemail. As Liz continued to watch the building, just down the street, Dani held the phone to her ear and listened.

Liz was so focused on the progress of the operation that, at first, she didn't notice Dani's expression. She glanced over to see Agent Brown watching her, a look of concern on her face.

"What is it?" Liz asked, feeling her stomach clench.

Dani hesitated, then shook her head. "That was from Agent Denzel," she said. She huffed. "I'm sorry to tell you, but Kotler has been abducted."

Liz felt her blood go cold. "Abducted?" She kept herself calm, though the nerves were starting to vibrate through her like micro-jolts of electricity. "Do we know anything? Who might have done it?"

"Denzel thinks it was someone named Travis Bell. He's an athlete or something, but Denzel doesn't have much else on him yet. And he says he believes Bell is working for Richard Kotler."

Liz took this in and nodded. "Ok," she said.

"Denzel is catching a flight to Salt Lake City," Dani continued. "That was Bell's last known destination. There's a team from Historic Crimes en route, and apparently some of the security force from the *Göbekli Tepe* dig site is traveling with Denzel."

Again Liz nodded. "Ok," she repeated.

Dani was studying her. "Are you going to be able to handle this? Do you need to break away?"

Liz shook her head, inhaling and exhaling, keeping herself calm. "No, I'm good. I'm worried, of course. But Roland would be my very first choice to deal with this. He can handle it."

Dani was still watching her.

"Dani, I'm ok. I promise. When this is over, when we have Young in custody, I'll fly to Salt Lake. If that's ok with you."

Dani nodded. "Of course."

Liz turned back to watching the building. She felt her heart pounding, but she breathed through it, focused on calming herself. She needed to stay in this moment, to stay clear. She and Dani had worked too hard to put this op into motion, and they couldn't afford any screwups.

This had to be done. And it had to be done right.

A black town car arrived at the front of Young's building, and as they watched, Senator Acosta emerged from the back seat.

"Ok," Dani said. "Here we go."

This was the part that made Liz the most nervous. They had arranged for Acosta to set up a meeting with Young at his offices. This sort of thing was common enough that it shouldn't raise any red flags for Young, and it gave them the opportunity to distract him and set him up for the takedown. It also gave them a way to solve a tricky problem.

Acosta couldn't wear a wire while doing this. She'd be found out almost immediately, as Young's personal security routinely scanned for devices. Acosta would even have to leave her phone with the security team in the lobby.

Effectively, this would have meant that the Historic Crimes team was going in blind. Thanks to a few key pieces of technology, however—courtesy of Ethan Patterson—they still had a way to see and hear what was happening inside.

Across the way from Young's building, hovering unseen in the shadows of the rooftops, was a floating array of micro-drones equipped with laser microphones that could translate vibration from the windows into sound, and then relay that back to the surveillance team. In addition, each unit utilized LIDAR and thermal mapping, as well as radar, to construct a 3D image of the offices and their occupants. Coupled with 8K resolution video, all of this data gave the Historic Crimes team the ability to be a fly on the wall, monitoring and recording everything, inside and out.

It was a frightening level of surveillance technology, and if Acosta hadn't used her influence to get a judge to sign off on it, the whole operation would have been delayed. As it was, Acosta had requested the tech as part of her personal security detail, provided as part of her station. In effect, the Historic Crimes agents were monitoring Senator Acosta, not Kendell Young.

For the Senator's own protection, of course.

It was a flimsy sort of reasoning that might not hold up in a court of law, if anyone pushed back too hard. But there were some special considerations at play, and enough intel to implicate Young in a number of crimes, thanks to everything Granger had provided.

This approach was more about timing and expediency. They couldn't afford to let this intel get dated. Or to fall into the hands of Young's people.

It was also about giving them the lay of the land, so they could breach Young's inner sanctum and avoid a protracted battle that might endanger their operatives, as well as Senator Acosta, and give Young the time needed to escape.

Everything was down to precise, highly calculated moves now. Only slivers for the margin of error.

This either worked, or it failed spectacularly.

Liz and Dani exited the sedan and made their way casually toward the building directly across from Young's offices. In the distance, Liz could see one of the two surveillance vans they'd requisitioned for this operation. Inside, she knew, they were watching, listening, and recording Acosta's conversation and interaction with Young, as well as anyone else in the building.

The second van was further away, and was the nerve center for operating the various drones, tracking Acosta's movement as she had moved through the city. Now they were to maintain their position, keeping the technology focused on Acosta as she moved through the building, tracking her as she interacted with anyone, but particularly Kendell Young.

All part of the plan.

Liz prayed to God it all worked.

She and Dani stopped, hovering in the entry of the neighboring building.

Liz tried to keep her mind off of Kotler and the danger he

was in. Wasn't Kotler *always* in danger? And hadn't he always managed to be fine, to pull out of it with barely a scratch?

That was Dan Kotler.

Into trouble, out of trouble, and usually something boyish and clever in-between. It was so routine with him that it was practically his brand. So, Liz reasoned, there was no reason to believe this time would be any different.

Dan was safe, because Dan was always safe, by the end.

It was cold comfort. Largely because of the state they'd both left things in, the last time they spoke.

Things between the two of them had been strained, and she was uncertain about where they would or even should go from here. She wasn't sure how she felt, to be honest. Except...

Except she *was* sure. Which was what made this all so damned frustrating.

She had told Kotler that she loved him. She meant it. And that didn't go away, simply because Kotler had taken a hiatus. She knew him. She knew his ways, and his nature. They were really only just discovering each other, and themselves as a couple, when all of this started. When Kotler had left to go try to make amends for the sins of his grandfather.

Because that's what this was, she now realized.

Kotler had spent his life making himself into someone who could redeem his family, in one way or another. He'd organized his life, traveled and trained, studied and worked obsessively to make himself into the sort of person he believed his parents would be proud of. What little boy wouldn't, given the circumstances?

But because Kotler was brilliant, because he was who he was, he took it to extremes that few people on Earth would have gone to. He took his father's interest in archaeology and history, and his passion for science, along with his mother's passion for physics, and he made these into cornerstones for his career and his life. He trained, physically and mentally, to make himself strong enough and clever enough to solve problems on his own. He made himself into what he believed was the person who could live up to his parents' legacy, without having to depend on anyone else.

Kotler was independent to the point of being disconnected from most of the world. Liz hadn't quite understood that, at first, but now it was clear. His relationship with her, with Agent Denzel, with his own brother—these were the closest relationships he had.

And look at them. As much as Kotler clearly loved and cared for them all, he seemed ready, at any instant, to walk away from them. If, that was, he deemed it was for their own good.

Kotler saw himself as a burden to everyone around him, Liz had realized. A burden he preferred to keep on his own shoulders, to protect the people he loved most.

That burden extended to making up for the injustice of his parents dying, leaving him and Jeffrey alone. It extended to making up for the sins of Cristoff Vellar, and the work done by Vellar-Kotler Genetic Research.

And once Kotler learned that his grandfather was the head of the Novensiles, he turned his obsession toward redeeming Richard Kotler as well.

Rather than try to make his grandfather proud, however, Kotler had focused on bringing justice for Richard's crimes. Or on bringing punishment and restitution for them. He aimed himself at tearing down Richard's plans and his work, repairing the Kotler legacy and putting it back on track.

This sort of balance, the pursuit of it, was who Kotler was. Liz knew that much about him. She'd loved that about him, too. The drive to understand humanity, the meaning at the root of human culture and society, was at the heart of Kotler's work and life. But the drive to balance the tragedy of his life with doing something good and positive in the world—that *was* Dan Kotler. It was the absolute core of his existence.

Liz shook her head.

This was not the time.

She was worried about Dan, but right now there were immediate threats to deal with. She had Acosta to worry about. She had an operation to run. She had a job to do.

There was an entire team, including Agent Dani Brown, depending on her.

"We good?" Dani asked, and Liz realized she'd been watching for the past couple of minutes.

"Time?" Liz asked, clearing her throat.

Dani nodded, as if Liz had answered her question. "Once we get the word from the surveillance team, I'll give the order. We have operatives in place around the perimeter, and on the roof."

Liz nodded as well. "Ok, then." She reached under her coat and drew her weapon.

She rarely carried it, but she thought that maybe she'd better change that habit. Circumstances had changed of late. She had new responsibilities, and new challenges. New duties.

A gun in hand might just be her new normal.

———

Acosta was nervous, but she was keeping it in check.

She'd been briefed by Agent Brown and Dr. Ludlum. She'd been told what to say, asked to memorize some prompts from a script, given a safe phrase to use, when it was time. She was made aware, again and again, of the risks and the danger. She had signed the waiver, when asked, without hesitation.

This scared her. But she was doing it.

Acosta had used her influence and her office to get the court order, to "enhance" her security detail with the resources of Historic Crimes. That part of the plan was crucial, she knew. It meant abusing her power a little... but given that she'd been robbed of that power for so long now, she felt it was justified. This little nudge could free her. It could also help to bring down a dangerous man, and maybe even the organization he controlled.

She had gone round and round with Agent Brown and Liz Ludlum, being drilled on what to do, how to take cover if things went bad, how to minimize the risk to herself. She had told them she was ready, and she mean it.

What she hadn't told Agent Brown or Liz Ludlum, or anyone else, was that she'd also been briefed by Granger.

Now that he'd gotten Cameron under heel, Granger had started dropping by her DC apartment to walk her through everything he was trying to accomplish. Over the past few days he'd visited her frequently to keep her updated on what was about to happen.

"They're doing a remarkable job of distributing and tracking the information I leaked to them," Granger had said. "I've been impressed. I'm starting to think I should have extended my invitation to join the Jani to Dr. Ludlum, instead of Dr. Kotler."

Acosta listened, quietly. She still wasn't sure how much she could trust Granger. But he was keeping her in the loop, in a way that no one else had, since all of this started. He was also listening to her, hearing her out on her concerns, on her thoughts.

Treating her like a person, instead of just a resource.

The conversation evolved from preparing her for what was coming to what she thought she might want to do, once all of this was over.

"Do you have any plans, regarding your seat on the Senate?" Granger had asked.

She thought for a moment. "Do you?"

Granger smiled and laughed lightly. "I see. You think I'm trying to put you under my thumb, the way Kendell Young has. That's understandable. In a way, I am."

Acosta hadn't expected him to be so candid about it, but she felt a slight dread at the confirmation.

"Don't worry," Granger said. "Unlike Young and the Novensiles, I will tell you exactly what I have in mind. If you want to hear it."

She studied him, then nodded.

"I want to see you reach your real, full potential, as a person of power in US government."

She arched her eyebrows at this. "That feels a little like smoke being blown up my ass," she said.

Granger laughed, loud and sharp. "Well, I can see why. But no, not entirely. We've watched you, since you appeared on our radar. It was clear from the start that you were recruited for this, to be a mouthpiece and a symbol. Used, frankly, by the Novensiles, as a way to further their agenda. What we noticed, however, was that despite being kept relatively powerless by Young and his people, you still managed to put things into motion that will ultimately bring the Novensiles down."

Acosta listened and felt a thrill of something go through her. Then she shook her head. "Flattery," she said.

"Manipulation, you mean," Granger said. "See how much you've grown?"

She considered this. "You're trying to say that because of all this, I've... maybe I've gotten better at spotting when I'm being manipulated?"

"Is that what I'm saying?" Granger asked.

Acosta knew instantly what he was doing, which in itself

seemed to prove the point. "You want me to be confident in what I think. To be independent."

"You are already confident and independent," Granger shrugged. "Now you're starting to realize it. I believe you could have a positive impact on this country's future."

Acosta again raised her eyebrows. "So you agree with my platform? That the US should be a socialist country?"

Granger didn't nod, or shake his head, or give any sign of either agreement or disagreement. Instead, he kept her gaze. And when he spoke, Acosta felt she had no choice but to focus on every syllable.

"Whatever your political philosophy, you will do this country, and the world, the most good by being decisive, resolute, and open minded to the truth."

Acosta discovered that her mouth was hanging open slightly as she listened. She closed it, cleared her throat, and sat back, turning her head to stare out of the window of her apartment. The DC skyline glistened, unperturbed by the plots and plans happening in her home. The world moved by, as if it couldn't possibly be aware of her.

"And what's the truth? That's all relative, right?"

Again Granger laughed. "*Relative*," he said, derisively. "No, the truth is the truth. It's our *interpretation* that's relative. You see socialism as the truth, the one way that the world can be set to rights. I disagree, but I also don't believe you're entirely wrong. As with most things, the answer, the reality, lies somewhere between two extremes. I believe that if you stop fighting on the front of proving your perspective is right, and start fighting to discover and nurture truth and goodness in the world, you'll be a great and powerful leader, regardless of what label you hang on your philosophy. That is my perspective on the truth, at least. Regarding you."

The conversation had gone on from that point, ranging

back into preparation for today's operation. More drilling. More things to memorize. But that small part of it, when Granger had told her what "truth" really meant... that lingered with her.

Acosta thought about that conversation with Granger now, as she rode the elevator up to Kendell Young's suite. She ran it through her mind, over and over, clinging to it, letting it become a fundamental part of her. She wanted it to be her own philosophy, because it felt so *real*.

She took a lot of flack from conservatives—over her stance on socialism, over her videos and posts on social media, over just the fact that she was young and female and idealistic. She'd started to fall into the trap of thinking that anyone who disagreed with her was wrong, or stupid, or bigoted in some way. Now she had a different way to frame it.

They had a different perspective on the truth.

Or they didn't yet know the truth. And it was up to her to pursue the truth so doggedly, focusing all of her passion and energy on that pursuit, that she could change the world for the better. It might take dragging everyone along with her, kicking and screaming. But it was her own values she had to adhere to.

Acosta had spent so long being shaped by outsiders, by people who saw her only as someone they could manipulate and control, this notion of her own power having real weight, real value, was enticing. It was also frightening. It made her realize that *she* was the one responsible for her decisions, her actions, her fate. She, alone, had to own that.

Even if someone else was trying to use her, she was still responsible for her own thoughts. They could control her life in all aspects but that one. That was her power.

She didn't know what Granger was going to want from her, once this was over. But she felt like she could trust him. He would manipulate her, that was a given. But not in the way

Kendell Young had. Granger was offering to tell her she was on a leash, and why. And he was letting her know that, on that leash, she could go in any direction she wanted.

In a way, he was telling her that she was, in some limited sense, free. Maybe for as long as she was willing to work for him.

The elevator opened and Acosta stepped out, making her way down the corridor to Young's offices. There were guards here, which wasn't entirely unusual. They recognized her and had been alerted to her presence by the staff downstairs. They let her pass without interference.

According to Liz Ludlum, the technology being used to track her should alert the surveillance team that there were people other than Kendell Young on this floor. She hoped that was true, knowing what was about to go down here. Because there were a lot of Young's people in the building. More than usual, by Acosta's estimate.

When she arrived at the end of the corridor, she found that the door was open. She passed through the receptionist area to yet another open door. The main suite.

Young was expecting her.

As Acosta stepped into the inner sanctum of Young's empire, she found him standing in the doorway to his apartments, just beyond the office space.

Acosta had been here, and in those rooms, hundreds of times now. The place had always felt restrictive and even dangerous to her, as if she were entering the den of some sort of beguiling monster, with designs on not only her life but on the world itself.

Which, it turned out, was the truth.

But now, for the first time, even as she felt nervous about what was happening, she felt also that she had more power than before. The confidence she'd discovered, in her chats with Granger, wasn't retreating in the face of her enemy.

A strange, warm calm came over her. A feeling that she had some control here. It was as reassuring as it was new.

She glanced at the windows of the office, knowing that out there, across the way and in the dark, there were eyes and ears. There was a team, waiting and ready. She was—well, maybe not *safe*. But protected.

But she was also empowered.

"I was a little surprised that you wanted to meet," Young said.

He was wearing casual clothes, an untucked button-up over jeans. He looked the way he did in a lot of his YouTube videos —fit, casual but still stylish, an easy affect. The face of the influencer, comfortable and relaxed, confident that he was in no danger. He had all corners covered. He had nothing to fear, especially from this girl he'd had on a tight leash for some time now.

Acosta smiled. "I hope you don't mind."

Young shrugged and his lower lip curled in an ambivalent pout. "I have some time. What can I do for you?"

This was where the script kicked in. Acosta had been given talking points by Liz and Agent Brown. And these had been shaped, somewhat, by Granger. Acosta knew the sorts of things that both the Historic Crimes operatives and the Jani needed to hear from Young.

She sighed, putting on an air of having thought long and hard about something, before coming to a decision. "I've been thinking about my role. With you, with your plans. I feel like I've been a little... resistant, pushing back. Making things harder. Not just for you, but for me. So... I was hoping maybe we could talk about it. Do you have anything to drink?"

Young had been watching her, and something passed over his features. An expression—maybe curiosity?

She hoped it wasn't suspicion.

"Sure," he said, hesitating only a second before leading her into his personal space, to the bar in one corner of the living-groom. He looked back over his shoulder. "You... prefer beer, if I remember."

She smiled. "I guess that makes me slightly uncultured."

He laughed, shaking his head. "No, I'm the same way. Beer and Red Bull. I still drink like a frat boy, even after all that's changed for me. I was never really able to get into all the snob-bery of booze. I like wine well enough. I don't have much taste for whiskey, unless it's mixed with a Coke."

She laughed, and he appeared mildly startled before laughing with her.

He went behind the bar, stooped, and when he stood again he held two cold, glistening bottles of Shiner Bock. "Texas beer," he offered.

She nodded, and he placed each on the bar, then used an opener to pop their tops.

"A buddy of mine got me to try this," Young said, handing her one of the bottles. "It's become one of my favorites. They don't sell it locally, so I have it shipped by the crate to wherever I am."

She took the beer and sipped, and had to admit she liked it. She smiled and held the bottle up and toward him. "To new opportunities," she said.

Again that expression passed over Young's features, but he nodded, raised his own bottle, and clinked a toast.

The two of them retreated to a lounging area, sitting across from each other in plush, white chairs. The view of the city spanned before them, framed by the massive, single sheet of double-paned glass that formed one full wall of the room.

There were no shades. No curtains. Acosta looked out toward the building across from them and saw no sign of the drones that she knew would be there.

This immense glass wall was the eardrum vibrating with every word they said. Agent Brown and her team were listening.

"So you seem a little different from the last time we spoke," Young said, observing her. He sipped from his beer before adding, "More... *actualized.*"

She raised her eyebrows, then laughed. "That's an interesting way to put it."

"Put it a different way," Young said.

She sensed something hard-edged in his tone, and it sent a tiny shiver through her.

Suspicious after all.

She'd have to be careful.

"Confident is the word I've been using," she said. As if to emphasize this she settled back in her chair, crossing her legs at the knees, forcing herself into a relaxed pose as she sipped from the beer and never broke eye contact.

Young watched, studied, made no indication she could read as to how he felt. Then she saw the tiniest shift. He also relaxed, just a bit. Or appeared to. "And what's made you so confident?"

This was what Granger had prepared her for. Agent Brown and Dr. Ludlum had given her a script, but Granger had given her a strategy.

"I got tired of the bullshit," she said, smiling.

"And what bullshit is that?" Young asked.

"You. Cameron. People on my staff who pretend to work for me, but are really there to handle me. I let all of it dictate who I was for a while. And now... I'm not."

"No?" Young asked.

She sipped and shook her head. "No," she smiled.

Young smiled as well. "So, if we're handling you—what makes you think we'd just let you change that? Wouldn't there be some sort of consequence?"

Acosta felt her heart racing, but she kept calm. "Only if my plans don't align with your plans," she said.

He was watching her, that was for sure. What he was thinking, she couldn't guess. So far his demeanor seemed more amused than anything. Intrigued, perhaps.

Again he made that non-committal pout and nodded. "Ok, then. What are your plans?"

Acosta uncrossed her legs and straightened, keeping her pose relaxed and, she hoped, confident. "I feel like I could do so much more than I am, but I've been getting in my own way. I don't really know what your plans are—for Historic Crimes or my Senate seat, or anything else. But it's pretty clear you have some. An agenda. I've just realized that I'm much better off being a part of it than trying to fight it. I can't get anything done if I'm constantly trying to take control of my own life. So... it's better to join them, if you can't beat them."

Young was again studying her. There was a slight smirk on his face, which could mean anything really. But she felt she had his attention, and that perhaps he was open to what she was proposing.

"You want to come to work for me," he said.

Acosta nodded. "And for... the rest. The Order."

Now Young's eyebrows went up. "Order? What Order?"

Acosta sighed. "Ok, I've read the reports. A secret order, that's been around and running things forever. What's it called? Jani. Knights of Jani. There are rumors, Kendell. About you. That you're not only one of the Jani, but you run the whole thing. I believe them."

Young laughed then, shaking his head. "Rumors aren't always the best foundation for making a plan," he said.

"Unless they're true," Acosta replied.

Young had raised his beer to his lips, his elbow resting on the arm of his chair. He rolled the bottle over his lower lip and locked eyes with her.

Again, her heart pounded. She could feel the adrenaline. The aftertaste of the beer started to become cloying, like an acidic coating on her tongue. She kept calm.

"Alright," Young said, nodding. "Let's say you're right. I'm a member of this 'Order.' And I'm not just a member, I'm a leader. Wouldn't that put you in some danger, coming here to confront me about it?"

"Does it?" Acosta asked. "I was hoping it gave me an opportunity to improve my life a little and join something bigger."

"How idealistic," Young said.

"Practical," Acosta replied. "Realistic. If I'm going to be a dog on a leash, I want to at least have a diamond collar and gourmet dog food."

Young laughed at this. "Good one," he said. He shook his head. "It seems like I've misjudged you, Arania. I had you figured all wrong. That's... unusual for me."

"No," she said. "You had me figured out all along. But I hadn't. I thought I was one thing, but now I see I'm another. And I see that, if you're willing, I can become something else entirely. Something better."

Young was smiling. "Ok," he said. "So, let's just lay things out. It's true. I'm a part of the Order. It's not the Jani, exactly. I mean, I am a Jani. But this has been... something else. Something outside even the Jani's reach. An... offshoot, we'll say. And I am leading them toward something."

Acosta continued to keep her breathing in check. "What is

it?" she asked, quietly, reverently. This part she didn't have to fake. The intrigue, the curiosity, was real.

"Reshaping the world," he said. "Reorganizing reality, in a way. Taking this country, and all countries, as our own, and remaking the world the way it should be. With us as... well, as gods, if I'm being honest. The name of our Order, the *Novensiles*—it means 'new gods.' That's exactly what we intend to be."

Acosta listened, and though she knew some details of this, the last part took her by surprise. "Gods?" she asked. "Like, white robes and staffs made of lightening?"

Young chuckled. "Not exactly. More like emperor gods. Like the Egyptian Pharaohs. We're still human, after all."

Acosta nodded. "Ok," she said. "Gods. Rulers. So... you're, what? Trying to overthrow the US government?"

"All the governments," Young said. "We will bring every last government to heel. We will control all corporations. We already control both, in a lot of places. We pretty much control the United States, too, it's just that there's a lot of competition. We're hardly the only secret order behind the scenes here."

This made Acosta smile, then laugh. She shook her head. "I'm not sure how much of this I can believe."

Young shrugged. "I have no need to convince you. I didn't arrange this little meeting, you did. If you really want to be a part of this, and not just a dog with a pretty collar, then this is the reality you'll have to accept."

"That you and the... what was it called?"

"The Novensiles," Young supplied.

"You and the Novensiles already rule? You've somehow gotten control of parts of the US government?" She said this last with some skepticism.

Young smirked. "We have you, don't we? You think you're the only Senator or government official we control?"

Acosta squinted at him. "No," she said. "I don't."

This was it. This, surely, had to be enough. Confirmation. Proof. It *had* to be.

But what if they needed more?

There was one last thing that Agent Brown and Liz Ludlum had prepared her for.

"What about Historic Crimes? What's your plan for that? There are a lot of players on that board. I've never been able to figure out what your game was."

Young sighed. "At first, it was something I inherited, from my predecessor. He... had an obsession. Trying to find artifacts, from around the world. And trying to find something hidden in certain archaeological dig sites. He created Historic Crimes almost like it was a family tribute, like the ultimate form of nepotism."

"For his grandson," Acosta said, nodding.

Something passed over Young's face.

Instantly, Acosta realized she'd slipped.

A beat passed.

Young paused, then sipped his beer. He placed it on a side table beside his chair and leaned forward, elbows on his knees. He smiled. "Lean forward," he said.

Acosta's heart was pounding now, a drum that she worried Young would hear. She kept control, kept her calm. She placed her own beer on the table beside her and did as she was asked.

She looked Kendell Young in the eye. She waited, smiling lightly, as if they were two potential lovers, about to kiss. Because Young was acting like that himself, as if he were about to whisper something sweet and gentle to her.

Maybe she hadn't slipped after all. Maybe the game was still going.

The smile disappeared, and Young's features became hard and cold. He reached out and took her hands and squeezed them painfully. "You don't get to be tired of this. You don't get to be anything I don't tell you to be. I own your staff. I own your seat on the Senate. And I own you."

Acosta nearly lost her resolve, as the pain from her hands made her afraid. Young was willing to hurt her, if he had to. Maybe even worse.

Granger had told her this would be the case. Agent Brown and Liz Ludlum had warned her that there was the potential for danger. Granger had assured her that the danger was real and had talked her through how she should react.

Own the fear. Own the danger. Be a force in that room, not passive. Kendell Young believes he controls everything he can see and touch and hold. But he has no control over your mind or your choices. When he uses fear to control you, turn that fear into power, and act.

She felt the fear fade. The pain reminded her of exactly what she was supposed to do.

She held her smile, expanded it, showed her teeth.

"Not anymore," she said, quietly, almost sympathetically.

She took her hands away, stood, and turned to the window. She could see Young's reflection, in the glass. He was watching her, maybe perplexed. Uncertain. She could read at least one thing in his expression.

He knew.

The game had just changed.

"I hope I can still count on your vote," she said.

A casual phrase. Out of place, but also not entirely random. It had been agreed upon, practiced, rehearsed.

It was the signal.

And in that instant, all hell broke loose outside of Kendell Young's offices.

Young stood up, turning toward the ruckus. He glanced at

Acosta as she turned to face him. His expression was easy to read now.

Outrage. Disbelief. The expression of someone who had been sure, only seconds ago, that he was in control, only to discover that things had gone sideways.

He started moving, stepping back, walking backwards while watching the door to his apartment.

A small army of agents suddenly burst into the room, shouting for Young to put his hands on his head, to get down on the floor.

"Face down! Now! Now!"

Acosta watched as Young leaped over the side table, knocking his beer to the floor, and rushed into his bedroom. The door closed behind him even as the agents rushed forward.

The door must have been reinforced, maybe even armored, because no matter how hard it was hit, it wouldn't budge.

"He's on the move!" someone shouted. "Secure this room, get the Senator to safety!"

Acosta was suddenly being moved along, agents on either side of her, led out of the suite and back down the corridor. They passed the elevator in favor of the stairs, and once in the stairwell she was surprised to discover that they were going up, not down.

"Where are we going?" she yelled over the din of combat and weapons fire.

"Roof!" one of the agents shouted. "We have an evac ready to lift you out of here, Senator."

"Where is Agent Brown?" Acosta asked. "And Dr. Ludlum?"

"We have orders to get you out of here, that's all I know!"

Acosta found herself being practically carried up the stairs, then out of a door that led to the roof. There was the roar of a chopper, settled on the helipad with its propellors spinning, and Acosta was moved to this with undeniable force and efficiency.

Once onboard she was strapped in and handed a pair of headphones with a small boom microphone that was positioned over her mouth. The headset helped cut some of the roar from the chopper as it started to lift off.

"Senator Acosta," a voice said in her ears. "We're taking you to a safe house. Agent Brown wants you to know that you'll be safe, and that you'll be debriefed when you get there."

"Take me to Agent Brown!" Acosta said.

"Negative, Senator," the voice fired back. "I have my orders."

"I am a United States Senator and I demand...!"

She found herself stopping short as the helicopter banked sharply, forcing her to push against the side of the craft's interior to keep herself from slamming into it.

When they leveled out, she leaned against the glass, peering down at Kendell Young's building as the chopper rose and moved away.

Did it work? Did they have enough on him? Had she done it?

She'd find out. Either Agent Brown would tell her, or Granger would.

Either way, no matter the outcome, Acosta felt something warm and liberating flow through her, like blood returning to a sleeping limb. It energized her, joining the adrenaline within her, making her feel invincible.

Making her feel powerful.

She had just shed the shackles of the man who had tried to rule her, and rule through her.

Whatever happened next, she knew that Granger had been right. She was coming into her own power now. There would be a change. She was no longer the lapdog of Kendell Young or the Novensiles.

She might still be handled, she knew. Granger had been blunt about that. But he'd also made it clear that if she cooperated, if she went willingly, she could be a partner, instead of a pawn.

That, she decided, was the best outcome.

The helicopter lifted her away, moving her out over the city that, now, she thought of as her domain. It all looked so new and hopeful from up here. It all seemed so full of possibility and opportunity.

The rules had just changed.

And so had she.

CHAPTER TWENTY-TWO

ANY HESITATION DENZEL may have felt about utilizing Ethan Patterson's private jet before was left on the ground as they lifted off for Salt Lake City. Anything that got him there faster was welcome.

He wasn't alone on the plane.

Sarge Canfield had insisted—in colorful language—that he was coming along. And he brought some troops. Six of his best guys were with him, all armed to the teeth and ready for anything.

It's like traveling with the Howling Commandos, Denzel thought.

There could be no more absurdly contrasted sight than Sarge himself, still wearing his camo pants and tucked-in A-frame shirt, pant legs shoved into his combat boots, an unlit cigar clamped in his teeth, lounging here in the posh and polished interior of a Gulfstream G650 private jet. Except, maybe, the sight of him sipping Champaign from a delicate flute, and eating *hors d'oeuvres* from a silver tray.

Likewise, his six mercenaries seemed out of place as well,

each in various states of ease, chatting and laughing and ready for battle.

They looked out of place, but Denzel was thrilled to have them all along, just the same.

He suspected things were going to get ugly on the ground in Salt Lake. And there were few people in the world that Denzel trusted as much as Sarge and his team, when things got ugly. Reinforcements from Historic Crimes—which meant a squad of interdepartmental agents and operatives—were on their way. But Denzel suspected that if it was just him and these seven men, they'd still get this job done.

Now the trick was to figure out where, in Salt Lake, Kotler actually was.

For that intel, Denzel was chatting with Ethan Patterson, via the plane's satellite uplink.

"My people have managed to gain permission to access Aireon, which helped with tracking Bell's plane," Patterson said.

Denzel shook his head. "I've heard the term, but I'm not entirely sure what it is."

"It's relatively new," Patterson said. "It's satellite technology used to track airline traffic and help find downed aircraft. The system was widely adopted in 2017, three years after Malaysia Airlines flight 370 disappeared."

"Ok, I've heard of that. And you just happen to have access to it, so we can use it to track Travis Bell's plane," Denzel replied, skeptical.

"My company supplied part of the satellite array," Patterson said. "I do have certain privileges."

"Lucky thing, then," Denzel said. "So were your people able to track Bell?"

"Definitely in Salt Lake," Patterson replied. "At a private air strip in the mountains. We've confirmed that with local air traffic control as well. I'm sending you the data from my team. And speaking of my team, I'm informed that you've brought along part of my security detail."

There was a wry note in Patterson's voice that told Denzel the billionaire was fully aware of how futile it would be to tell Sarge Canfield he couldn't tag along.

"I'm happy for their help," Denzel replied.

"And you're welcome to it," Patterson said. "I've been in contact with Agent Brown, and I've briefed her on the position of the Oversight Committee. She's aware of where you're headed and who will be with you. Your reinforcements are on the way. But you should know that Historic Crimes has had a bit of a shakeup in management this evening."

"Anything I need to be aware of?" Denzel asked.

"I'll let Agent Brown give you full details," Patterson said. "For now, just know that I am the new head of the committee."

That told Denzel just about everything he wanted to know. The implications of it, in terms of what it meant for Historic Crimes, would remain to be seen. So far, in its short history, the fledgling task force had seen a fair number of shakeups and reorganizations. Somehow it always managed to recover. Denzel just wasn't entirely certain if it should.

A conversation for another day, however.

"Understood," Denzel replied. "Everyone safe?"

"Everyone but Dr. Kotler," Patterson said. "Bring him home, Agent."

They hung up, and Denzel checked to find that, as promised, he had received details on where they were headed. Satellite imagery accompanied the report and helped paint a picture. Not one that was entirely helpful, however.

Sarge suddenly plopped down in the seat across from Denzel, half a dozen appetizers stacked on a napkin in his hand. He popped one of these into his mouth and spoke around it as he chewed. "We got our marchin' orders?"

Denzel nodded. "Patterson's team has identified what they think is a compound, deep in the Wasatch Mountains. A private airstrip was cut into the rock there, and satellite imagery indicates that it's close to an entrance of some kind. Not much sign of a compound above ground, but the kind of people we're dealing with tend to prefer caves and tunnels, I've noticed."

"And I'm sure they've rolled out the welcome mat," Sarge replied.

"This could get ugly," Denzel nodded. "I know you're determined to come along, but I do have agents en route. We'll be coordinating on approach." He hesitated, knowing that what he said next really didn't need to be said. Or really wouldn't matter, at any rate. "You don't have to put your men at risk."

Sarge waved this off as he popped another appetizer into his mouth. "My boys are always at risk. It's their job. And Kotler was under my protection when that ninja fella took him. That makes this personal."

Denzel sighed and nodded. "Alright then. As long as you follow my orders."

Sarge affected a phony salute, "Sir, yes Sir!" he said, grinning, and then shoved the rest of the *hors d'oeuvres* into his mouth all at once.

* * *

Kotler had worked under worse conditions.

The room his grandfather had set him up in was essentially a computer lab, with dozens of machines running God-only-knew what sort of applications. Essentially, Kotler was seated at one of several laptops, spread across multiple tables.

It was almost like a university classroom.

Except, in the area where an instructor would stand before a whiteboard and conduct a lecture, there was nothing but a railing that overlooked the menagerie of maturation tubes on the floor below.

In addition, if this were a classroom, Kotler would end up with a failing mark. So far, he wasn't learning anything new.

After a few hours of puzzling over the encryption, thinking through all the possibilities, all the facts and trivia he knew about his parents, Kotler was still coming up dry. A dangerous situation, considering that just outside the door to this place, Travis Bell hovered. Waiting.

Kotler stood and stretched. He moved through the room, rotating his neck on his shoulders, shaking his arms to get the blood moving. He needed some sort of stimulation, or distraction. There was relatively little in this space to provide either. And so he inevitably found himself standing at the railing, staring down into the glowing, green grid formed by the maturation chambers.

He sensed movement and glanced back toward the door.

Bell was nowhere to be seen, but Kotler knew that was by design. He had no doubt that if he tried something—hopping over the rail to make an escape, for example—he'd find himself flat on his back and sporting new bruises. Or worse.

Bell was there, whether Kotler could see him or not.

Kotler had no intention of trying to escape this way, however. Not yet, at least. It was one of the possibilities he kept in his back pocket, just in case. But gazing down, now, at the floor below, with dozens of dangerous-looking objects jutting upward and outward, he doubted he'd survive a leap over this railing anyway. It would take someone of Bell's skill to do it without being impaled, bludgeoned, or worse.

Kotler sighed.

So far he'd actually been treated well enough by his grandfather and the people in this facility. His movements were severely restricted, of course. He was accompanied to the restroom, if he needed it. And if he otherwise tried to leave the room, Bell was waiting, threatening with just his existence. But at the very least, his grandfather had provided coffee, snacks, and, Kotler was pleasantly surprised to learn, an exquisitely expensive selection of whiskey.

In particular, Kotler spotted a 30-year-old Balvenie Scotch that seemed very promising as a means of mental escape, if physical escape continued to elude him.

He walked over to the table burdened with concessions, ran a finger over the Balvenie, and opted instead for a cup of coffee.

Best to keep his mind sharp and focused. He had a puzzle to solve.

And an escape to plan.

With coffee in hand, Kotler returned to the laptop he'd been using and stared once more into the black abyss of the screen, with its green, blinking, taunting cursor.

The cursor that mocked him.

It held the key to his parents' legacy. It prevented his grandfather from achieving world domination.

A slow-blinking, green-glowing, double-edged sword of dissonant angst.

Kotler had solved a lot of puzzles in his life and took great pleasure in doing so. It was a passion, a hobby, and a profession, at this point. But some puzzles could only be solved with dangerous consequences as a result. And this was certainly one of those.

Still, for the moment at least, Kotler had very little choice, and even fewer options.

The problem was, there was almost literally nothing to prompt or inspire him toward finding an answer. The display contained nothing but the damnable cursor and a string of ambiguous text:

PROJECT CODE: CHIMERA
ENTER ENCRYPTION KEY: _

AT LEAST THE MYSTERY OF "MANTICORE" had been solved.

The project code—*chimera*—was a reference to Greek mythology. It was a creature thought to be composed of the parts of several other animals. Traditionally, a chimera had the body and head of a lion, with the head of a goat protruding from its back, and a tail ending in the head of a snake. In some depictions, it had wings resembling those of a giant bat, or perhaps a dragon. The latter seemed most appropriate, since the creature was also reported to breathe fire.

In appearance and in theme, the chimera very much resembled the manticore, with its human head and lion's body.

Beyond the mythological reference and general physical similarities, however, there was something else about the project name that provided a tantalizing hint. There was another meaning for the term *chimera*. One that Kotler's father would have been very familiar with, as a geneticist.

In biology, a chimera was a single organism composed of cells originating from more than one genotype. Essentially, one living creature with two sets of DNA.

Chimerism, as Kotler remembered it, was more common in the animal kingdom. But humans could be chimeras as well. Most often, human chimerism could occur in pregnant women, who absorb cells from their unborn fetus. The opposite could be true as well, with the fetus absorbing cells from the mother.

The result, bizarrely, could be a woman giving birth to her own twin.

Or, from a slightly different perspective, her own *clone*.

It was the sort of perfectly symmetric and enigmatic double-meaning that would have appealed to Berrett Kotler, and would have been indulged by Alexandria Kotler, for her husband's sake. Too perfect, really, to pass up.

Kotler had run with the theme as well, trying every instance of chimeric mythology he could think of as a potential key. The sphinx, minotaurs, centaurs, pegasus, even extreme long shots such as *Quetzalcoatl* and a whole host of more obscure hybrids. He'd even tried *Hercules* and *Heracles,* since they were technically hybrids of gods and humans.

That didn't work, but it inspired a new line of possibilities. For a brief instant, he thought he might have had the perfect solution in Romulus and Remus—the twin sons of Roman mythology, born from the union of a human woman and the Roman god, Mars, and suckled by a she-wolf. It was as pure a combination of related themes as he could have imagined.

He'd really thought he was on to something with that one.

None of it worked, however. Every entry brought him an error, and a refresh to that damned, blinking cursor, glowing in a green that was a little too similar to the maturation chambers spanning the floor below.

This was impossible.

Kotler knew what was at stake here, that if he couldn't solve this, he would effectively be of no use to Richard. It was absurd, at this point, to think Richard would keep him alive, out of some sense of familial obligation. Worse, Kotler feared he might send his new surrogate grandson, Travis Bell, on a hunt for everyone Kotler ever loved, out of retaliation. He couldn't put it past his grandfather, considering all the man had done.

So not solving this—that wasn't an option. But damned if Kotler knew how he was going to do it.

He leaned back, sipping coffee, staring at the cursor, repeating the same circle of thoughts and frustration and urge to make the leap over the railing anyway. A punctured spleen or broken neck certainly couldn't be worse than this.

"I take it you've made little progress," Richard's voice said from the doorway.

Kotler looked up to see his grandfather, standing with his hands in his pockets, looking frankly amazing for a man in his 90s. Or even for a man in his sixties.

"Not stalling, are you?" Richard asked.

Kotler shook his head. "No. Not stalling. But stalled."

Richard continued to watch him for a long moment, then nodded and moved into the room. He made his way to the railing, hands still in his pockets, and as he faced outward he turned slowly, scanning his domain. After a moment, he faced Kotler.

"You know, you won't believe me, but I always meant for this to be your legacy." He shook his head, then added, "Well, your father's legacy. But then he married your mother..." he shook his head, then lifted a hand, placating Kotler before he could say anything. "No, I know. 'Don't invoke their names.' I heard you the first time. But he was my son, you do understand. And when they were married, I saw less and less of him."

"I can't imagine why," Kotler replied. "Thanksgiving with a megalomaniac who heads a secret organization bent on world domination? It practically screams 'cozy family holiday.'"

Richard looked at him and laughed. "You always were a funny one. Even when you were only a child, you had a quick sense of humor. Got you in a lot of trouble, as I recall."

Kotler leaned back and put his hands behind his neck and sighed. "So do I."

Richard leaned against the railing. "Actually, getting into trouble was more or less your thing. Do you remember that time I took you and Jeffrey to the caverns? The walking tour?"

Kotler smiled in spite of himself. "I do," he said. "That may actually be the last time we spent any time with you."

Richard considered this. "You know, I think you're right. One last hurrah. Your parents..." he stopped, looking at Kotler. For the first time, Kotler read some real, genuine caring and concern on the man's face.

"Died," Kotler finished for him. "Probably about a month after that."

Richard didn't speak for a moment, then nodded. "It... was devastating."

Kotler had lost his smile, and had sat forward, more rigid, more guarded. "Yes, it was."

Richard shook his head. "I did it wrong, Daniel. I'll admit that. I should have taken you in. I should have... done something."

"If I remember right," Kotler said, "You died around that time, too."

Richard's eyebrows arched. "Is that what Cristoff told you?"

Cristoff Vellar—Berrett Kotler's business partner, and the guardian of Daniel and Jeffrey Kotler, after the death of their parents. "Where *is* Cristoff?" Kotler asked. "I haven't seen him since the events at Vellar-Kotler. Did he... is he still alive?"

Richard nodded. "Alive and well, and right here in the facility."

Kotler felt like sighing in relief.

Cristoff had been the closest thing to a father Kotler had left for many years. It was he who had helped Kotler get on the path that led to where he was now. Though, as Kotler thought about it, this wasn't such a great path at the moment.

"I'd love to see him," Kotler said, almost wistfully.

"Maybe once you've finished your homework," Richard said, a slight note of wry irony in his voice.

Kotler looked at him and shook his head. "What made you remember the trip to the caverns?"

Richard shrugged. "Look around you. This place may have some upgrades, but it's got enough of the original stone to at least invoke a memory or two." He chuckled at his own joke, then shook his head. "But no, the real reason is that when we went on that trip, you disappeared. Do you remember that?"

"I got lost," Kotler said.

Richard scoffed. "*Lost*, sure. You purposefully went off on your own. Put the whole staff of that place in a panic. Everyone started searching, scouring every side tunnel, every crawlspace. But I didn't panic. I knew you were alright. Do you know how?"

Kotler had leaned forward, resting his chin against his intertwined hands. He shook his head.

"Because you were always getting in and out of trouble like that. From the minute you could walk, you were off and getting into something you weren't supposed to. We were constantly finding you in dangerous places. Your father told me they had to put a grating with a padlock over the fireplace to keep you from climbing up the chimney. If there was a tight spot, with imminent danger, you were in it."

"So you just figure your grandson would be ok because he was always in trouble anyway?" Kotler asked.

Richard laughed. "No. I just figured I knew exactly where you'd gone. When we entered the caverns, the tour guide pointed out a tunnel. Not much more than a hole a little larger than a basketball, as I remember. It was the natural shaft that the discoverer of that cavern had used to gain access to it, for the first time.

Almost a hundred and fifty feet of narrow, claustrophobic, spider-clogged gap that you'd have to be insane to climb into. That's why no one had ever bothered putting any sort of gate or barricade over it. Who, in their right mind, would ever go in there?"

Kotler couldn't help himself. He smiled, and chuckled a little, leaning back once again in his chair.

His grandfather was also chuckling, shaking his head and glancing out over his shoulder to the chambers below. "You, Daniel, have so many gifts. You're the brightest mind I ever knew. I've always been proud of you. But when your father died, I couldn't face you anymore. You, specifically. Jeffrey, I could have taken with me. And perhaps I should have. Who knows what he could have become, with the right influence? Level-headed, that boy. You? You were just too much like..." he hesitated, stalled.

"Like you?" Kotler asked.

Richard smiled, wide. "I'm sure that isn't much of a compliment."

"I don't even see it as accurate," Kotler replied.

Richard never lost the smile, but nodded. "I can understand why. Still, when all of this started, the plan was to use your father's work as a way to entice him into the Order. I backed everything he did. Approached Vellar from the beginning and gave him the seed money he and your dad needed. Your father never knew that."

"You helped them found Vellar-Kotler?"

Richard shrugged. "I had suggested Kotler-Vellar. But yes. I think Cristoff pitched the name as a way to rebel, and your father went along with it because he really had very little ego. And from his perspective, Cristoff was supplying the funding, after all. I let him have his tiny little victory."

"So you've had this in mind, all these years?" Kotler asked, motioning toward the larger chamber and shaking his head, incredulous.

"Well, more or less. Cloning was such a new science back then. Everything was so uncertain. But so much promise! I saw the potential, and I knew that with time, and the right motivation, your father would crack the whole thing. That was why I kept connecting him with people, nudging him from behind the scenes. Researchers, archaeologists, other geneticists. I even introduced him to your mother, though I hadn't quite considered the ramifications of that one. She ended up being a distraction."

He held up a hand, again placating Kotler. "A good woman, ok? I will admit that. Just because I had other designs for my son doesn't mean I can't recognize how he felt about her. And she *was* brilliant. That's why I connected the two of them in the first place. Berrett... he was a scientist, but he tended to think in terms of metaphor and story. He took to genetics like he was born for it, but history—the evolution of ancient cultures was as fascinating to him as the evolution of individual species. I'd like to think I had something to do with that." Richard was gazing off into some distant memory, a regretful half smile on his lips.

Kotler felt something click within his mind. A connection—two synapses linking, perhaps.

His grandfather turned and was once again looking out over the chambers. He shook his head. "You need to figure this out, Daniel," he said, his voice regretful and quiet. "You just need to."

He turned back, looked at Kotler, and then walked toward the door and out of the room without another word.

Kotler said nothing and did not track him as he left. He was staring at the damned cursor.

Thinking.

Realizing.

He'd been going at this all wrong.

He'd been looking at this the same way his grandfather had —from the perspective of Berrett Kotler, and his interests. The hints of mythology, the in-joke and double meaning of the term "chimera," the link between manticore and other hybrids... that was certainly his father's influence.

But it was his *mother* who had created the algorithm.

His mother, the physicist.

His mother, the lover of mathematics and numbers.

The key wasn't a phrase. It was a *numerical sequence.*

And Kotler thought he knew exactly what it was.

More than that, he now realized exactly what information was on that hard drive.

Now... he just had to figure out what to do with this knowledge.

There was an eruption of noise from the corridor outside of the room. Shuffling, activity, people shouting orders.

Kotler rose from his chair and went to the door where he was immediately blocked by Travis Bell.

"There's nothing for you to see here," Bell said. His tone was calm, practical, matter-of-fact.

Kotler studied him.

The man was ready to act at all times. His body was honed and trained, and even relaxed he could call upon it to commit explosive action, or sudden violence.

As disciplined as he was, however, he was not entirely in control of his body language. Kotler could see a tension in the way Bell held himself. Something was going on. Something that Bell thought he could help with. Instead, he was stuck here, babysitting Kotler.

If Bell was primed to leap into action, Kotler could think of only one reason why.

This facility was under attack.

Denzel was here. And, if Kotler knew his partner, he'd brought reinforcements.

Kotler saw the muscles in Bell's jaw tighten, along with his neck and shoulders. He was preparing to force Kotler back into the room, back into his seat.

It likely would not be a gentle nudge.

Kotler was skilled in hand-to-hand. It had been part of a long, hard regimen of training. Part of how he had prepared himself to face a world in which his mother and father could be taken from him, in which anything he loved might be taken, if he couldn't fight for it.

He *could* fight, if he needed to.

Bell might be able to beat him. He'd certainly done it the first time. But he'd also brought the fight to Kotler, unexpectedly, and Kotler had made the error of underestimating him.

That wasn't going to happen again.

He wasn't sure if he could beat Bell in a strict hand-to-hand scenario, but he thought he might be able to shift the odds in his favor. He would use his other weapon—his intelligence—to create some advantage.

For the moment, he backed off, and went back to the laptop where he sat and pretended to puzzle over the encryption key. Though, that puzzle was no longer a concern.

He'd solved it. And it wasn't entirely what he or Richard Kotler had thought.

His mind was on a new puzzle now, however.

He was working out the best way to take down Travis Bell, and to find his way to Denzel and the rest of the Historic Crimes operatives.

He had the answer to the chimera puzzle. Now it was time to find a way out of this room.

CHAPTER TWENTY-THREE

LIZ WAS SEATED in the local van—the one parked in front of Kendell Young's building—coordinating with surveillance, talking to the remote van via radio and getting any intel they could give her on where Kendell Young had disappeared to. It had taken several minutes for the team to breach Young's bedroom, through a door reinforced by steel. When agents entered and cleared the space, they found a hidden, single-person elevator in the back of his closet.

"He's in the wind," Dani said, stepping into the van and leaning over to look at the monitors.

"We have the drones circling, top and bottom," Liz reported. "Agents are working a grid for two blocks in every direction. So far there's no sign of him leaving the building."

Dani nodded. "We have the exits blocked both on the ground floor and on the roof. There's a parking garage below the building, and that's secure. I'm having agents sweep floor by floor."

Liz nodded. It was down to beating the bushes, trying to

flush him out so he could be taken down. It should only be a matter of time.

But something about it didn't quite add up for her.

"Young always seems to have all the angles covered," Liz said. "I can't imagine he'd leave himself vulnerable in a situation like this. He's been pretty good at keeping himself insulated and protected."

Dani was watching her. "So what are you thinking?"

"I'm thinking he's got another way out. We need to have someone drop down that elevator shaft from his bedroom."

Dani nodded. She picked up her radio and issued orders, and seconds later got confirmation that a team was gearing up to make a descent.

Liz turned to one of the other agents. "Can we find any sort of city planning documents? Blueprints? Maybe something that could indicate any service tunnels going to and from this building?"

"I'll start a search," the agent replied.

Liz nodded and then stood. "I need to stretch," she said.

"I've got this," Dani replied, nodding to the array of surveillance equipment and the personnel manning it. "Could be a long night."

Liz agreed, and as she stepped out of the van, she raised her arms above her shoulders, and rotated her neck and torso, feeling her muscles stretch and loosen.

It had *already* been a long night.

The raid had gone more or less as planned, but as they had listened in on the conversation between Acosta and Young, Liz had noticed that Acosta occasionally went off script.

Some of it had to be improvising, adjusting to what Young was saying and asking. That was understandable and expected. But Liz couldn't shake the feeling that there was something else. Acosta had suddenly developed a new air of confidence and inner strength that she hadn't quite demonstrated before. And she had some inside information that couldn't quite be explained.

Unless...

Granger.

The moment Liz thought of it, she knew she was right. Granger had gotten to Acosta and had done some coaching of his own. He had given her intel and had prompted her on how to use it.

Acosta was new at this sort of thing, however, and had over-stepped. It was understandable. It could have cost her, and this operation, under different circumstances. But for the moment, it seemed to be working out.

But what did it mean, that Granger had taken a personal interest in Acosta?

Liz could think of only one possibility, and it wasn't entirely good news.

Granger was recruiting Acosta into the Knights of Jani.

The Jani seemed to have tendrils running deep into the various governments of the world anyway, but it certainly wouldn't hurt to have a popular up-and-comer join their ranks. Especially one who was still perceived as a national hero, after the ordeal of being abducted and then leading the escape and rescue of her fellow Senators.

And then there was her role with the Oversight Committee for Historic Crimes.

Recruiting Acosta would give Granger a direct line into the workings of the task force.

There were implications upon implications because of this, Liz knew. Too many paths and permutations to be able to see the entire picture. She would have to outline this for Dani, to see if there was something the two of them needed to do, to safeguard the fledgling operation, or to otherwise dismantle it.

If they had no other choice, it would be better to shut Historic Crimes down than to let it become one more tool for the Jani or whoever else might be behind the curtain.

Though, shutting it down had been tried once before. More than once.

Historic Crimes was something of a phoenix, rising from its own ashes.

Still, there were only so many times they could be saved by miracles. Obviously they had some benefactors, but the deeper Liz looked into the roots of Historic Crimes, the more she wondered if it even *should* exist. There were layers of agenda, built into the DNA of the task force. There might be no way to unravel them, and there was certainly no way to know what their influence truly meant.

Liz was thinking about the best way to broach the subject with Dani, regarding Granger recruiting Acosta, when the door of the van opened again. Agent Brown leaned out.

"I just got a call from headquarters," she said. "While we were running this operation, someone managed to penetrate the facility where the Jani operatives were being held. They... *liberated* all of our prisoners."

Liz felt her guts twist. "Granger," she said.

Dani nodded. "That's what I think. I'm headed there now, to deal with the fallout. I need you to take over here. We have to find Kendell Young. This is our shot."

Liz nodded.

Dani left the van and went to the sedan, parked only a few feet away. In moments she was gone, leaving Liz to watch her taillights fade, and to think about what the hell she was going to do now.

Kendell Young was in the wind.

Acosta was once again compromised, which meant Historic Crimes was compromised.

Granger had just taken back the resources he'd given them.

This was a lot more than she'd ever signed on to deal with, as head of Forensics.

Her life had changed in startling ways.

"Agent Ludlum?"

Liz turned to see the agent she had set to the task of finding city planning documents.

Agent Ludlum.

She was rarely called that. She'd been *Dr. Ludlum* for so long. Or simply Liz. Informal titles within the walls of the FBI. But now, in her role as second-in-command for Historic Crimes, she might have to rethink that part of her identity.

"Yes," she said, shaking herself, getting with the present moment. "Did you find something?"

"There's a maintenance tunnel that connects to the basement of the building. It should be accessible from the parking garage, but our people haven't been able to find it. We think the access was sealed off."

"That sounds like the perfect escape tunnel," Ludlum said.

The agent nodded. "We think so. The team in the elevator shaft are reporting that they've put boots on the ground at the bottom. No sign of Young, so far. What are your orders?"

Ludlum thought for only a second before answering. "Pursuit. How many are on the ground?"

"Four agents."

"I want four more down there as quickly as possible. Groups of two, in case they need to split up."

The agent nodded and turned back into the van, relaying her orders.

Her orders.

She had been in charge of the labs for a long while now. She'd had a sort of quiet authority, never trying to impose too much on the people who worked under her. She'd become accustomed to it, at least. She treated her Forensics team with respect, and they honored that by doing their jobs without the need for micromanagement or heavy-handed leadership.

But giving orders such as these? Asking good men and women to risk their lives?

This was new. Different. Heavy.

This was frightening.

She swallowed, felt her heart thump, and then climbed back into the van, preparing for the long night ahead, and for whatever would come after that.

CHAPTER TWENTY-FOUR

DENZEL LED THE WAY, though he was the first to admit he had no idea where they were going.

Flanking him, Sarge and his six mercs operated like a surgical strike team, coordinating without the need for radios or even speaking, gesturing and signaling their way to key positions.

Denzel had given orders to the reinforcements outside and knew that they were also moving into the facility. There had been three branches from the main entrance once they'd made their way in. Denzel and Sarge took the center tunnel, and the rest of the Historic Crimes task force branched off into the remaining two.

Radio silence would be the rule until they'd engaged the enemy.

That engagement happened faster than Denzel would have liked.

As he and his team breached a door at the end of their tunnel, alarms screamed. Denzel and his men took up positions, and just in time. A flood of enemy combatants filled the space ahead of them, and the air was suddenly alive with noise, smoke, and flying ammunition.

Sarge was hollering obscenities as he and his men returned fire. To Denzel's thinking they were taking dangerous risks, moving from cover and out into the open as if sheer force of will was enough of a barrier to block bullets. It would be a miracle if none of them took a hit.

It seemed to be working, though. Denzel was never one to argue with results.

He took out his radio and chirped the signal that he had agreed upon with the two squad leaders. Three quick taps and wait.

Four taps, the signal from the B squad.

Five taps, the signal from the C squad.

Enemies had been engaged on all fronts, then. They could end radio silence.

"We got armed combatants with higher ground!" B squad informed them.

"Coming your way!" C squad's commander reported that they'd met light resistance coming in and had emerged on the floor above B squad's entry. The two were now pressing the enemy from both sides, coming to meet in the middle. The enemy's position was giving them an advantage for the moment, but that was about to end.

Now it was down to Denzel and Sarge to fight their way through the front door.

"I need eyes on Kotler!" Denzel shouted into his radio. "Top priority!'

So far, there had been no sign of Kotler, which was worrisome. If it turned out that he wasn't here, or worse, they might be out of leads. Denzel felt confident that they could take down this facility, at least. But beyond that...

Sarge's men managed to create a gap, and Denzel followed

as all seven men went barreling into the enemy's front line, guns blazing. It was as inspiring as it was terrifying.

The enemy had pulled back, digging in deeper in the facility. Denzel was getting updates from the other two squads, reporting essentially the same.

Something within this facility was getting a lot of protection. Denzel figured that was a good enough compass to go by. "Keep pushing!" he ordered. "Whatever they're protecting, that's bound to be where Kotler's being kept!"

They pushed. Reports came back as each squad cleared and secured the next section, and the next.

The fighting dipped somewhat as they drove deeper into the facility, but never quite let up all together. And then, as Denzel's squad entered a set of tunnels that seemed to be more intentional-design rather than reliant on the natural stone, things suddenly heated up again.

Denzel and his team were forced to take cover.

"Hot bed! Hot damn!" Sarge yelled, ejecting a clip from his rifle and slamming a new one into place.

"We need to get past this!" Denzel shouted.

Sarge dropped back, letting his men hold the line as he surveyed their surroundings. "There's an offshoot right there," he said, pointing with the stub of his cigar. "Right past these pansies taking pop shots at us. I'll get my boys to push back hard, and you and me go hit that tunnel. They can come up behind after they've mopped up this mess."

Denzel took a quick peek at where Sarge was pointing, ducking back as bullets ricocheted near his head. He glanced at Sarge and nodded.

Sarge yelled his orders, and as if they'd been holding back to keep the fight fair, suddenly his men were simply *unleashed*. They yelled, in growls that could be heard even over the din of gunfire and its echoes from the stone walls, and then lurched from behind cover as if the very notion of being shot was absurd.

The enemy was as baffled and startled by this as Denzel, and fell back briefly, creating the gap he and Sarge needed to reach the side corridor.

They sprinted for it, firing at the enemy to provide additional cover, and in short order they hit the corridor at a dead run.

The sound of combat still echoed behind them, but here they were safe. For the moment. There appeared to be no one down this branch.

They kept up a brutal pace, moving at speed. When doors started to appear, they rotated doing checks, each covering the other during inspection.

Occasionally they startled unarmed non-combatants—mostly scientist types. Men and women rushed in a panic, hiding among lab equipment and overturned tables.

Kotler wasn't among them.

They ordered everyone to stay put, and no one seemed willing to refuse that order.

Denzel and Sarge pushed on, checking more rooms as they went.

In the third such room, Denzel spotted a familiar face.

He rushed forward, weapon raised, "On the floor! Now! Hands on your head!"

The figure did as ordered, shakily complying.

Denzel took a pair of cuffs from his back pocket, and clicked them onto the man's wrists, twisting his arms behind him. He pulled the man to his feet and pressed him against the wall.

Cristoff Vellar.

Last seen during the raid at Vellar-Kotler Genetic Research. Liz Ludlum had reported that Vellar had gone with

Richard Kotler, though it was unclear whether this was against Vellar's will.

"Where is Kotler?"

Vellar shook his head, his expression perplexed. "Daniel? I... I don't know! I wasn't even aware he was in the facility!"

"What about your partner? Richard?"

Again Vellar shook his head, but his expression darkened. "Richard is *not* my partner. I'm a prisoner here. I have no idea where he is."

Denzel relaxed and let Vellar stand away from the wall.

The room they were in seemed sparse, but it did have some computers and equipment. Denzel didn't pretend to know what anything here could do, but he knew that Vellar was a geneticist. His story was likely true—according to Agent Brown and Liz Ludlum, Vellar had been an unwilling pawn in Richard's plans.

That didn't make him any less culpable. But it might make him a more willing asset.

"We have to keep moving," Sarge said from the door. He had his weapon trained on the corridor, peeking out with his rifle propped against the doorframe.

He was right.

For the moment, things were clear. They were able to take their time with this search. But the dial could turn at any instant. They had to press this advantage while it was there.

Denzel swore and turned Vellar around. He took off the cuffs. He would need Vellar to have some freedom of movement, to keep from becoming a burden to them. "You're coming with us," he said.

Vellar nodded. "If it gets me out of here, absolutely. Also... I want to help. If Daniel is here..."

"For now, you do everything I say, and nothing else. If it

comes to it, I will not hesitate to shoot you. Do you understand?"

It was mostly a bluff. Denzel couldn't think of any real justification for shooting an unarmed man who, by every indication, was as much a prisoner as Kotler was. But Vellar didn't know that, and he nodded shakily.

It was problematic, having him with them. But he was too valuable to leave behind.

"Let's move," Denzel said, shoving Vellar out of the door, to follow Sarge down the rest of the corridor.

Kotler had to be here somewhere, Denzel knew. They had to find him.

They *had* to find him.

KOTLER COULD HEAR THE FIGHT.

It was hard to miss it, echoing up from all corners. The chamber room, below, was undisturbed, so far. But Kotler suspected that would change soon enough.

And if *he* suspected it...

He stared at one of the darkened corners of the laptop's display, into the reflection on the glass, and confirmed what he'd known would be there.

Bell was moving toward him, as quiet as a ghost.

This is it, then.

For the past fifteen minutes or so, Kotler had been mentally preparing for what was about to happen. Which did not mean it was going to be easy. In fact, he expected it was going to hurt. A lot.

It might even kill him.

Bell was close, and Kotler put his hands down, seemingly relaxed and casual, palms against the edge of the table, fingers resting lightly on top. He had backed away from the table by several inches earlier, sitting so that his back was straight and his legs were bent, ready, like coiled springs.

To Bell—at least, Kotler hoped—it should look like nothing had changed, and that Kotler was completely unaware of his approach.

When Bell was within a couple of feet, Kotler exploded upward.

With a push and a spin, Kotler rolled to rest his backside against the edge of the table, kicking the chair outward as he moved, so that it rolled quickly toward Bell.

Easy to deflect, easy to dodge, and Bell did both in a fluid motion. No challenge whatsoever.

But it had bought Kotler time. Seconds. Precious seconds.

As he'd moved, Kotler had closed and lifted the laptop—an Apple MacBook, 17-inches in diameter, built from two pieces of solid, extruded aluminum. With the lid closed, the edge of the laptop was about half an inch thick, and the device itself weighed around five pounds.

Now, with the heft of the laptop in both hands, Kotler brought it up in an arc, swinging it as he pivoted his torso and shoulders. As Bell dodged the rolling chair, he was opened up to the swing, and the laptop connected with the side of his head, with an impact that made Kotler's palms hurt.

Bell spun, dazed, and Kotler pressed his advantage.

Not wanting to waste the momentum of his movement, Kotler spun on his heel, a full 360 degrees, and brought the laptop back around for another strike with Kotler's full weight and inertia behind it.

This time the edge of the laptop connected with the back of Bell's head, snapping his chin to his chest and sending the man sprawling to the floor at Kotler's feet.

Kotler wasted no time. He dropped the laptop on top of Bell and sprinted for the door.

He was maybe three feet away when his feet were suddenly pulled out from under him.

Slapping the floor face-first, Kotler felt things slide toward black, but shook himself and forced himself to turn and look back over his shoulder.

Bell had swung around somehow—faster than Kotler could have ever expected—and was lying on his stomach, hands outstretched and clamped on Kotler's ankles.

Enough is enough, Kotler thought.

He rolled, forcing Bell's arms to cross, and then rolled again, pulling himself free.

Bell was on his feet in the next instant, moving as if gravity had no hold on him.

Kotler rolled again and was on his feet as well.

They faced each other, only a small gap between them.

Bell was already poised, in a fighting stance Kotler immediately recognized, but could hardly believe. As he watched, Bell started to sway and dance, occasionally dipping and hopping onto one hand, swinging his legs in a windmill motion.

Capoeira.

Kotler knew the style—a Brazilian fighting form, created by African slaves. The style had been adapted from dance moves, to help mask and hide the training, so their masters would never suspect.

Rebellion and revolution, right out in the open.

It was a formidable fighting style, and one that was difficult to defend against. Especially when it was performed by someone as physically proficient as Travis Bell.

In a flash of feet and hands, Bell suddenly swept toward Kotler, an avalanche of striking limbs, making several hits to Kotler's chin, chest, and upper thigh.

Each hit was like a hammer landing, and Kotler's leg felt numb for a moment.

He rolled to the side, spinning away to try to avoid another flurry of hits. Bell adjusted, like some mad pinwheel, corralling Kotler backward and deeper into the room.

Further from the exit.

That was his plan, of course. Kotler realized it immediately. Bell was pushing him toward the railing, where Kotler would have no safe way to escape.

It would either be death by beating or death by fall.

Kotler would have to do something to shift the balance of this, if he hoped to survive. Otherwise, he was about to go over the rail, into the maw of obstacles below.

There was no defense in Kotler's repertoire of training that was going to prevent these hits.

So he wouldn't.

Taking a deep breath, Kotler crouched into a fighting stance, one leg outward, one foot back, resting against the rail, giving him a gauge for his position. His arms were up, right arm down to guard his torso and lower body, left arm up to guard his neck and head. From his stance, Kotler could strike, if he needed to. He could punch or kick, but could also block and move.

He had no intention of doing any of these things.

Bell poured into him, and Kotler felt every hit like a miniature car wreck. These were profound strikes, if not precise, and Kotler gritted his teeth against the pain.

He was going to lose this fight, hand-to-hand. If Kotler had ever doubted it, the question was now resolved. Bell was simply better than him. When it came to physical force and prowess, Bell had the upper hand.

It was time for Kotler to shift the balance.

The gap between them closed to nothing, and Bell's advantage of reach drained away. With Kotler only inches from him, the sweeping moves weren't as effective.

Bell was an expert, though, and immediately switched fighting styles. Now he was attacking Kotler in forms that were more familiar—forms Kotler knew, himself.

They wouldn't matter. Kotler was no longer fighting.

As Bell landed one more hit, this time to Kotler's ribcage, Kotler rolled with that as well. In the process, he grabbed Bell, pulling him into a bear hug, slamming himself into the man and head butting him to throw off his rhythm and balance.

Just enough. Kotler needed *just enough*.

And then Kotler turned, with Bell in his arms, and tilted the two of them over the railing.

Bell realized what was happening, too late. He flailed, struck Kotler in the side of the head, but was otherwise powerless to do anything as the two of them plunged downward, finally colliding with one of the jutting arms of a piece of lab equipment.

Kotler felt another hit, this time from something hard and metallic, right to his jaw.

It was like a punch from a robot. It dazed him, and he must have blacked out for a moment.

When he opened his eyes, he was sprawled uncomfortably and painfully over something mechanical. He felt it humming and vibrating beneath him.

It took a long moment to extricate himself, to climb down and stand, swaying slightly, on the floor.

He heard a gasp and moan.

Looking up, he saw Bell.

The man was now impaled by part of the machine they had landed on, hanging in a macabre-looking display as metal rods protruded through his back and out through his chest, his stomach, his neck.

He was alive.

He stared at Kotler, his eyes full of pain and hate. Blood flowed from a dozen wounds, and the man couldn't move a muscle, but his hate could practically be felt, it was so palpable.

There was a loud noise from across the room, startling Kotler to look that way, and one of the doors burst open with a small explosion. Smoke billowed into the environment, immediately drawn away by the exhaust fans overhead.

A man—huge and imposing, hair as red as a robin—stepped into the room. He spit on the floor and held up a rifle in one hand, aiming at the distant ceiling. "Clear!" he shouted, in a voice like cascading gravel.

Sarge Canfield.

Kotler could have wept, seeing the bristled mercenary, standing there like a G.I. Joe action figure come to life.

And behind him, sweeping into the room with his weapon leveled, was Denzel.

Kotler tried to take a step, tried to wave for their attention, but the action was too much for him. He was done. He wasn't sure what sort of wounds he had—he hurt in every place his mind was willing to probe. But before he could catch himself he went down, sprawling on the ground.

When both men saw Kotler, they rushed to him.

"Medic!" Sarge shouted, and another man raced forward, slinging a pack from his back and dropping beside Kotler, starting to cut away his shirt and administer treatment.

"Kotler," Denzel said, leaning down beside him. He was quiet. Concerned. "You look like hell."

Kotler tried to laugh, but everything hurt.

He coughed, felt his lungs and ribs and chest burning, then laughed anyway.

CHAPTER TWENTY-FIVE

It was obvious that Kendell Young had made his escape. They had managed to curtail a lot of his known resources, in an attempt to cut him off. But it was possible—likely, even—that he had more resources to call upon that weren't a matter of public record. He was the head of the Novensiles, after all. Who could really predict what sort of arsenal he had at his disposal?

Ludlum had stuck it out to the bitter end, hunkered along with the surveillance team, occasionally fielding questions from agents on the scene, giving orders as needed.

But after several hours she called it.

With some final orders, mostly regarding securing the building and starting the deeper, forensic sweep, she turned the operation over to one of the agents who had arrived just an hour or so earlier, fresh and ready to keep things on track.

Ludlum needed some shut eye.

She'd ridden in with Agent Brown, so she had to catch a ride home from someone else on scene. She had considered taking an Uber, but the idea of possibly having to engage in idle chit-chat, having to practice social hospitality after a night like this, made her cringe.

When she got back to her apartment, she planned to sit and use whatever leftover adrenaline there was to write her report, while all the details were fresh. Then she would shower and sack out. She'd circle up with Agent Brown in the morning, and help assess the damage and next steps resulting from the liberation of the Jani from their holding facility.

After being dropped off in front of her building, Liz made her way up, starting to feel a little heavy. The adrenaline had started wearing off. Writing her report was going to take some effort. And maybe coffee.

She opened the door to her apartment and dropped her keys on the small table in the entryway.

There, on the floor by the little table, was her grandfather's medical bag. The bag he'd left her when he died. The bag that symbolized, for her, everything she'd wanted to do with her life and career.

As big as that bag was, with all of its forensic and medical gear inside, it wasn't big enough to contain everything she felt right now. It couldn't contain what she was starting to realize, about herself and about this job.

Something had changed for Dr. Liz Ludlum.

It was as if, tonight, *Agent* Liz Ludlum had been born. As if, for the first time, she suddenly *understood* the weight of her new role with Historic Crimes, instead of simply *feeling* it.

She wasn't yet sure how to articulate it, but she knew that there'd been some kind of shift. And that it had really been coming for some time.

It suddenly hit her that tomorrow she'd have to find a flight to Salt Lake City. She could hardly believe she'd forgotten—Dan was in trouble.

But wasn't he always?

She knew that it was mostly the exhaustion talking, coupled with the weight of too many revelations and too many new responsibilities. She was worried for Dan, and wanted very badly to see him, to make sure he was safe. But she also knew that, when it came to Dr. Dan Kotler, things tended to work out.

She had faith in him. For the moment, it was the one thing keeping her from breaking down into tears.

She would make arrangements tomorrow. First thing. After a good night's sleep. For now, she needed to take a minute, to breathe, to regroup. Whatever change she'd just witnessed emerging within her, she still needed to process it all. She didn't know how she'd manage to sleep tonight, worrying about Dan, worrying about where Kendell Young had gotten to, worrying about what came next. But she needed it. She needed to rest.

She froze as she stepped from the entry and into her living room.

The adrenaline suddenly returned.

Kendell Young stood, leaning against the bar separating the living space from the kitchen. He had a gun in his hand, but it wasn't pointed at Ludlum.

It was pointed at Dani.

Agent Brown looked like she'd been through hell. Her face was bruised, her lip and nose were bleeding. Her hair was down, hanging in a chaotic web around her face and matted with blood.

She was tied to one of Liz's dining chairs, with what looked like a lamp cord. Her head slumped forward, chin to her chest, and only a faint movement and a low groan indicated she was still alive.

Liz immediately started to take a step toward her, wanting to help.

"I think that's far enough," Young said.

Ludlum halted, looking to Young, her hands at her side.

Her weapon was in the shoulder holster, hidden under her jacket.

She never carried it. Not until today. She was supposed to, but before things had *shifted*, she'd always been *Dr. Liz Ludlum.* Now...

She could *feel it.* Could she reach it? Before Young shot her dead, right here?

"Good," Young said. "I always knew you were smart, Liz. One of your best qualities. A strong woman. Both of you, strong woman with some clear leadership traits. The two of you made for great optics. I was looking forward to seeing how the media portrayed you both." He shook his head, regretfully. "Now, take a seat. There on the sofa."

Liz glared at him, but did as she was told. She was careful to sweep her hands over her jacket as she sat, making sure the button was done, hiding the gun.

"You know, when I asked my people to make sure I had a way into your place, I never thought I'd need to use it personally," Young said. "I honestly thought, when the time came, that I'd have to hire someone to do this. But you've made it something personal. You and Agent Brown here."

"You brought this on yourself, Kendell," Liz replied.

He laughed and nodded. "Maybe. I do blame myself. All the time and work I put into joining the Jani and then taking over the Novensiles—I made the mistake of starting to think that I'd won. That's always when things fall apart, you know. See, you haven't *won* until it's *over.* And it's *never over.* The campaigns go on forever. That's the point. Marketing is life."

"This isn't a marketing campaign," Ludlum said. "You've hurt people. Murdered people."

"Never directly," Young smiled. He shook his head and

held up a hand. "I know, I know... semantics. I ordered things to happen, and people got hurt because of it, yada yada. I knew that was going to be the case, going in. It was part of the gig. When I managed to boot the previous Chairman from his seat, and take over the Novensiles, I had to strike a bargain. I was new blood. Some among the Novensiles were suspicious of me. So I had to agree, with myself more than anyone, that anything that happened was on me. My responsibility. That was my power, you see. I *owned* my role. All of it."

He shifted position, lowering the gun so that it rested at his side, rather than pointing at Agent Brown. Ludlum almost sighed in relief.

"Tonight, you forced me to make a new decision. I had to walk away from my plan. That hurts. It's going to force me to adjust, to pivot. But that's business for you," he laughed. "You took my plan, but you didn't take my power."

"Where are your people now?" Ludlum asked.

She was taunting him.

He knew it.

The smile flickered, but stayed. He nodded. Sniffed derisively. "I'm on my own. You got me. In all the chaos of the evening, I had to leave a lot of resources behind. I have more, of course. But... well, this does effectively end some of my reach." He shook his head. "Damn, I'm going to miss being a public figure. For a while."

"For a while?"

He shrugged. "You think a few lines on a transcript will be enough to bring me down? I'm one of the wealthiest YouTubers in the world. I'm an *influencer*! I have strings tied to world leaders and CEOs. I can *spin*, baby! Six months. A year, tops. Actually, by the end of the week I'll have evidence that shows how I was framed. AI voice synthesizers and deep fake videos were used to set me up. People love that sort of thing."

He laughed, glanced at Dani and shook his head. "Honest to God, Liz, do you think anyone's going to believe *the FBI?* Over *me?* I tell people what shoes to buy and a company goes from obscure to Fortune 100 in an afternoon. I will tell these people that the mean bullies in government want to bring me down, and the next day I'll be nominated to run for President. This is less than a setback for me. All I have to do is lie low just long enough that people get antsy."

Ludlum listen to it all. The whole diatribe. She realized that Young was right. Their evidence, the work they'd put into building this case, it was all going to come to nothing, once he left this room.

Left this room, that Liz and Dani would never leave.

"What about Granger?" Ludlum asked.

Reaching. Casting for something. Anything.

The smile faded slightly, and Young sighed. "You know, I've never met him? I hear about him all the time. He's famous in Jani circles. Rumors are that he's actually the head of the Jani. Calling all the shots, pretending to be a foot soldier. But no matter how often I asked, I could never get him to meet with me."

"Maybe not," Ludlum said. "But he's the one who brought you low tonight. Agent Brown and I built a case, but it was Granger who turned Acosta against you. He gave her what she needed. And he's set all of this up to dismantle your network." She shook her head, then added. "I don't know how. This goes into levels too deep for me. But he has mountains of data on you and everyone you work with, and he's put things into motion. You can kill the two of us, but the rest of Historic Crimes is coming for you."

Young laughed, loud and hard. "*Historic Crimes.* Good one. The grammar error that became a branch of law enforcement."

He laughed again, finding his own joke particularly clever. "You know, I only took on the charter for it because it was something the Novensiles already had on the books. The Chairman was backing it. Wouldn't let up on it. It's not like we weren't finding artifacts and historical documents by other means. But he just *poured* resources into Historic Crimes. Like it was personal to him. It *was* personal. Someone involved was his family. His grandson." He shook his head. "Never could figure out who. The Chairman is what, sixty years old? Whoever he set this up for, they have to be around my age. And I'm definitely not the guy!" He laughed at his own weak joke.

Ludlum listened, stunned.

He doesn't know.

It seemed impossible, but somehow Richard Kotler, in his role as the Chairman, had managed to keep his relationship with Dan a secret. He'd also masked his real age, keeping the work at Vellar-Kotler off the books.

Young had taken over all of Richard's assets, when the power shift occurred. But he didn't have Richard's intel.

She laughed.

"What's funny?" Young asked, his own expression light, mirthful, playing along.

Deadly.

She shook her head. "You," she said. "The *influencer*. As much as you've managed to pull off, it's all been dumb luck. You're not an *influencer*. You're just as much a pawn as everyone else! You're a conman, being run by his own con!"

It was the first time since she'd met Young that she saw, genuinely and truly, that something had hit him, hard. The shell of confidence he'd built around himself had always seemed impenetrable. But her words broke through to hit something raw and unprotected within him.

The smirk disappeared. His eyes flashed. His muscles tensed.

And Liz knew she'd gone too far.

"No!" she shouted.

But too late.

Far too late.

Young raised the gun, aimed it at Agent Brown, and fired.

"Dani!" Liz said, rushing toward her.

"Sit down!" Young shouted to her, standing straight and aiming the weapon at her now. "*Sit back down!*"

But she was not going to listen. She would never do anything this man said, ever again. She'd gladly die first.

She was kneeling beside Dani, pressing her palm against the wound in the Agent's chest. Dani looked at her, pain in her eyes, her mouth working. Her breathing was labored. She coughed.

Blood sprayed in a mist, flecks of it landing on Liz's shoulder, her neck, her face.

Blood now oozed from the corner of Dani's mouth.

The shot had punctured her lung.

Liz transferred her left hand to Dani's wound, leaving her right hand free.

It moved. It slid under her jacket.

"I said *sit down!*" Young shouted, putting a hand on her shoulder, attempting to roughly turn her, to push her back.

Liz used the momentum to roll back and away, to turn. She drew the weapon, aimed, and fired. One motion. Instinct more than marksmanship.

Young's eyes widened, and he staggered back.

His own weapon dropped, clattering to the floor.

As Ludlum rose to her feet, her weapon still trained on him, steady as stone, she watched as Kendell Young reached up to put his hands on the wound in his own chest. He pulled his fingers away, revealing bright red blood.

Ludlum's aim—her instinct—had been true.

A shot to the heart.

Young's blood pulsed freely from the wound, soaking his shirt, spreading like a macabre rose over his chest and stomach as he slowly slumped to the floor.

He was dead before his body had settled.

Liz immediately ran to the front entrance and retrieved her grandfather's bag. She raced back to Dani and used a scalpel to cut her free from the chair, lowering her to the floor. She opened Dani's shirt, and started working, pressing gauze against the wound, trying desperately to clear the blood enough to see what she was working on.

It was bad. It was very bad.

She fumbled in her pocket and took out her phone, and with blood-covered fingers she managed to dial 911. She reported exactly what had happened, told the operator she was a Federal agent, kept her voice calm and steady despite wanting to scream in hysterics.

Help was on the way, stay on the line, is the victim breathing?

Liz couldn't say.

She dropped the phone to the floor, not bothering to disconnect. It was best if they could hear. Maybe. Yes, that was best.

There was a cold intelligence at work within her now. There were two of her: Liz Ludlum, and Dr. Ludlum. Agent Ludlum had done her work, and now it was down to these two.

Liz wanted to cry, to weep for her friend.

Dr. Ludlum wanted her to stay calm, to work, to use their hands to save Dani's life.

As she leaned over Dani, she put pressure on the wound

with one hand, making a compress from the remaining gauze. It was all she could do. Hope, hold out, keep pressure on the wound until someone got here, with more tools that might help.

That was Liz Ludlum's hope.

Dr. Ludlum could see the truth.

"It's ok," she tried to smile. She stroked Dani's hair with her free hand. "It's ok. You're going to be ok."

She didn't believe the words herself, and she could see that Dani didn't either.

"Liz..." Dani said, her voice ragged, quiet, rattling with blood. It sounded terrible. It sounded like something Liz would remember for the rest of her life, in long and sleepless nights.

"Shh, it's ok," Liz repeated.

"Liz... I was right. You... really are," she coughed. More blood. Agony on her face. But then, a smile. Pained. Small.

"You really are... good... at this."

It was the last thing Agent Dani Brown ever said.

Her eyes were open, but Liz saw the life fade from them, like a machine powering down. Whatever there was of Dani, within this damaged shell, slowly faded. She was staring beyond Liz now, out into some void, some darkness beyond.

Or some light.

Liz knew there would be light.

Tears ran in streams down her cheeks. She let go of the compress—it wasn't necessary now—and brought Dani up and into her lap. She sobbed, but quieted herself. This was not the time for that. That grief would come later. Right now, she had to say goodbye.

She rocked her friend, back and forth, stroking her hair, telling her, still, that it was going to be ok. It was all going to be ok.

It wasn't a lie.

It was a promise.

The last thing Liz could do for her friend—a vow she could make, on Dani's behalf, as the sounds of ambulance and police sirens screamed from the streets outside.

A battle cry. A rallying cry.

Liz Ludlum—Doctor, Agent, Friend—was going to do whatever it took to honor Agent Dani Brown.

This wasn't the end.

It was the beginning.

CHAPTER TWENTY-SIX

KOTLER HOBBLED ALONG, waving off any attempts to slow him down, with an annoyed grunt.

The facility was secured. The enemy was subdued. Prisoners were freed, and the wounded were being treated.

Travis Bell among them.

He would get to live. God only knew how, or why, but there it was. He'd live in a cell, and there would be some long-term damage to adjust to, by Kotler's estimate. Pain would be a constant for Bell in the years to come.

Good, Kotler thought.

"Where's Richard?" Kotler asked as he moved toward the grid of maturation chambers. These were still online, and there were people on their way here who would assess everything, and decide what to do with these sleeping gods and kings.

It was going to be a challenge. This operation represented something unprecedented. Figuring out what to do here, what was appropriate and just and right—the ethical and moral implications alone were mind-boggling.

"We haven't found him yet," Denzel said.

Kotler paused, then picked up a laptop that was lying nearby. He made an angry, guttural sound as he threw it against the wall, then winced. His body protested, reminding him that he wasn't in top shape.

"Kotler, calm down," Denzel said. "You're pretty banged up. You need to ..."

"I need to find my *grandfather!*" he shouted.

And then he relaxed. He breathed. "I'm sorry," he said.

Denzel shook his head. "Understandable."

"No," Kotler replied. "I trained my whole life to make sure I could have some control over myself. The only thing I really could control. But now I'm learning, I failed at that. All along, I was fooled. *He* had control. He orchestrated everything, and it's all been for this." Kotler waved at the chambers, pulsing green and foreboding.

He paused.

"Thirty-eight," he said.

"I'm sorry?" Denzel asked.

"There are thirty-eight chambers. I gave him thirty-six samples, but there are thirty-eight chambers in this room. He wouldn't tell me who or what was in the final two."

"Ok," Denzel said. "When the squints get here, we can ask them."

Kotler gave him a look.

Denzel sighed. "Or we can go find out," he said.

They moved again, and Kotler started scanning the digital displays attached to each chamber.

There were some familiar names here. Names that, until today, represented figures of mythology and history, rather than living entities. But as Kotler inspected each chamber, the reality of it all was dawning.

Whatever final piece had been locked away behind his mother's encryption, whatever secrets she'd managed to keep hidden, Kotler could see that Richard had actually achieved his goal. Things were much further along than expected.

These were living beings. Fully mature. Sleeping, perhaps, but alive.

Ready to enter the world.

"What was Richard after?" Kotler asked.

"On that hard drive?"

Kotler looked to Denzel, nodding. "It looks like he had everything he needed to get this to work. So what was missing? My father's research was supposed to hold the key to influencing human evolution. Was he planning to alter these clones, somehow?"

Denzel shook his head. "I can't even pretend to know."

Kotler couldn't either. There were aspects of this that weren't yet clicking into place.

Mysteries upon mysteries.

Kotler started moving again, going from chamber to chamber, row to row.

When he reached the final two chambers he stopped and stared.

The first figure, he knew, was his grandfather. Or the body his grandfather planned to rob for parts, at least. Or maybe he was trying to find a way to just replace his own body altogether. Anything seemed possible at the moment.

The second body, however...

"Kotler," Denzel said. "Isn't that..."

"Dad," Kotler said, quietly. "My father."

Berrett Kotler, surrounded by the gel-like compound that filled each of the chambers, infused with a green luminescence that gave his skin a slight pallor.

He was alive, but it looked like no life Kotler could recognize.

Too far.

Richard Kotler had gone too far.

This was the product of something sick and demented. It looked like his father, but Kotler could only see it for what it was: A monster. A thing. A cruel joke.

"Where is he," Kotler said, his voice quiet, infused with cold rage.

"We'll find him," Denzel said, his own voice a low tone of shock and disbelief.

"We got him," one of the agents reported.

Kotler and Denzel were already moving as the agent briefed them.

"Northwest sector. He and an armed force are pinned down. They were making their way to an exit that led to the runway. Big set of hangar doors."

"How many?" Denzel asked.

"We've had eyes on Richard Kotler and eleven armed combatants," the agent replied. "We can't be sure whether there are more or not. There are cameras in that sector, but most have been taken out."

"Anything waiting on the runway?" Kotler asked.

"Negative," the agent replied. "Other than our own birds and the jet that Bell flew in on. All secured."

Kotler looked to Denzel. "Reinforcements."

Denzel cursed. Turning to the agent he ordered, "Get on the horn with air traffic control in Salt Lake. See if they've spotted any aircraft on the move locally. Anything that seems out of the ordinary. Military included. And make sure we have men posted up top, ready for anything."

"Yes sir," the agent replied, and hurried off.

"I need to get to that sector," Kotler said.

Denzel shook his head. "No way."

"Roland," Kotler said, his voice cold and hard. "I need to get to my grandfather. You want to end this? I'm giving you the way."

"How so?" Denzel asked.

"I have everything he's after," Kotler said. "The clones. The technology." He hesitated. "They key to unlocking the hard drive."

Denzel stared at him. "You cracked it?"

"I believe I have," Kotler said, waiting.

"This isn't protocol," Denzel replied.

Kotler smiled. "This is Historic Crimes. A new frontier. Who can really say what the protocols are?"

Denzel cursed under his breath and pulled something from behind his back. He handed Kotler a gun.

Kotler blinked.

"Got word from Patterson. Things have changed a bit. He couldn't give me the full details, but he did give me some go-ahead. You're an agent, according to the updated Historic Crimes charter," Denzel said. "Not FBI. But entitled to carry a weapon and a badge."

"I get a badge?" Kotler asked, grinning. "Let me see it!"

"They're being made," Denzel said, rolling his eyes. "Until then, you get a gun and you'll like it."

"But it's just not as fun without the badge," Kotler pouted.

The two of them started moving then.

Kotler's body ached to hell, but as he moved, as the adrenaline kicked in, he could feel himself loosening up. There would be Epsom salt baths and painkillers in his future. But for now, he was on the move.

Finding the northwest sector was easy. Just as with Rome, all roads led there. And as Kotler and Denzel approached, they could hear the occasional exchange of gunfire, accompanied by the whine of bullets ricocheting from stone walls.

"It's insane that we're firing guns in this compound," Kotler said.

"It's the best way to get the bullets into the bad guys," Denzel replied.

Kotler blinked. "I'm sorry, did you just make a joke? In the middle of a tense situation?"

"You've been acting like General Patton with a toothache for the past few hours. Somebody has to fill in the gaps."

Kotler chuckled and nodded. "Fair enough."

They approached the hot zone and rendezvoused with the agents there. After a quick debrief, Kotler peeked into the space, trying to get an assessment for what came next.

"I'm going to go in," he said.

"The hell you are," Denzel replied.

In answer, Kotler shoved the weapon into the waistband of his pants, at the small of his back, then raised his hands and stepped brazenly out into the open.

"Grandfather!" he shouted.

And waited.

No bullets rained down on him. No shots were fired at all,

Kotler stepped further out into the space.

The room was a hangar of sorts, doubling as a garage and workshop. Here, on the ground floor, Kotler could see rolling tool boxes dotting the area, as well as the occasional truck and, at the far end, a dismantled helicopter. Two large bay doors dominated that end of the room. Presumably they led to the airfield outside. Likely camouflaged in some way.

It was the only exit out of this room.

There was a catwalk lining the rim of the room, a floor above them. Armed men and women were in position along the rails, taking cover behind more tool boxes and other objects, top and bottom.

They had the high ground. They watched Kotler as he moved, the barrels of their weapons tracking him, like dark eyes that never blinked.

"Grandfather!" Kotler called again.

A moment later, Richard Kotler emerged from behind a set of three large, wooden shipping crates. He and two armed guards moved slowly, edging toward Kotler, meeting him out in the open.

Kotler didn't need to look back to know that Denzel and the other agents had their own weapons trained, ready. He would be in their way from this vantage point. Richard's men had a better shot of Kotler than the agents had of Richard.

That was fine.

This was Kotler's fight.

"I see you've had better days," Richard said, a light smile on his face.

"So have you," Kotler replied, just as genial.

Richard shrugged. "I've had worse. Though I'll admit, this isn't quite how I'd seen the day ending. I think I put too much trust in Travis Bell. Should have occurred to me that he might lead our enemies right to this place."

"Well, don't be too hard on him," Kotler said. "He's convalescing."

Richard took this in, nodding. "Alive, then. Good. He was a good man. Very skilled."

"Yeah, he's got a few new holes in his body, but I think he'll recover well enough to sit in prison and tell us everything we need to know about the Novensiles, and what you've been up to."

Richard laughed again, this time sharp and loud. Kotler could almost feel the agents tense behind him.

"You know better than anyone that a man like Travis Bell is never going to give you anything useful. And the Novensiles..." Richard shook his head. "Unfortunately, I'm no longer affiliated. This operation was my own."

"No doubt," Kotler said. "Has been for a very long time, I suspect."

"Very long," Richard agreed, nodding. "I'm starting to see I was wise to keep you out of it. You've managed to ruin everything."

Kotler shrugged. "All in a day's work."

Richard chuckled and shook his head. "Just more climbing into chimneys for you, isn't it? More adventure. More risk. I wonder when you'll figure it out?"

"And what am I figuring out?" Kotler asked.

"That you're whole life, you've been nothing better than a willful child, determined to do everything your own way. You think that after your parents died, you found a purpose. That Cristoff empowered you to become something that would honor your folks. What he really did was indulge you, until your fantasy, your delusion, became your reality."

Richard shook his head, smiling. "You're a boy, Daniel. A petulant child. No real relationships. No real purpose. You're on the outs with academia and the very institutions you claim to admire. Hell, if not for me, you'd probably be in a cell somewhere right now. You've always been so *independent*, but the reality is you're nothing without me. I made you, as surely as I made all those men and women of power, in the chambers."

"You cloned my father," Kotler said. He was ignoring everything Richard said. Or trying to. He couldn't help wondering how true it might be. But for now, there was something else driving him.

Hate.

He hated this man. He hated everything he stood for.

His grandfather. His own blood.

No, Kotler thought. *Not my blood.* By this time, Richard Kotler had altered his own biology so much, he could barely be called human, much less Kotler's family.

His grandfather really had died, all those years ago. Kotler was now staring at the thing that killed him.

"Your father," Richard said, sadly. "Yes. I... thought that if I could bring him back, maybe..."

"What?" Kotler asked, suddenly curious.

"Maybe he could fix this," Richard said, softly. "Fix... me. You. All of it."

Kotler laughed. "Fix what you've broken," he said. "How pathetic."

For once, anger flashed in Richard's eyes. "Well, I suppose that makes us a pair."

Kotler knew what he meant, knew that it was supposed to be a blade, slicing through him, cutting him deep.

Instead, it cut him loose. Set him free.

"You're under arrest," Kotler said. "I'm short the badge at the moment. But it turns out I'm an agent with Historic Crimes. The thing you built to manipulate me into helping you do all this is the very thing taking you down. How's that for irony?"

Richard laughed. "And how do you propose to impose your newfound authority?" He motioned to his people, poised to shoot at any second. "You may have me pinned in here, for the moment. But I have you in my sights. I can have you gunned down before anyone on your side knows it's happened."

"True," Kotler nodded. "But we know you're waiting for reinforcements. Which, by the way, aren't going to make it. That isn't why you're going to surrender, though,."

"Ok," Richard nodded. "Give me a reason. Make it a good one."

Kotler smiled. "Manticore."

He saw it in Richard's features. A myriad of emotions played on the older man's face, his eyes brightening at the word. Hope, then frustration. Fury. Then cunning.

He's going to try to manipulate me, Kotler thought, in disbelief. *After everything, he still thinks he has me.*

"We can bring them back," Richard said, his voice low. He locked eyes with Kotler. This conversation was between the two of them. It was a bargain. A Faustian deal, dressed like a Thanksgiving turkey and laid out on the table. "Both of them. Your father... your mother. With Manticore, I can awaken them. *Truly* awaken them. Restore them to who they were, Daniel. I can make them the people you and Jeffrey knew."

Kotler's heart flipped and pounded.

He'd known Richard would try something like this, but he hadn't been as prepared for it as he'd thought. He hadn't expected how he would actually feel.

Tempted.

"Daniel," Richard continued. "What Berrett discovered... it's the key. The key to *everything.* This goes beyond... all *this.*" He waved at the catwalks above, the armed personnel bearing down on them, waiting for the order to kill Kotler. "This is immortality. And more. We can live forever, with abilities that once only belonged to the gods. We can be gods ourselves! And your parents can live again. Manticore can restore them. Their memories. Their personalities. It's all locked within their DNA, Daniel. And along with it, the secrets of godhood."

Kotler listened.

His parents. Restored. Just as he'd known them.

No, he thought. *Not as I knew them.*

Changed. A mockery of the people he knew and loved. Abominations that would be the first in a line of beings who could disrupt the balance of nature, of life. Creatures who would end the age of man, and usher in some repulsive, new age of unending life with no purpose greater than admiring itself.

"Sorry, grandfather," Kotler said. "My father and mother died decades ago. You should have died with them."

Richard studied him, watched him.

Kotler had thought maybe he'd react, to call down hell on his grandson, to see him fall in a pool of blood at his feet, even if it cost his own life.

Instead, Richard turned, raising his hands. "Surrender!" he shouted. "Lay down your weapons!"

There was a brief pause, and then the sound of weapons clattering to the metal catwalks above.

Richard's people began filing down the steps, out of the pockets of cover around the room, grouping in the middle of the hangar with their hands on the backs of their heads, sinking to their knees as Historic Crimes agents rushed forward.

Kotler and Richard stood, staring each other in the eye as activity flourished all around them.

"A gift," Richard said, smiling. "For all those birthdays I missed."

"A ploy," Kotler replied. "You're playing your last card, hoping you'll find a way to turn this around and get your hands on Manticore."

Richard shrugged. "Stranger things have happened. I'm living proof."

Kotler could hardly argue with that.

Richard put his hands on the back of his head and sunk to his knees, just as Denzel stepped in beside Kotler.

Denzel held a pair of handcuffs out, and Kotler took them. He stepped behind his grandfather, locking the cuffs on the older man's wrists.

Within the hour, everyone in the hanger was arrested, searched, and moved.

The reinforcements, apparently either catching wind that the operation was a bust or never intending to arrive in the first place, never appeared.

It was over.

Richard Kotler's reign was ended.

Whatever that meant for the future, Kotler couldn't guess. But for now... here and now... it was done.

Kotler and Denzel walked out of the compound, through the large bay doors that were slowly opened, and into the sunrise lighting the Wasatch Mountains.

EPILOGUE

ETHAN PATTERSON STOOD at the podium where only weeks before Kendell Young had stood. His eyes passed over the room, and Ludlum noted that they paused on her for longer than expected. As if he was trying to make sure, one last time, that she was alright.

She'd had a lot of talks with Patterson over the past few days. A lot of conversations in which he seemed to be measuring her, gauging her. And, to be fair, counseling her.

She hadn't known Ethan Patterson very well before this. But now, somehow, he felt like a friend. A confidant.

She'd known, of course, that he was considering whether she was up to this task.

She had assured him she was. And she had told him why.

She was doing it for Agent Danielle Brown.

For Dani.

"This task force has had one of the roughest beginnings I've ever encountered. I've been a part of a lot of startups, and a lot of committees and programs. In business, in government. I've never encountered a situation quite like this one. So much chaos and tragedy and... so much pain."

He looked toward Ludlum again, lingering only an instant before continuing.

"The loss of Agent Danielle Brown—known as Dani, to those who cared for her most and knew her best—is, simply put, devastating. I knew her only a short time, but I've read her file and seen the results of her career. She rose quickly, as an agent with the FBI. She served her country with exemplary honor and capability. She was, by every description, the finest example of an agent and a human being."

There were nods throughout the room. Liz had made sure that the heads of every sub-department of Historic Crimes were present for this, along with the members of the oversight committee. The room was packed. And most of the people here had known and served with Dani, some for years.

Senator Acosta sat across the table from Ludlum. She looked genuinely saddened by Dani's death. And Ludlum thought this was sincere.

She felt wary about the Senator, knowing that she was a tool of Granger and the Jani. But she also felt she knew Acosta better than most. The Senator wasn't a bad person, Liz believed. She was someone coming into her own strength and power.

An ally, hopefully. Though one who could only be trusted so far.

"Historic Crimes was founded under a veil of deceit and manipulation," Patterson continued. "It's mission was a good one. But behind the mission, dark forces sought to corrupt it, to manipulate it for goals that would, frankly, have changed the face of the Earth, and the destiny of humanity itself."

"Considering this, it is all the more remarkable that this team, the agents and civilians who have worked so diligently toward this mission—not once has this team wavered from the *true* course. There may have been something dark at work, at the root of this task force. But that darkness was overcome by the good people who are a part of it. Proving, to this day, that though your roots may be planted in tainted soil, it's the fruit you produce that shows your true character."

As he'd spoken these words, Ludlum noted, he had looked directly at Dan Kotler, seated at the far end of the room.

Liz hadn't had a chance to talk to Dan. Not for days. Not since his return from Utah. Part of it had simply been the fact that so much had happened in such a flurry. Decisions and arrangements had to be made. Dani's family had to be contacted, and Liz had insisted it was her job to do that.

Dani's funeral would be in a few days.

Ludlum had arranged it all. Dani would be laid to rest with honors. Even the President was set to attend, along with a pantheon of government officials. It would be big enough to be a news story. Big enough to become part of history, in at least some way.

It was less than Dani deserved, but it was a good start.

Beyond that, Ludlum knew that Kotler was dealing with a lot of his own grief and trouble. His grandfather was in custody. His family name was on the lips of law enforcement and government officials, in some frankly unflattering ways. Kotler was getting some rough treatment, Liz figured.

She would catch up with him. They would talk.

The rest of Patterson's speech outlined the plans for Historic Crimes, moving forward. He was taking over Young's position, he announced. And he was using his own connections and influence to undo some of the damage Young had caused. He would do things differently. He would be transparent in his leadership.

"My friends in Congress and among the various agencies

have worked with me to alter the charter for Historic Crimes, to eliminate what we saw as weaknesses, meant to be loopholes that Kendell Young and his people could exploit. No such loopholes exist, as of today. And, further, the new charter includes an upgrade. Historic Crimes will not be a task force, after all. As of today, Historic Crimes is its own, fully empowered, autonomous law enforcement agency—a new branch of law enforcement with broad powers, and tight oversight. And led by the one person I believe is best suited for the role."

He looked to Ludlum, who stood.

She was nervous.

She felt like throwing up.

She felt like a fraud, and worried that everyone in the room would roll their eyes and revolt as soon as the announcement was made.

"On behalf of the oversight committee, endorsed by the President of the United States, by decree of Congress, I have been empowered to bestow the rank of Director of Historic Crimes upon Dr. Elizabeth Ludlum."

Liz was suddenly startled, as the entire room rose to its feet in a rush, everyone present standing and clapping and cheering, celebrating Liz's sudden promotion.

She looked around, amazed. She had half expected silence. Disapproval.

Every soul in the room was smiling. Celebrating.

Her eyes locked with Dan's.

He was on his feet as well. Smiling. Clapping. As they looked at each other, he nodded.

Ludlum took a deep breath, letting it out quickly, and as the room quieted down, she gave the speech she'd written.

She thanked everyone. She assured them that she would do her best to lead them. She praised the team for the work they'd done, and she promised that in the work ahead, their loyalty and competence would be honored. There was much to do, and she was absolutely honored to be doing it with them at her side.

And then, to close, she talked about Dani.

Agent Danielle Brown would be forever memorialized. Her name would be permanently emblazoned on the new headquarters, which Ethan Patterson would detail for them.

A building in her name. The Danielle Brown Memorial Building. Future home of Historic Crimes.

To Liz, it wasn't a big enough gesture. But then, for her friend, nothing would ever be big enough.

That was why she intended to take up Dani's work, to lead Historic Crimes as it expanded and grew, and to honor her friend by making this new branch of law enforcement the finest example of justice that the world had ever seen.

Ethan Patterson finished the presentation with closing remarks, and an unveiling.

"As a standalone branch of law enforcement, we are entitled to our own symbols." On the screen behind him, an image appeared.

A badge, made of gleaming, black gunmetal, shined to a glint. On etched scrolls it read, "Historic Crimes. Special Agent."

In its center was a seal. The official seal of Historic Crimes. And surrounding it, a Latin phrase:

AD SERVE HISTORIA, PRAESIDIO HOMNIBUS

"Dr. Kotler," Patterson said, motioning toward him. "As our resident expert in languages, would you be so kind as to translate this Latin phrase?"

Kotler, looking mildly amused, stood, hands in his pockets,

and nodded. He cleared his throat, and intoned, "*Ad serve historia, praesidio homnibus.* To serve history, and protect humanity."

The room once again erupted in cheers, and Liz watched as Dan sank back to his chair, still looking amused.

Patterson wrapped things up, giving final, inspiring words, as well as instructions for what would be expected, over the coming weeks and months.

It was all touching. All motivating. All good.

It scared Liz Ludlum to think of what it all meant. To imagine the path ahead—it was intimidating. It was frightening.

It was for the memory of Dani.

And to honor that memory, Liz would take on any challenge.

Kotler had waited until everyone had gotten their chance to shake hands with the new Director. He'd wanted to see Liz for the past several days, but this... all of this.

Upon returning home, and multiple debriefings, he'd realized that it would be awhile before Liz would want to see him. If she wanted to at all.

Kotler had plenty to keep him busy.

He was grilled over everything he knew about the chambers, about his grandfather, about the Novensiles and the Jani. And, of course, about the information on the hard drive.

He refused to give anyone the key.

Even under penalty of perjury, under threat of lifetime imprisonment, he had refused. In the end, Ethan Patterson's intervention had helped calm people down.

Not his influence, but rather his insistence that Kotler was protecting the world by refusing to unleash this mad science upon it.

The secrets on that hard drive were too dangerous to exist.

Denzel had cornered him on it, at one point. "You know the key," he said.

Kotler had nodded. "I do."

"But you're not going to unlock it?"

"Never," Kotler said. "If they'll let me, I'll smash the thing to pieces myself."

Denzel had accepted this. And Kotler had been serious. If they'd let him, he would have smashed the hard drive.

As a *symbolic* gesture.

Because what he'd not told anyone, and never would, was that he'd uncovered a secret about his father's research, and about the hard drive.

Kotler's mother, a dedicated mathematician and physicist, had locked that drive up so tight that it would be impossible to crack, even with modern technology. It would take the most sophisticated computers on the planet, working in tandem for thousands of years, to make any progress at all on cracking it.

But cracking it wouldn't reveal anything, anyway.

Because Kotler was willing to bet—as absolutely *certain*—that there was nothing on it.

The information Richard Kotler had been seeking was actually hidden in plain sight. Just as Berrett and Alexandria Kotler had agreed.

Manticore.

Berrett was passionate about archaeology.

But Alexandria was passionate about *numbers*.

Kotler had double checked, when he'd had a moment, and found he was right. *Manticore,* when translated into numbers using a common telephone keypad, turned out to be 626842673.

The exact sequence of digits used as the reference number in the database being stored at the Kotler Memorial Library.

Kotler had once again searched the database using this sequence, and now that he knew what he was looking for, he found it. Right out in the open, as it were.

Richard had used the information in this database to find the sarcophagus that had held the 36 genetic samples of gods and kings. He'd also found the various sites that Kotler's parents had used to disperse the various bits of research, to keep it all hidden.

What Richard hadn't realized—what only Kotler could possibly have put together—was that the final secret was spelled out by combining all the various components and boiling them down to a purely numerical sequence.

The locations of each site were tagged with mythical creatures.

Each creature's name corresponded to a numerical sequence.

Each sequence corresponded to a set of records within the database.

And when they were put together, they revealed all of Berrett Kotler's data and research. Every bit of it. The only cohesive version of it that had existed in more than 30 years.

Kotler erased all of it.

He'd never tell anyone what he knew. There could be other copies of the database floating around. He would never reveal this secret, for the sake of his parents, and for humanity.

Ad serve historia, praesidio homnibus.

To preserve history, and to protect humanity.

Kotler knew that synchronicity happened, but until Patterson had asked him to read the Latin inscription on that seal, he'd never been so certain that there was some guiding force out in the universe. And sure, maybe this would all turn out to be a coincidence. But it had certainly felt momentous.

"Hi."

Kotler turned to see Liz standing in the doorway of the conference hall.

She looked tired. Tired, but somehow strong. Stronger than ever, he thought.

"Hi," he responded, smiling. "I'm... I'm sorry. I wanted to talk sooner, but to be honest, I wasn't sure it was my place. I..."

She moved forward and suddenly shut him up.

She kissed him.

It was a long, hard, kiss. A kiss with a lot of meaning behind it. Clear meaning, Kotler thought.

For once.

For once we're both being completely open and honest and unencumbered.

When the kiss ended, they smiled at each other.

"So," Kotler said.

"So," Liz replied.

"You know, technically you're my boss. This could be wildly inappropriate."

"You're fired," Liz said, and kissed him again.

They left then, deciding that it was time they had some dinner, and beyond time for them to have a long chat.

They talked about their relationship. About Dani. About Kotler's grandfather. About Senator Acosta and Granger and the Jani.

They came back around to the two of them, and what they planned, and what they hoped for.

"I can't promise that I'm not going to be able to stay out of trouble," Kotler said. "Apparently, that's just who I am. It may be genetic."

"Dan," Ludlum replied, "if that was going to be a problem

for me, we wouldn't be here. But look... I already lost someone I cared about in this. Things... just changed. Everything's changed. Historic Crimes just got a lot bigger. So did my job. I don't know exactly where this is going, but..."

"But you want to see it through. For Dani."

"And for me," she said. "And you. For my grandfather. It's hard to explain."

"I get it," Kotler said. "And I'm with you. Historic Crimes is something kind of special and amazing. I'll be here to help out. I know it's bigger now. Your time and attention will be split. But I'm here. I'll help."

She nodded. "So will Roland," she said. "I've asked him to be my Deputy Director." She made a face, a cringe. "I know he used to run this whole thing... and he was my boss. I feel kind of weird about it. But it was Ethan's idea, and I really feel like I'll need the help."

Kotler nodded. "He's the right man for the job, for sure. He won't mind you being in charge. I don't think he likes being in charge, actually. He'd rather be out in the field."

"He'll be able to do some of that," Liz said. "I need him to keep one of our biggest assets in line."

Kotler blinked. "You're talking about me now, aren't you?"

Liz smiled, laughed, and nodded. "There's no bigger asset than you."

"Ouch," Kotler smiled.

They continued to chat as the evening wound on. Kotler marveled at how this woman, such an incredible and brilliant person, would have anything to do with him.

She was right. Things had changed.

Whatever came next was anyone's guess.

And Kotler was ready for it.

A NOTE AT THE END

Most of this book was written post-apocalypse.

I'm not sure when you're reading this, but there's a good chance that the global pandemic is still in progress. People may still be "social distancing," restaurants and businesses may still be closed or only partially opened. That's certainly the scenario as I write this. The world went and ended a couple of months back.

Welcome to the new world.

So when I use the term "apocalypse," I know that stirs up all sorts of negative connotations. You picture fires, floods, meteor strikes, maybe even an army of zombies. Or a virus. That's certainly on our minds.

But I tend to use "apocalypse" in the sense of its original Greek origin: "A revelation, or an unveiling or unfolding of things not previously known and which could not be known, until they have been revealed."

Or, to put it a little cleaner, "The end of one world, and the beginning of another."

When you study history, you start to see certain patterns.

We humans kick along just fine for a long stretch and then *boom*. Things go wrong. And not *just* wrong, but *epically* wrong. Life-altering, culture-altering, *civilization-altering* per shaped. And then...

Well, we start over.

One of my deep interests is "comparative mythology." If you've been one of my readers for any length of time, you've seen the phrase. In a nutshell, it's the study of like-themes and commonalities between various mythologies, even those that would, seemingly, have had no influence on each other.

This is a fun thing to have an interest in, especially when you write archaeological thrillers. Because there's just so much to explore, and it's all so bizarre!

For instance, every major mythology, from every culture on Earth, shares a flood myth. Look into the mythologies from Egypt, the Celtics, the aboriginal tribes of Australia, and the Mesoamerican cultures of Central and South America. Look at stories from Native American cultures, too. Name a culture, study its myths and legends, and things get soggy at some point.

Likewise, certain stories of the gods seem to migrate from one culture to the next, with eerily similar details.

Osiris might be the most easily spotted. A "dying deity," who rises from the dead and ascends to the heavens... that's going to sound oddly familiar to a lot of Westerners, for sure. But it gets even weirder when you learn that Osiris rose "three days after his death and burial."

Oddly, the story of Osiris finds some parallels among the Aztecs—a culture that should, in no way, have any connection to the mythology of Egypt. But just as Osiris was killed and placed in a floating box, sent down the river and on to the sea (where it is said to have landed in Canaan, later to be known as Phoenicia), the Aztec god figure, *Quetzalcoatl*, was similarly dispatched. His legend says that he was tricked into his demise, and his body was sent out into the ocean, riding on sea foam to the horizon.

The similarities between those two gods, and indeed both the Egyptian and Aztec cultures, do not end there. In fact, I could easily fill an entirely separate book with just a bullet list of comparisons.

Maybe someday I will.

But it's not hard to find the parallels. And sometimes the implications of those parallels make you feel pretty uncomfortable.

As a born-and-raised Christian and to-this-day Believer, for example, I start getting a tiny bit of the sweats when I see the Christ myth played out, line for line, in cultures that predated Christ's birth by several thousand years.

That always made me uncomfortable, actually, until I one day discovered that the early Christian church tended to borrow *heavily* from the mythology of other cultures, as it spread across Africa, Asia, and Europe. In fact, if you think of any Christian tradition, whatsoever, there's a very (very) good chance it actually has its roots in someone else's culture, and wasn't a part of the original Christian faith at all.

The explanation for this is pretty simple: *It was good marketing.*

Ok, so maybe not so simple. But I can explain. And, as essentially "a marketing guy," I find this fascinating.

Basically, as the early church grew, instead of trying to contradict and stamp out the beliefs and traditions of other cultures, it instead tended to incorporate and appropriate those traditions into itself.

Thus, the celebration of Easter, marking the pagan period of renewal and rebirth, became the celebration of the resurrection of Christ. Celebrations of the winter solstice became the Christmas holidays. And even that most recognizable symbol of

Christianity itself—the cross—can be found in Celtic cultures that predate its use by Christians by at least 3,000 years.

When details such as these are brought up, there are those among us who like to crow and point and call out the faith as a sham. But (and I know I'm a little biased here), it's anything but.

Early Christianity was more concerned with spreading the Gospel of Christ, than with spreading the *accuracy* of Christ's story. It was more important to get these sweeping, distant cultures to understand the message than it was to get the details right. In large part, those details *simply did not matter*.

When we look back at the appropriation of these symbols and traditions now, it seems like an attack of some sort. But instead, it was a way to end conflict and get everyone on the same page. Because even as Christianity sought to persuade cultures to shift from their beliefs and focus on the "one God," it also brought along vastly beneficial principles, wisdom, and knowledge.

Medicine. Peaceful philosophy. Concepts of equal rights. Concepts of law.

A lot of what we think of as morals or ethics came from the spread of that faith. And the incorporation of ideas from other cultures helped to make that spread palatable and acceptable.

I know, I know... I can almost hear the protests from those who have no love for Christianity, and blame it for all the ills of the world. So be it. Let's just agree to disagree, or whatever lets us carry on in peace. I won't change your mind, you won't change mine. But in terms of the analysis of Christianity's impact and influence on global culture, it can be fascinating to study. I recommend it.

But here we are again, back at the current apocalypse. And more pointedly, at this book's origin, which started before and finished after the pandemic became the pandemic.

It all comes down to living in a camper.

So, some of you may know that my wife and I, and our tiny little dog, have for some time planned to move out of our apartment and start living full-time in a small camper, as we travel the US for a few years. This isn't our first time doing this. We sold our home, back in 2013, and bought a motor coach. We lived in that for about two years, while we traveled.

This time, we decided to downsize. We bought a tiny little camper, about 19-foot, and a pickup to tow it. And from around September 2019 until April 2020, we started downsizing our lives, packing, storing, and preparing. The plan was to move into the camper on April 7th.

Almost to the day that the US was asked to put itself in quarantine.

What could we do? Our lease was ending. Our time was running out. So, we started pushing to get things settled as quickly as possible, with the plan that we would hunker down with Kara's parents for a bit, until things seemed to get back to normal.

In February, I flew to San Francisco for an author's conference. February 13th through 18th, I was there. And when I returned, I was sick.

I can't say for absolute certain, at the time of this writing, that I contracted COVID-19. I do know, now, that the earliest deaths connected to the virus, in the US, have been discovered to have been in that exact area, at that exact time. And when I flew home and started showing flu-like symptoms, the epidemic was just starting to show itself here in the States.

You should know, I never get the flu. And if I do, I'm usually up and about by day three at the most. This time, I was down, with high fever and a persistent, unproductive cough, as well as a complete lack of energy, for nearly four weeks.

My wife, Kara, caught it and recovered much faster.

But we have since learned that people with certain pre-existing conditions, such as heart defects, are more prone to the illness. I happen to have a congenital heart defect, which necessitated getting a pacemaker back in 2010. So there's that.

It doesn't actually matter whether I had COVID or not. What matters is that right smack in the middle of writing this book, I got taken down for the count for a month. And then, following on the heels of that, I had a month of heavy workload for the publishing company I work with. And when the smoke cleared on that, I still had packing the apartment and moving into the camper to deal with.

Actually, moving to God only knew where, by that point.

So there were a lot of things that helped to delay me from getting this book finished on the timeline I had originally planned. But I think, somehow, that may have ended up working in my favor.

For one thing, when I have to stop and come back to a book, I tend to re-read and re-write everything that I'd done before. This lets me get familiar with the story again, and to rebuild momentum. But it also helps me add to the word count, while polishing and editing.

This has proven so beneficial, I've made it an official part of my "edit stack."

I was always doing this, in one way or another, but now I make it a more intentional process. I write, and I loop back. I read. I rewrite. And I try to do this at least twice, before I send the book off to my team of editors, who find all the stuff I somehow missed through two passes of edits and rewrites and a bunch of scans by editing software.

This book has benefited from that process quite a bit. Not only did I find and fix a lot of typos and other errors during those passes, but I became inspired to expand on certain scenes and certain ideas. I came up with new character arcs. I even came up with a new idea for the "brand" of the whole thing, that will allow me to write more than just Dan Kotler stories.

You may have noticed a heavy emphasis on "Historic Crimes."

This will become the overarching brand for a large chunk of my fiction, going forward. And it opens a path for me to write new characters and new series, without alienating the readers who came to me through Kotler.

I love Kotler. I love Denzel. I love Liz Ludlum. And now I can create more characters I love, and see where their adventures take me, without worrying that people will be disappointed by not having more Kotler books right away, as I craft new stories.

So there's that.

Another side effect of the delay in finishing this book came in the form of Senator Acosta.

I'm going to confess something, and you can take it for whatever you like: I wrote Acosta with a plan.

I had always intended for her to evolve as a character. And through her, I had always intended to explore certain political ideas, as they relate both to me, the author, and to my characters.

That said, I've been pretty amused by the reviews, when it comes to that character.

Reviews of *The Hidden Persuaders* could be particularly cutting. That was the first book to introduce Acosta, and I literally pointed out that she was a (highly) fictionalized version of Congresswoman Alexandria Ocasio-Cortez. Commonly known as AOC.

Look, I don't fault anyone for their perspective on AOC, or the Left, or Socialism. I have my own opinions and views, but I respect everyone's take. I can show you, line for line, how dangerous and dumb socialism is, but I'd never convince you, if you think it's great. So let's not fight.

My take on AOC, though, wasn't really meant to be some kind of attack on her or her ideology, or on those who really, really like her. I like her, too. I think she's a pretty fresh face and perspective in US government. I can't agree with her on something like 99% of her platform. But I'm actually really glad she's there. Because our government is some kind of weird, sick, dying animal that needs a challenge to get itself back into the fight.

So Senator Acosta, meant to be a parody of sorts of AOC, was me introducing a character that let me explore AOC's platform and perspective from the inside.

This is how we learn and grow.

But the one-star reviews that flooded my way because of that character were simply amazing.

I won't quote anyone directly, because I don't want anyone to become a target of negative comments or bullying. But the gist of the negative reviews seems to be, "I really enjoyed this book, until I read the author's note at the end and realized he was picking on AOC. Politics have no place in thrillers!"

I've been accused of being preachy, of being bigoted, and of being racist, all because of that one character.

In the next book, I started developing her more, giving her more muscle, and making her more a part of the Kotler mythos.

That didn't entirely salve the hurt for some readers.

More "author's politics interfere" reviews. Stars withheld as punishment. Comments along the lines of, "The books are good, but the author needs to keep his politics to himself."

Something, by the way, I find wholly ironic.

And now, this book.

I don't know what kind of reviews I'll get. I don't know if the readers who felt suddenly and irrevocably betrayed by the previous two books will even give this one a shot, to see the character redeemed. But I gotta be honest...

I genuinely do not care.

If you read a book and love it right up until the last few pages, when you learn a character was a parody of someone you like, and you then decide to go "punish" me with a negative review, there's nothing at all I can do to make that better for you. I'm definitely not going to apologize—especially when I've been playing out a plan to redeem that exact character over a three-book story arc.

I'd like to point out, as well, that the "redemption" of that character was not "she turns from socialism and becomes a Republican." In fact, that would have been the most boring thing I can think of.

Also, for the record, I'm not a Republican (or a Democrat).

I'll let you guess my political persuasion, if you like.

What it all comes down to is this: If you've read this far, even if you might be a little annoyed with me, then this book, and all the books, are for you. You are the one I care about. You are the only one with an opinion that matters.

It just doesn't particularly matter to *me*.

I applaud people who have the courage and strength to stand by their own convictions, and to speak truth to power, and to let bullies know they won't be tolerated. If I am perceived to be one of those bullies—well, that I *do* care about. I have no intention to browbeat anyone into doing what I want or believing what I believe. I just want to write fun stories, to inform and inspire, educate and entertain.

I serve you. That's what I'm trying to do.

For someone to say they loved a book, otherwise, but they have to give it a one-star review, publicly, because a fictional character displeased them... wow.

That's like leaving a one-star review on Star Wars because Darth Vader seemed mean.

Anyway, that's their business. It was clearly something they felt so strongly about that it ruined their experience with the book, and they are more than entitled to that opinion. The one-star reviews—that's part of life for an author. So are the biting comments.

I still love them, even though. I still write for them, even though.

But here we are, in the midst of an actual, literal apocalypse, and this book that straddles the before and during. There's so much in here that, I believe, was influenced by my experiences. No direct, one-to-one correlation or themes. But the feeling of change and growth, that's in here.

I hope you felt that.

I hope it moved you.

With the death of a major character, and the transformation and evolution of two more characters, plus the evolution of Historic Crimes itself, I'm looking forward to seeing how this changes things in the future. I'm looking forward to seeing what you think. And I'm looking forward to telling all new stories.

This apocalypse is going to reveal a bold new world.

Let's go play in it.

Kevin Tumlinson
Sugar Land, Texas
May 4th, 2020

ALSO BY J. KEVIN TUMLINSON

Dan Kotler

The Coelho Medallion

The Atlantis Riddle

The Devil's Interval

The Girl in the Mayan Tomb

The Antarctic Forgery

The Stepping Maze

The God Extinction

The Spanish Papers

The Hidden Persuaders

The Sleeper's War

The God Resurrection

The Demon Core

Dan Kotler Short Fiction

The Brass Hall - A Dan Kotler Story

The Jani Sigil - FREE short story from BookHip.com/DBXDHP

Dan Kotler Box Sets

The Book of Lost Things: Dan Kotler, Books 1-3

The Book of Betrayals: Dan Kotler, Books 4-6

The Book of Gods and Kings: Dan Kotler, Books 7-9

Quake Runner: Alex Kayne

Shaken

Triggered

Compromised

Aftershock

Historic Crimes Crossovers

The Man Below

The Outsiders Gambit

Evergreen

Evergreen: Book 1

Evergreen: Trace Contact

Citadel

Citadel: First Colony

Citadel: Paths in Darkness

Citadel: Children of Light

Citadel: The Value of War

Colony Girl: A Citadel Universe Story

Sawyer Jackson

Sawyer Jackson and the Long Land

Sawyer Jackson and the Shadow Strait

Sawyer Jackson and the White Room

Think Tank

Karner Blue

Zero Tolerance

Nomad

The Lucid — Co-authored with Nick Thacker

Episode 1

Episode 2

Episode 3

Shorts & Novellas

Getting Gone

Teresa's Monster

The Three Reasons to Avoid Being Punched in the Face

Tin Man

Two Blocks East

Edge

Zero

God Mode

Collections & Anthologies

Citadel: Omnibus

Uncanny Divide — With Nick Thacker & Will Flora

Light Years — The Complete Science Fiction Library

Dead of Winter: A Christmas Anthology — With Nick Thacker, Jim
Heskett, David Berens, M.P. MacDougall, R.A. McGee, Dusty Sharp
& Steven Moore

YA & Middle Grade

Secret of the Diamond Sword — An Alex Kotler Mystery

Wordslinger (Non-Fiction)

30-Day Author: Develop a Daily Writing Habit and Write Your Book
In 30 Days (Or Less)

Watch for more at kevintumlinson.com/books

HERE'S HOW TO HELP ME REACH MORE READERS

If you loved this book, you can help me reach more readers with just a few easy acts of kindness.

(1) REVIEW THIS BOOK

Leaving a review for this book is a great way to help other readers find it. Just go to the site where you bought the book, search for the title, and leave a review. It really helps, and I really appreciate it.

(2) SUBSCRIBE TO MY EMAIL LIST

I regularly write a special email to the people on my list, just keeping everyone up to date on what I'm working on. When I announce new book releases, giveaways, or anything else, the people on my list hear about it first. Sometimes, there are special deals I'll *only* give to my list, so it's worth being a part of the crowd.

Join the conversation and get a free ebook, just for signing up! Visit https://www.kevintumlinson.com/joinme.

(3) TELL YOUR FRIENDS

Word of mouth is still the best marketing there is, so I would greatly appreciate it if you'd tell your friends and family about this book, and the others I've written.

You can find a comprehensive list of all of my books at http://kevintumlinson.com/books.

Thanks so much for your help. And thanks for reading.

ABOUT THE AUTHOR

Kevin Tumlinson is an award-winning and bestselling novelist, living in Texas and working in random coffee shops, cafés, and hotel lobbies worldwide. His debut thriller, *The Coelho Medallion*, was a 2016 Shelf Notable Indie award winner.

Kevin grew up in Wild Peach, Texas, where he was raised by his grandparents and given a healthy respect for story telling. He often found himself in trouble in school for writing stories instead of doing his actual assignments.

Kevin's love for history, archaeology, and science has been a tremendous source of material for his writing, feeding his fiction and giving him just the excuse he needs to read the next article, biography, or research paper.

Connect with Kevin:
kevintumlinson.com
kevin@tumlinson.net

facebook.com/jkevintumlinson

x.com/kevintumlinson

instagram.com/kevintumlinson

bookbub.com/authors/kevin-tumlinson

amazon.com/Kevin-Tumlinson/e/B007POXGEG

KEEP THE ADVENTURE GOING!

GET MORE THRILLS FROM AWARD-WINNING AND BESTSELLING AUTHOR, KEVIN TUMLINSON!

★★★★★ "Half way through I was waiting for Harrison Ford to leap out of the pages!"
—Deanne, Review for *The Coelho Medallion*

★★★★★ "Kevin has crashed onto the action-thriller scene

as only an action-thriller author can: with provocative plot lines, unforgettable characters, and enough adrenaline to keep you awake all night."
—Nick Thacker, author of *Mark for Blood*

★★★★★ "Move over Daniel Silva, James Patterson, and Dan Brown."
—Chip Polk, Review for *The Atlantis Riddle*

★★★★★ "Move Over Indiana Jones, there is a New Dr. in Town!"
—Cycletrash, Review for *The Coelho Medallion*

★★★★★ "[Kevin Tumlinson] is what every writer should be—entertaining and thought-provoking."
— Shana Tehan, Press Secretary, U.S. House of Representatives

★★★★★ "I discovered Kevin Tumlinson from The Creative Penn podcast and immediately got his novel, Evergreen. I read it in like 3 seconds. It's the most fast-paced story I've encountered."
—R.D. Holland, Independent Reviewer

★★★★★ "Comparison to Clive Cussler is a natural, though Tumlinson's 'Dan ' is more like Dan Brown's Robert Langdon than Dirk Pitt."
—Amazon Review for *The Coelho Medallion*

FIND YOUR NEXT FAVORITE BOOK AT
KevinTumlinson.com/books